HEIR

FOURTH IN THE IMMORTALS OF INDRIELL SERIES

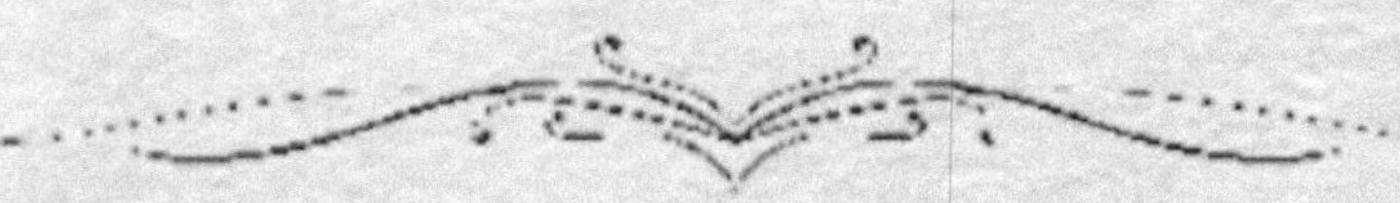

MELISSA A. CRAVEN

PRAISE FOR IMMORTALS OF INDRIELL

2016 RONE Award Winner – Best Book Cover
2016 YA Books Central Finalist for Best Indie
2015 Dante Rossetti YA Awards Finalist
2015 International Book Awards Finalist
2015 USA Best Book Awards Finalist

"I loved that Emerge wasn't the usual vampires, shape shifters and werewolves but an entirely new concept." Amazon reviewer ★★★★★

"Just when you think Allie's journey is coming to an end... Craven shows you just how wrong you were. You should NOT miss the end of this book." Amazon reviewer ★★★★★

"Craven has skillfully developed an Urban Fantasy set in a real life, believable context. I can almost believe this ancient race of Immortals actually lives among us." Hub Pages Reviewer ★★★★★

"Emerge is a story that begins as a single snowflake and ends in an avalanche. Craven has put together a story that unfolds again and again, revealing characters of unusual depth." Amazon Reviewer ★★★★★

"Craven has a talent for keeping her reader's attention as she reveals Allie's story, layer by interesting layer. And when you get to the last page, you're left wanting more!" Amazon Reviewer ★★★★★

"The immortal characters in "Emerge" all have a special gift, but so does the author. Craven's is a superpower that we can all benefit from: storytelling." Amazon Reviewer ★★★★★

Heir: Immortals of Indriell Book 4

By: Melissa A. Craven

Midnight Hour Studio INC

Atlanta, Georgia

For more information contact: Hello@Melissaacraven.com or visit the author's website at **Melissaacraven.com**

*Previously published as Emerge: The Heir (Immortals of Indriell Book 4) © May 28, 2018

Cover design by: Daqri Combs (Covers by Combs)

Edited by: Chase Night and Rebecca Jaycox

Interior design by: @BooklyStyle

ASIN: eBook

ISBN: 9798562713353 Paperback

ISBN: 978-1-970052-15-2 Hardcover

First edition for print November 12, 2020

Printed in the United States of America

A FREE OFFER

In Heir, find out what happens for Allie and her friends four years after the end of Judgment and Captive. And then download your FREE copy of SCHOLAR and discover everything there is to know about the Immortals of Indriell. **Loyal subscribers will also receive bonus chapters and a short story.**

Visit **bit.ly/ScholarOffer** to download now

For Dad
Thank you for being the kind of father my friends wish they had

EMERGE
Family Tree

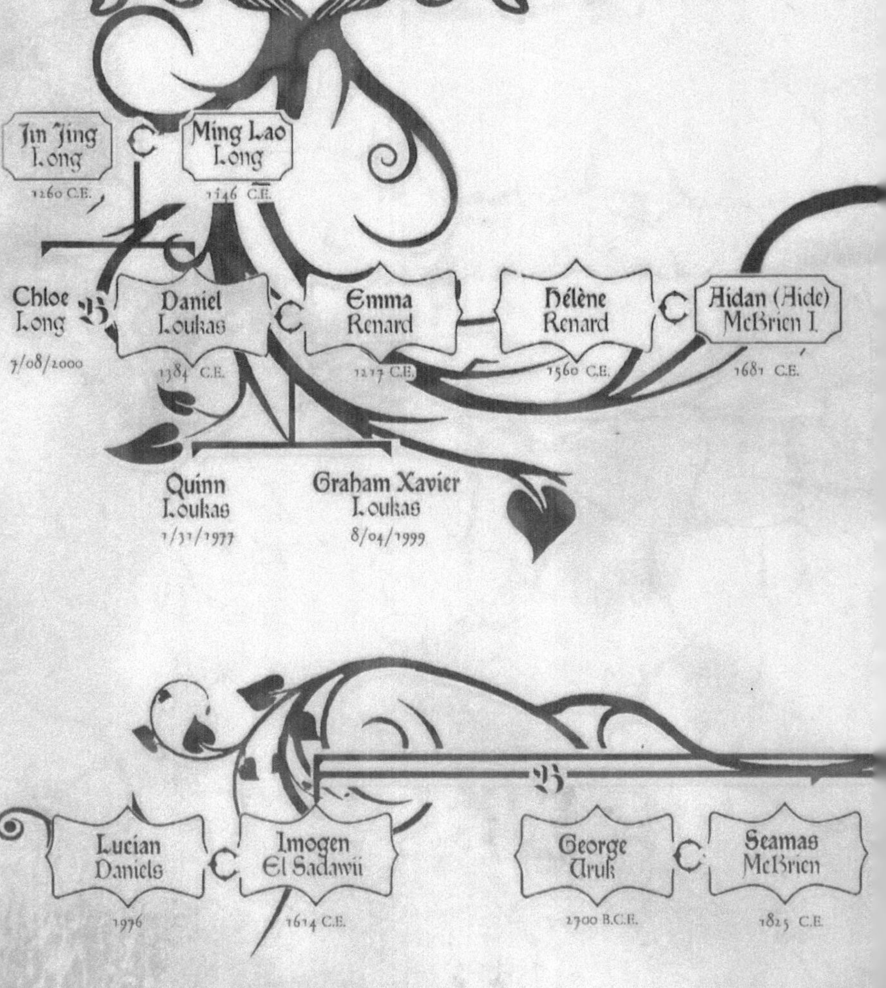

Jin Jing Long
1260 C.E.
C
Ming Lao Long
1146 C.E.
Chloe Long
7/08/2000
B
Daniel Loukas
1384 C.E.
C
Emma Renard
1217 C.E.
Hélène Renard
1560 C.E.
C
Aidan (Aide) McBrien I.
1681 C.E.
Quinn Loukas
1/31/1977
Graham Xavier Loukas
8/04/1999
Lucian Daniels
1976
C
Imogen El Sadawii
1614 C.E.
B
George Uruk
2700 B.C.E.
C
Seamas McBrien
1825 C.E.

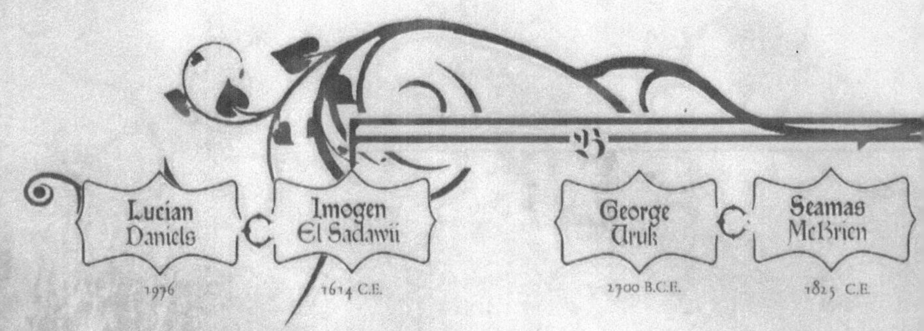

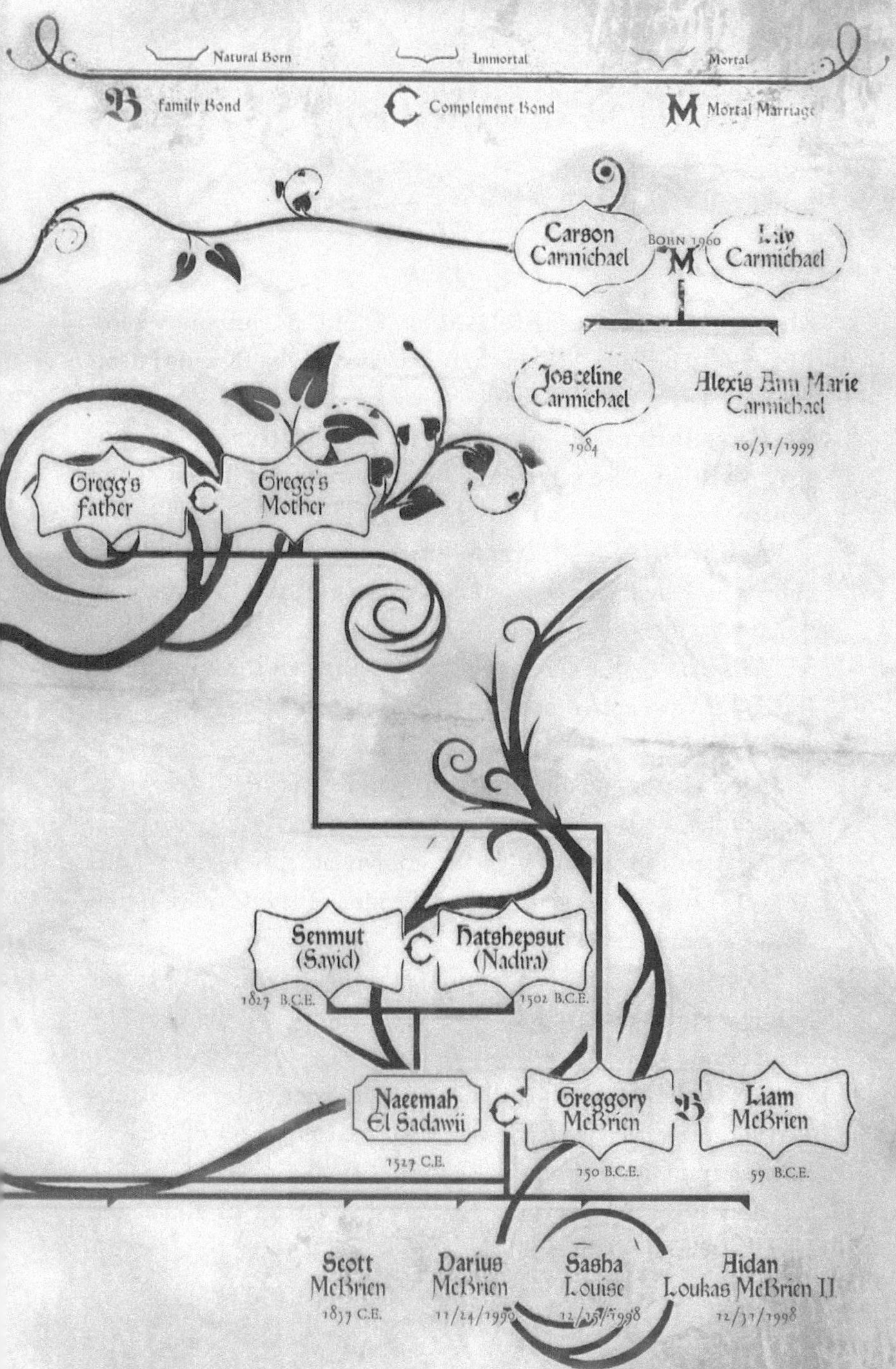

Natural Born
Immortal
Mortal
B family Bond
C Complement Bond
M Mortal Marriage
Carson Carmichael
Born 1960
M
Liv Carmichael
Josceline Carmichael
1984
Alexis Ann Marie Carmichael
10/31/1999
Gregg's father
C
Gregg's Mother
Senmut (Sayid)
1827 B.C.E.
C
Hatshepsut (Nadira)
1502 B.C.E.
Naeemah El Sadawii
1527 C.E.
C
Greggory McBrien
150 B.C.E.
B
Liam McBrien
59 B.C.E.
Scott McBrien
1837 C.E.
Darius McBrien
11/24/1990
Sasha Louise
12/25/1998
Aidan Loukas McBrien II
12/31/1998

Additional Cast List for Heir

Alexis (Allie) Carmichael – Child of prophecy and adopted daughter of mortal parents, Lily and Carson Carmichael

Kassandre – Allie's natural mother. Syntrophos to Greggory McBrien. Also served as Chief Justice of the International Senate

Ashar – Allie's natural father. A dream walker, also known as Navid. Served as Chief Justice of the International Senate

Alísun – Allie's ancient grandmother and last queen of Indriell. Was captive of Marcus Servius for almost two-thousand years

Alexander – Allie's ancient grandfather. Also known as the Scholar

Marcus Servius – Also known as the ancient Lord Teigan. Livia's "adopted" father. Leader of the Coalition and owner of Soma

Porcia – Livia's adopted mother and wife to Marcus Servius (Porcia and Marcus have never completed the Complement bond)

Livia McBrien – Allie's natural sister. Also known as Alivia. Former leader of Soma, "adopted" daughter of Marcus Servius and Complement to Liam McBrien.

Kahlynn McBrien – Adopted daughter of Liam and Livia McBrien

Dean McBrien – Son of Aidan (Aide) McBrien I and Hélène Renard. Cousin to Sasha and Aidan McBrien II. Former Soma slave

Tessa St. James – Former Soma slave. Girlfriend and equal of Dean McBrien

Lennox McBrien – Former Soma slave. Adopted daughter of Seamas McBrien and George Uruk

Jayesh Basu – Friend to Sasha McBrien and current leader of Soma

Naomi Hauser – Friend to Aidan McBrien and daughter of Greyson Hauser, long time friend of the McBrien family

Emma Renard—Mentor to Allie Carmichael. Complement to Daniel Loukas. Mother to Quinn, Graham and Parker Loukas

Alex Parker Loukas – Two-year-old natural born son of Emma Renard and Daniel Loukas. Godson to Alexis Carmichael.

Known Syntrophos pairs

Alexis Carmichael and Darius McBrien

Sasha McBrien and Quinn Loukas

Greggory McBrien and the ancient, Kassandre

Author's Note

Heir takes place four years after the events of Judgment and Captive. Allie's ancient roots play an important role in this new addition to the series. I have included the original backstory of the Queens of Indriell as a refresher for those who need it. Look for it at the back of the book in the table of contents.

My upcoming book, Betrayal will circle back to the timeline between Judgment and Heir, and will be a dual point of view novel between Allie and Aidan. I hope you enjoy this look into their future before we go back to learn how their journeys have led them to this point.

—Melissa A. Craven

PROLOGUE

From the private journals of
Alexander, the Scholar

I am the ghost of history, one of the oldest living Immortals and Complement to the last queen of Indriell. I am the man no one remembers. It is my destiny to witness and record history. That is my role as the Scholar.

I don't take many things seriously, but my duty to knowledge is one of them. I document the events I witness through the omniscient power of my gift, and I do not dare alter the details of what I've seen. But sometimes I must ... fudge it. The banishment of the first mortals was one of those dark times. As our history recalls, Queen Alísun exiled the mortals from Indriell to prevent the disease of death from spreading. And then she dismantled Indriell, erasing all traces of her nation from the face of the earth. As the taint of mortality began to subside among the Immortal children, the queen sent her remaining subjects into the world to watch over our mortal brethren, for the world belonged to them now.

But that's not quite how it went down.

For thousands of years, we've taught our children this bittersweet fairytale version of Indriell's history. In reality, we've fed them a pack of lies. But the best lies are rooted in truth. Just as my lovely wife recorded a false prophecy to protect the identity of our granddaughter, I recorded a false history to protect our people from the crimes of their ancestors.

The queen banished the mortals, not to protect the Immortals from the threat of death, but from the witch-hunt that was happening despite our best efforts to stop it. We were dangerously close to another war. Most wanted to wipe out the scourge of the mortal children, bathing them in fire to rid the world of death. Mortals gathered in huge numbers to protest, creating the very foundation of the Coalition. The hatred between the races escalated. And so Queen Alísun banished the mortals to protect them from those who would see them slaughtered.

Our mortal son, Kristopher, led the banished from Indriell. That was the last we saw of him, but I kept my eye on him through the power of my gift. I watched him grow into a strong and courageous man, but Alísun was like a wounded animal when he left. Driven by hatred for those who had given her no other choice but to forsake her only child, the queen destroyed Indriell. Once a beautiful place of lush green forests and fertile plains as far as the eye could see, the queen and her council transformed Indriell into the wild and dangerous jungles of South America. They leveled cities and towns. Raised mountains, rivers, and forests filled with dangerous creatures. They made it uninhabitable for those accustomed to the luxuries of Indriell.

The remaining Immortals scattered across the world while Alísun and I sought a quiet life together—a time of peace after years of war, strife, and sorrow. When our daughter, Kassandre, was born, we finally put the past behind us and looked to the future.

As our numbers grew and the Coalition zealots became a

problem, the Immortal Senate was born. A governing body we desperately needed. They became a successful substitute for the Indriell queens.

Until they weren't.

I've seen our world change so many times. I've watched Immortals adjust and adapt with each passing generation. I've seen them flounder and stumble, and I've seen them survive the darkest of times against all odds. We are approaching one of those times. The Senate has grown corrupt and threatens our future, particularly that of our children, whom they have exploited time and again for personal gain.

We are at a crossroads unlike anything I've seen since the days of Indriell. The future lies shrouded in darkness, yet we will face it together as a unified community. We can no longer stand quietly on the sidelines watching others rule in corruption. It is time to act. It is time for the resurrection of the ancient queens.

—Alexander, the Scholar

CHAPTER

1

"Here you go, Gramps," Allie placed the worn leather journal on the table beside her grandfather's favorite armchair.

"Done with this one already, Allie-girl?" Alexander reached for the book.

"Are you kidding? It was fascinating to read about the sack of Carthage from someone who actually witnessed it. I sobbed like a baby when Grandma Alísun was taken by the Coalition after." Allie flopped onto the sofa across from him, exhausted after a long afternoon with Emma. "I never realized she spent so many years in a Coalition prison until Marcus got her out of there and took her captive himself."

"At first it was a relief to know she was finally free from that awful prison. But Marcus's prison was worse in so many ways."

"But grandma was able to know Livia. At least from a distance." Allie was often jealous of the relationship her sister had with their grandmother.

"Watching her granddaughter grow up was a comfort to her during the final years of her captivity. Truth be told, I'm a little jealous." Alexander lowered his voice. "But I'd never tell her that."

"What else you got for me, grandpa? The destruction of Pompeii? The fall of the Roman Empire?"

He winked. "I'll send you home with a few more of my private journals if you like reading the aimless musings of an old scholar."

"Aimless musings?" A smile tugged at her lips. "You should write thrillers, old man."

"Who says I don't?"

"Auntie, are they here yet?" Kahlynn McBrien raced into the common room and pounced on Allie's lap. The seven-year-old girl was getting too big for such entrances, but Allie refused to be the one to tell her to stop.

"Almost, kiddo." Allie smiled at the excitement in her niece's cornflower blue eyes. "They're on the ferry right now. I can see them just over there." Allie pointed across the room where the spectral shapes of her visions were taking form. Her newest visions weren't always easy to decipher. They mostly looked like red, orange, and green people-shaped blobs, like one would see through an infrared lens. But Kahlynn didn't need to know that. Allie could see a couple that vaguely resembled Liam and Livia standing on the deck of the ferryboat making its way to Kelleys Island this very moment.

"Are you excited? I can't tell if you're excited." Allie folded her arms across her chest in mock seriousness, ignoring the shifting, indistinct forms floating around her. She still struggled with this newest manifestation of her clairvoyance, but she'd found a way to keep the spectral figures isolated to her peripheral vision, only allowing them out in moments like this when she wanted to examine them. She'd learned to cope with her gift, but when it first began to evolve, it was impossible to function like a non-crazy person.

"I can't believe it's finally official. I have a mom!" Kahlynn zoomed around the common room like a Tasmanian devil, until she finally settled down beside Allie on the sofa to wait for Liam and Livia to return from their honeymoon.

Allie couldn't believe it either. She loved her sister, but they'd traveled down a long road littered with the broken glass of heartache, betrayal, and forgiveness before they finally arrived where they were now. Livia was unrecognizable from the hateful woman she had been the night she became a captive of the McBriens four years ago. And an incredibly long four years it was. Allie could hardly remember what it was like to think of Livia as an enemy and not a sister.

"What do you think, Grandpa Alex?" Allie shot her grandfather a wink. "She's not nearly excited enough. And I'm not sure her new mom is even going to recognize her after a month away."

"She's grown so much, her dad might not recognize her either," Alexander said, putting on his most serious Scholar face.

"He wouldn't dare," Kahlynn said in a huff. "Liv—Mom would kill him."

Allie admired the way Livia and her new daughter had bonded so quickly. Allie suspected she saw the girl's innocence as something to protect. Kahlynn was everything Livia should have been if circumstances hadn't taken her from her family at such a young age.

"Are they here yet?" Kahlynn asked again.

"Not yet, but I think we have other matters to discuss, don't we?" Allie eyed her niece with a frown. "Out with it, kid. What do you got for me?"

The girl emptied her coat pockets of chocolate bars, potato chips, and snack cakes she'd pilfered from the kitchen when Naeemah wasn't looking.

"Did you forget your great-grandpa?" The Scholar gave the little girl a wounded look.

"No way, Gramps." Kahlynn handed him a fist full of beef jerky.

"You two are diabolical." Darius shook his head as he watched them from kitchen doorway. "Using the kid to feed your bad habits."

Allie beamed at the sight of him, the Syntrophos bond igniting between them like a living thing. "You're just sad because she didn't bring you anything." Allie tore into a bag of potato chips, sharing a secretive smile with her niece.

"Alísun doesn't think jerky qualifies as real food." Sighing, Alexander leaned back in his overstuffed armchair. "I beg to differ." He cracked open a beef stick and inhaled the spicy scent. "It's the best food there is."

"You two are dangerous." Darius came to sit beside Allie. "What kind of trouble did you get up to yesterday? Your cover story of 'going out to dinner' was total BS."

"We went skydiving," Alexander said.

"In the dead of winter?" Darius asked.

"It was awesome." Allie leaned across the side table to give her grandpa a high-five. Of all her Immortal family, she'd slipped into her relationship with Alexander as if she'd known him her whole life. He was so easy to love, and it didn't hurt that they were pretty much the same person.

"So that's why my heart stopped for no reason yesterday afternoon?" Darius said. "Give me a heads up next time you two decide to get destructive."

"Sorry, Dare." She squeezed his hand. Their bond hummed with the satisfaction of reunion.

"Where are they now, Allie?" Kahlynn asked eagerly.

Allie glanced around, checking for the ghostly images still wandering about the room. "Oh, it looks like they're in the tunnel. You'd better go if you want to meet them in the hall."

Kahlynn shot to her feet and raced across the common room. "Daddy's home!"

Allie took a deep breath, pushing the spectral figures back

into her peripheral vision now that she no longer needed them. Her chest heated with the use of her power, casting her world with a tinge of green light as the forms reluctantly receded. Just as she exhaled, she thought she saw some familiar faces among the shapeless blobs but couldn't be certain. It was a struggle to force the visions out of her main line of sight, but once she managed it, they stayed there. She could still see them, but it made it easier to function if they weren't right in front of her face.

"Where are my girls?" Liam's voice echoed across the vaulted hall as he raced to scoop Kahlynn up into a big bear hug and kept moving into the common to envelop Allie in his arms—Kahlynn clinging to him like a monkey.

"We missed you," Allie said, burrowing into her brother's side. A month was a long time to be away from her brother and sister—who were now married. To each other. "Where's your sister-wife?" She grinned up at him.

Liam rolled his eyes. "We've told you a thousand times, your sister is *not* my sister. That's not how this works."

"My mortal brain just can't see it like that."

"The natural bond between us would have been as brother and sister-in-*law*, but because we met first and neither of us knew Livia, we bonded as brother and sister instead because that was the only way we could understand our relationship. It does *not* make Livia my sister and my wife."

"If you say so, bro." Allie slapped him on the back. She got it. It made perfect sense, but she liked messing with him.

"Stop teasing him, Allie," Livia said as she entered the room. "Even though he does make a rather large and easy target." She winked, reaching to hug Allie. "I missed you way more than I care to admit." Livia gave her an extra squeeze, almost cutting off her circulation.

"Missed you too, Liv." Allie gazed into her sister's silver

eyes. Those eyes used to be so full of hate and resentment, but now they sparkled with happiness. Livia was still a guarded and severe woman. She probably always would be, but Allie also knew her sister didn't feel like she deserved the life she had now. Allie sometimes still felt a lingering resentment toward the woman her sister used to be, but Livia was not that woman anymore. She'd redeemed herself and deserved whatever goodness life had in store for her now.

"Can I have the munchkin now?" Livia held out her arms. "I need to squeeze her."

Liam beamed as he passed his daughter to her mother.

"I missed you ... Mom." Kahlynn buried her face in Livia's shoulder.

Livia wrapped her arms around the girl, inhaling the scent of her hair. "I missed you, too, Munchkin."

"What'd you bring me?" Kahlynn glanced up at her mother.

"Your mom has plans to spoil you rotten with all the presents she brought home from our honeymoon," Liam said. "But I need to get a report on your behavior before you get anything." Liam grasped Kahlynn's hand as he turned to Allie. "Give it to me straight, Auntie Allie. Was she a holy terror for you or your parents?"

"I don't know what you mean. Kahlynn's a perfect angel," Allie insisted.

"Right. I forgot who I was asking." Liam shook his head. "What new bad habits have you taught her?"

Allie gave him an affronted look. "We did homework together every night after training and when I had class, she was on her best behavior for my parents."

Liam rolled his eyes and turned to Darius for a translation.

"Behind all that waffle about angels and best behaviors,

Kahlynn was her usual mischievous, prank-loving self, but she was mostly good. It's these three together that can't be trusted." Darius gestured at Allie and Alexander. "Vince and Kayla helped with babysitting during our few evening classes, and she spent most of her afternoons with Lily and Carson after school and training."

"I see." Liam frowned. "Didn't we talk about that before I left?" He turned to Allie with an accusing glare. A glare that would make most people tremble in fear.

"We did, but I decided you're an ass," Allie said, folding her arms over her chest. "The munchkin loves Vince and Kayla, and they are happy to babysit—for free, I might add. So don't get your undies in a twist about it."

"Fine." Liam grumbled. He'd always had a difficult time trusting Allie's mortal friends with his daughter. He felt like they had a little too much interest in her.

"By the way, what'd you bring me?" Allie cocked her head and smiled.

"Aren't you too old for presents by now? You just had your twenty-first birthday."

"As long as I live, I will never be too old for presents, Liam. And my birthday was months ago. We'll be gearing up for my twenty-second soon."

"I may have gotten you a little something." His serious demeanor thawed with the half smile he reserved just for her.

"I'd settle for an open tab at your bar," Allie said, grinning. "The law says I'm old enough."

"As far as I'm concerned, I'm the law inside my bars, and they are no place for you or your friends. And no, you don't get an open tab. Are you nuts?"

"If you got me a snow globe, I'm going to divorce you."

"He got you a leather jacket in Milan," Livia interjected.

"You'll love it. I got you a fully stocked wine fridge for the cottage."

"Wine and leather, that's more like it." Allie wrapped her arm around her sister's waist. Her hair stood on end as an icy prickling sensation swept through her. *The Ice Queen's here.* Allie and her grandmother—Queen Alísun of Indriell—hadn't always seen eye to eye. Allie loved and respected her grandma, but the queenly side of Alísun made for one intimidating Immortal.

"Relax, Allie. Your face is going to freeze like that." Livia turned to greet their grandmother.

"It's so good to have both my girls home again," Alísun said softly as she hugged her granddaughter. "I trust you've had a relaxing honeymoon?" Leaning back, she gave Livia a once over.

"It was wonderful," Livia replied.

"You both deserve it." The queen turned to her new great-granddaughter. "Kahlynn, darling." She bent down to her level. "Run along to the kitchens. Emma and Parker have a treat for you."

"Bring me some," Allie whispered before Kahlynn ran off to find Emma and her two-year-old son, Parker.

"Now that we're all together for once, I'd like to call a family meeting in the yard," Alísun said. "Navid will meet us there."

"I'll catch up with you later," Darius said, squeezing Allie's hand.

"Nonsense. You are my granddaughter's Syntrophos, Darius. You are family," the queen said.

"Uh, thank you. Ma'am." Darius was always flustered whenever the queen spoke directly to him. Allie felt the same way but for different reasons. Whenever the queen looked at her, Allie felt like she was disappointed with what she saw. Alísun was an ancient prophetess who foretold of Allie's birth thousands of years ago. Allie couldn't help but think there was no way she'd ever measure up to her grandmother's expectations.

Chapter 2

Allie elbowed Darius in the ribs as they followed the queen down the underground corridor leading to the yard. The royals had taken up residence there for the last several years. "Stop fidgeting," she whispered.

"Why am I here?" he asked.

"I don't even know why *I'm* here." She smiled nervously, waving at Navid as they crossed the grassy lawn. Navid spent most of his time in the yard after his accident in the dreamworld a few years ago. He was still recovering and getting better every day, but it had taken a toll.

"Gather round everyone." The queen gestured for them to sit around the picnic table at the pavilion beside the small underground lake. She and Alexander had a little cabin in the woods just a short way down the hiking trail, and Navid lived alone in the nearby cottage along the lake. He spent his days relaxing and fishing at the dock, enjoying the peaceful environment in the safety of the underground. The low stress level was just what he needed during his recovery.

"Welcome home, darling," Navid said, taking Livia into his arms. "It's so wonderful to see our family growing again." He cast his eyes around the small group. Alísun and Alexander stood at the head of the table while the others took their seats.

"These last few years have been such a joy, getting to know my family again," Alísun began. "For so long, we've been scattered across the globe. It's been wonderful learning what it's like to be a family together." A rare smile lit her face, transforming her from the proverbial ice queen into the warm, kind grandma Allie preferred. "We welcome Liam, Kahlynn, and Darius with open arms, and we are honored to have you join our small family." The warm moment faded as Alísun returned to the reason she'd called them together.

Perching on top of the table behind her, Alísun was casually dressed in jeans and a white t-shirt, yet she still managed to look like a queen on her throne. "I dissolved the nation of Indriell so long ago sometimes I can hardly remember those days. The royal family ruled the Immortal world for thousands of years before my birth, but I was the one who destroyed it." Alísun's eyes held a shadow of the tears she'd shed for her people. "It was one of the most difficult decisions Alexander and I have ever made. And we have been party to some difficult decisions." She grasped Allie and Livia's hands.

"My reign was vastly different from my parent's and grandparent's. I inherited a broken nation at war. I inherited chaos and death. But as a child, I learned of the old ways. Liam, as Complement to a princess of Indriell, you would have held a position of honor on the queen's council. Darius, as a Syntrophos to an Indriell princess, you would likely have commanded the queen's army."

The color drained from Darius's face, and Allie squeezed his hand in sympathy. In moments like this, she felt really bad for him. He'd never asked for any of this, yet he found himself in the midst of more drama than he ever bargained for.

"In ages past, the queens had multiple children," Alísun continued. "Long before our fertility rates declined. In the old days, a queen would name her heir, choosing among her children for the rightful queen to rule the nation. Someone who would bring the Immortal race into the future as a thriving, peaceful community. Her other children would be given high offices in service to their future queen. Many sons of the Indriell queens served as their sister's second—an ally and trusted advisor."

Alísun sat back, resting her hands on her knees. She seemed a million miles away, haunted by the past. "But those days are gone," she said sadly. "During my reign, the world changed. We did heinous things that ultimately gave birth to the mortal race. Alexander and I had another child once. A son. Kristopher." She glanced at her husband. "For years we watched him grow into a beautiful, strong prince. But we worried, like all parents did during those days. Would he be like me and the other children of my generation who were among the first to experience an Awakening, or would he be afflicted like so many other post-war children? On his sixteenth birthday, we knew. Kristopher was mortal. My only son. I loved him despite his *disability*. But my duty was to my people, both Immortal and mortal alike. You all know the true reasons I destroyed Indriell. History says I did it to protect the Immortals from the disease of mortality, but I did it to save my mortal subjects from those who would see them annihilated. I destroyed my inheritance and never looked back. Until now." Alísun drew a shaky hand across her forehead.

Alexander laid a sympathetic hand on her shoulder. "After we left Indriell and our numbers grew once more, the Senate ultimately took the place of the Indriell queens."

"And they've done a remarkable job." Alísun gave a weary sigh. "I was content to fade into the history books and leave our world in their capable hands."

"But they are like turds spinning around the rim of a clogged toilet now," Alexander said.

"Eloquently put, as usual, Husband." The queen managed a ghost of a smile. "The Senate has grown corrupt. There are other entities now, like Soma and their Amrita front, that threaten the future of our children. And our government is their best customer." Alísun shook her head in dismay.

"I have never officially renounced my title. As long as my line exists, Indriell still exists. There is a chance our family still commands enough respect that others would look to us to lead again. It could mean war. It could mean the beginning of another dark time in our history, but I believe it is a necessary risk. I can no longer stand on the sidelines watching others rule in deceit."

"You're going to resurrect Indriell?" Livia asked.

Alísun nodded. "In a manner of speaking, yes. But I am old. This modern world is not mine to rule. This world is for the young. We cannot expect to return to the old ways. It would never work. We must set a new course for the coming generations."

"And how do you plan to do that?" Allie asked, glancing nervously at Livia.

"If I were to publicly name my heir, it would speak of the royal family's intention to step forward as leaders again. Should the people respond positively to the act of the naming, it would be our royal right to intercede where we feel the Senate is failing."

Allie reached for Darius's hand under the table. "Not it," Allie whispered. *Please don't let her choose me.*

"And what does that mean?" Livia asked, ignoring Allie's quiet freak out.

"What that means and what happens from there is for the heir to decide. After the naming, it would be her decision." Alísun attempted to catch Allie's gaze, but Allie cast her eyes down at her hands twisting in her lap.

"And you are ready to make this announcement public?" Navid asked.

"Not public. But I have chosen my heir. I am ready to name the new first princess of Indriell, for our family's ears alone ... for the moment.

Allie closed her eyes and tried to swallow. *This is not happening*. Her heart hammered in her chest, her power churning deep inside her as she reached for Darius's hand like a lifeline.

"I have chosen Allie as my heir." The queen's words fell with a resounding thud in Allie's mind. Ancient power filled her words with finality. "I chose her even before she was born," she added softly.

Allie gasped, a tear splashing on her hand still entwined with Darius's.

"Look at me, Allie," Alísun said. This was her grandma speaking, not the ice queen. Allie lifted her gaze to meet her grandmother's.

"I am so sorry, my darling. But you are the child of prophecy. You are destined to lead us. I have always known you would struggle to accept this mantle. I have given you as much time as I dare, but I have faith that you will soon come to understand you are the right person for the job."

"But Livia is the eldest," Allie said, desperate to find any excuse to avoid this madness.

"She is, but that has never been recognized as significant when it comes to choosing an heir. Livia will be your champion. Your second in command. She will be the one you trust as much as you trust your Syntrophos and your future Complement. Her hard life has prepared her for this role as much as yours has prepared you."

"I'm not ready for this, Grandma," Allie choked. "Please,

it's too much. I can't be the right one. You need someone like Navid. Someone older and wiser. I will screw this up."

"The naming is complete," Alísun murmured, sadness etched across her features. But in the next instant, the queen steadied her voice and lifted her chin. "Alexis Ann Marie Carmichael, you are my heir and the first princess of Indriell. The question now is what will you do with it?"

"That old nut-job has lost her damn mind." Allie swerved across two lanes of traffic to catch her exit for the Shoreway.

"Could you slow down?" Darius gripped the edge of his seat. "Just down to about eighty would be great. I'd like to get back home in one piece."

"Of all the things she's said over the years, that was just ... she's senile. She has to be. Do ancients get Alzheimer's, do you think? We should have her checked out."

"She isn't the crazy one, Red."

"She's just—she creeps me out." Allie shivered. "When she gives you that ice queen stare, it's like she's looking right through you, seeing all of your inadequacies like the gunk on the bottom of her shoe."

"Yet, she still named you her heir."

"Because she's crazy."

"Because she loves you."

"I know grandma Alísun loves me. It's the queen part of her that causes all these problems."

"She believes in you, Allie."

"That's great. When your grandma believes in you, it should be like she thinks you're going to be the world's greatest graphic designer. It should not be, hey, your batty grandma thinks you're going to be the next dictator of the world."

"That's not what she said."

"First princess of Indriell, Darius. What am I supposed to do with that? If she knew me at all, she would know that is the absolute last thing I would ever want."

"Can you imagine for one second how that might be appealing to a queen who wants to choose the right leader for her people? That she might want someone who wasn't power hungry? Someone who recognizes the burden of ruling for what it is? She chose you because she believes you are the right person to follow in her footsteps."

"Aren't you supposed to be on my side?" Allie glared at him. But she knew he was right. Allie should be honored that the queen chose her. And she truly was honored, but under that humbled feeling was a fear so intense, she couldn't even process it.

"Of course, I'm on your side. Don't you think I'm crapping myself over this, too? I'm the Syntrophos of the first princess. When you become queen, I'll be expected to lead your council or army, or some other shit I'm not prepared for. I'm a cop, not a politician."

Allie's eyes shifted to meet his as she exited the Shoreway, speeding down the ramp into Cleveland traffic. He was just as freaked out by this as she was, yet he was still trying to calm her down.

"We are the *worst* people for this job." A worried frown creased her forehead.

"Right? Can you even imagine?" Darius forced a laugh.

"She can't be serious, right? She just can't be that crazy."

"I'm afraid the queen doesn't have much of a sense of humor, princess."

"You want to keep your face looking pretty, never call me

that again." Allie glanced in the rearview mirror as she changed lanes.

"Allie, she's looking at the big picture. The woman is a prophet, and she's seen literally everything that has ever happened. She's almost eight thousand years old. She's not just Immortal; she's a legend. I imagine she knows what she's doing. I *hope* she knows what she's doing," he added with a note of alarm in his voice.

"It should be Livia. Livia is so much stronger and better prepared for this. And older. An experienced leader."

"Yeah, Liv with all the experience leading her evil minions into the mass market slave trade." Darius arched a brow at her.

Allie shot him a dirty look. "You know she never had a choice in that. And she's still more experienced than I am," she muttered, clutching the steering wheel with a white knuckled grip.

"But she's not you, Red. Alísun's not going to push you into this. She knows you well enough to know you need time to wrap your mortal brain around what she's offering. The naming was just for the family. This isn't happening right now and probably won't any time soon."

"You're right. As usual." She released her death grip on the steering wheel and reached for his hand. It was instinctive—the urge to touch him when she was upset. The bond craved it. "I just can't see myself ever accepting this role. There has to be someone better suited for this."

"The queen chose you."

"And we're back at the question of her sanity." Allie sighed.

"She sees something ahead. Something bad." Darius clutched the safety handle as Allie slammed on the brakes for a red light.

"Me and my mortal brain just aren't ready for this." Allie

shook her head. She liked her quiet, normal life. She'd worked hard and sacrificed too much to see it change now.

"Did you even listen to what she said?"

"I was kind of busy trying not to freak out." Allie swerved across two lanes of slow-moving traffic and back again to avoid the shifting, blob-like figures standing in the road. In her current state of mind, she'd let her focus drop, and her visions were commanding too much of her attention. Some of them even had faces. Faces she knew she should stop and study, but her head just wasn't in the right place for that.

"When she talks about the banished mortals, she thinks of them as her children. Her son was one of the original mortals. I've only ever heard one other Immortal talk of them with such reverence and respect. And she's sitting right next to me, driving like a maniac. Seriously." He put his foot on the dash. "You should not be driving right now."

"I'd be happy to be part of something bigger," Allie said, ignoring Darius's concerns. "She's right; things do need to change. But why do I have to be the force behind that change? What's the rest of our world going to think?"

"Since when do you care about what other people think?"

"I just want to go home and focus on school, Dare." Allie threw her hands up in defeat.

"Keep. Your. Hands. On. The damned wheel, Alexis Carmichael."

"It's our last semester, and I want to enjoy it. I just ... I can't think about this right now."

"You say enjoy, I say endure. I can't wait 'til this education crap is behind us." Darius scrubbed his hand over his face.

"This will not be the only time I go to college, Darius. I like learning, and I have multiple lifetimes ahead of me. I will go back to school. Often."

"Well, the next time you decide to further your education,

can we just make me your loser live-in boyfriend, so I don't actually have to get another degree?"

"You majored in Photography, Darius." Allie arched her brow. "And I do most of your homework for you."

"It sounded fun at the time and an easy way for us to take a lot of the same classes, but photography requires way more talent than I actually have," Darius said. "When we're done, I'm going back to being a homicide detective."

"You didn't have to quit the CPD," Allie said. It bothered her to no end that he'd sacrificed the job he loved just to be with her, doing something he hated.

He shot a grin at her. "You know I needed to be near you, Red."

"I never expected you to give up your career for me. You could have kept your job, and we could have seen each other in the evenings and on weekends."

"That would have driven us both insane." He took her hand. "I can't be away from you like that."

"I wouldn't have liked it either, but I want you to be happy. I want that more than I want my own happiness."

"I am happy, Allie. More than I've ever been. We agreed; college first and then when you get your first job, I'll go back to detective work."

"Or assistant to the queen in training," Allie muttered.

CHAPTER 4

"Are you even going to sleep tonight?" Darius rubbed a hand across his tired eyes.

Allie violently fluffed the pillows on her bed back at the sweet little lake cottage they shared with Sasha, Quinn, and Santi near campus. "Probably not but you need to sleep."

"Just because I need to sleep doesn't mean you have to." Darius stood in the doorway of their adjoining rooms, dressed in black pajama pants and a soft gray t-shirt.

Allie cracked a smile. "How many times have I told you that same thing?"

"A million." He crossed the room to flop down onto her freshly made bed. "But it's only because neither of us wants to be sleeping when the other is awake." He reached for her hand, pulling her down beside him.

Allie curled into his side. "You'd think after all this time, we wouldn't still feel the need to be within arm's reach of each other."

"It makes for a long day when we have separate classes." He sighed, maneuvering them so Allie lay in the crook of his arm. For nearly four years, they'd structured their course schedules so they never had to spend more than a few hours apart. The rest of the time they were in class together.

"You could have majored in the graphic arts with me, so we'd have the exact same schedule."

"They would have kicked me out in the first semester. The art history classes alone have been my nemesis, yet you insist on taking them every single semester." He rolled his eyes.

"Hey." Allie flipped back toward him. "Those are the easiest classes for us to take together. And I happen to love art history."

"Professor Wilson actually asked me to stop taking his classes." He laughed, absently tracing the lines of the tattoo along her throat. He stopped at the neckline of her t-shirt, but the tattoo continued, snaking down her side from her jawline to her hip, concealing the worst of the scar she'd received the night she was shot with a Coalition bullet. "Are you okay, Red?"

She nodded.

"I know you're mad as hell about this heir business, but behind all that fire and brimstone you're throwing around with those fiery green eyes of yours, I know you're just scared."

"Terrified." Allie closed her eyes. She wouldn't admit it to anyone else, but she was frightened beyond anything she'd ever felt before. "What if I actually end up being a freaking princess? Or worse, a queen?"

"I don't think it's something you can really escape," Darius said. "You're a royal; it's who you are whether you like it or not.

"Royal-schmoyal." Allie settled onto her side pulling Darius's arm around her. "I'm the heir of a dead nation."

"Just take a deep breath and remember we don't have to deal with any of this now. Nothing may ever come of it anyway."

"You're right. Grandma said it's my choice what to do with my title. I can't see myself ever reaching for that kind of power."

"And we have bigger things to worry about right now." He heaved a big sigh.

"What could possibly be bigger?"

"I have to graduate in a few months. You'll be fine, but it'll be a miracle if I actually make it."

"You'll make it if I have to drag your dead carcass across the finish line. Go to sleep, Dare. We're okay." Allie kissed his palm.

"You sure?" His midnight blue eyes were filled with concern as he gazed down at her.

"I'm sure."

"I'm like four feet away if you need me."

"Go to bed." She shoved his face playfully.

"Night, Allie. Love you." He crossed the room to the double doors that never closed between them.

"Love you, too." Allie rolled over, turning her bedside lamp off. It was nice having him so near. They were closer than she could imagine any two people being, but their Syntrophos bond made it easy. Too easy sometimes. In the beginning, it was awkward, and their feelings were so confusing. They craved each other like air, but their desire to remain close had also remained completely platonic.

Darius was her ride or die guy. If he killed someone, she'd be the one reloading the smoking gun, no questions asked. His love was like her morning coffee. It was a given. She never had to question it or worry that it wouldn't always be there. Just like his loyalty. From the moment they met, Darius was the one who reminded her to have fun and never take life too seriously. He was the one who encouraged her to reach for her dreams, but he was also the one to tell her like it was. Darius didn't sugar coat things. He was her rock. And despite the intimacy their bond demanded, there were no romantic feelings between them.

The love she shared with Darius gave her almost everything she needed. Almost. But she still craved romance, like any girl. But that kind of love had walked out of her life years ago without a backward glance.

It still hurt. Even after all this time.

Goodnight, Aidan... wherever you are.

Allie ran through the dark corridors, up and down stairs, checking every door as she went. They were all locked.

Sweat beaded her brow, and her heart thumped in her chest as she ran, her bare feet pounding against the cool marble tile. She rounded a corner in the never-ending sea of hallways, catching a glimpse of a dark shadow at the other end.

She pursued the shadow, desperate to lay eyes on him. To finally understand why she chased him. She'd raced through these halls so many times; she knew the labyrinth by heart. Darting down a narrow corridor, Allie reached the other side of the building, cutting off her phantom shadow. She would see him this time.

He ran toward her, his face guarded in shadows as he looked over his shoulder, expecting to find her behind him.

Allie reached for the hood of his jacket and as she felt the fabric in her hands, he dissolved into nothing.

"Aidan," she gasped as she sat up in bed, her heart still pounding from the same old nightmare that had haunted her for years. Tears soaked her pillow, and her heart shattered all over again.

With a deep breath, she tossed the covers aside, despite the chill of the late winter night. She glanced into Darius's room, hoping she hadn't disturbed him. His breath came in the familiar even pattern of sleep.

She lowered herself back against the pillows, checking the time. Three in the morning. Nine o'clock in Germany where Aidan lived. At least he had the last time she'd heard anything about him. Her heart still ached with missing him. She hid it well, but it still hit her hard in these moments of solitude. She'd moved on. They both had. She'd created a life for herself. The normal life she'd always wanted. As normal as a young Immortal's life could ever hope to be.

They were both doing the college thing now. She'd been content with that for these last few years, but now that she was in her last semester and the next chapter of her life was on the horizon, she thought of him more often than she cared to admit. What would happen when they both left college behind?

Would he even want to see me again? Would I? The night he'd chosen to end their telepathic connection was one of the most horrifying moments of her life. She'd worked hard to put it behind her, rarely letting herself think about him. He'd left her with no other choice but to move on.

I want you to have your own life, Allie. We're young. We both need time to figure out who we are. Without each other. His final words had echoed in her mind for months after he left. The sentiments had been her own. It was ironic that her reasons for why they should never have been together in the first place ended up being his reasons for leaving.

From the moment they met and she finally knew what it was like to truly have a friend, her greatest fear had been that loving Aidan would ruin everything. It seemed she was right all along. Those few short weeks after she'd admitted she loved him were some of the happiest Allie had ever known. But things changed. Aidan was different, withdrawn and distracted. She knew he still loved her or had when he first chose to leave for what was supposed to be one semester abroad. But then he'd failed to keep his promises to see her during their months apart. And then he just never came back. Stopped answering her calls. Changed his number. The son of a bitch ghosted her.

At the time, it gutted her, but after four years, it just made her sad that she couldn't look back on what they'd once had with fond memories. It was all tainted with unanswered questions.

In her worst moments, she'd thought that once he'd finally gotten what he'd wanted from her, she no longer held the appeal she once had, and the kindest thing he could do was leave. But in the quiet of a still night after dreaming of him, Allie knew he wouldn't have left if he hadn't had a good reason. Not after everything they'd been through together.

The not knowing gnawed at her from the inside out. Having zero closure and a wealth of unanswered questions made it so much worse than it should have been.

She'd seen it happen to other couples. High school romances tended to break apart when college and circumstances set two people on different paths. It sucked, but you got over it and moved on. Despite her dreams, she had moved on. But more than anything, she missed the friendship she'd shared with her equal. So many times she wished she could go back and unsay her professions of love. Then Aidan might still be here with her.

She had Darius now. He was her Syntrophos, and she loved him dearly. She was grateful for the time they'd had together to dive into their relationship with zero distractions.

But he just wasn't Aidan.

Chapter 5

The thump of Allie's foot against the punching bag was always such a satisfying sound. Working out her aggression on the poor, unsuspecting bag, she never held back. Darius had to make her a special punching bag with a double layer of thickness after she'd ruined several by putting her foot right through the canvas.

Since bonding as Syntrophos, she and Darius were both stronger than they were before. The bond linked them in a way that gave them access to each other's gifts—it was what made a Syntrophos pair so dangerous. She would never be able to use Darius's gifts directly, or he hers, but the connection allowed their individual gifts to influence and sometimes merge with the other's, giving them an unprecedented range with their collective abilities. Allie's gift for lending strength and stamina had given them each a near constant bolster of strength.

Back in the comfort of her own home and the gym she shared with her friends and Liam's family, Allie's temper shifted into high gear. At a time when she should be looking forward to the next chapter of her life—after finally finding happiness within herself—everything was changing. Again. It was the story of her life. Allie's fist landed with a loud thud, reverberating across the renovated barn that was their gym. She sent the punching bag swinging from the old hayloft and tossed her thin gloves aside. She never used traditional padded boxing gloves or shoes. Ming Lao had taught her to fight with the barest protection, so in a real fight, she would be saved from broken fingers or toes.

Allie gave the bag one last kick as it arched back toward her. The memory of Ming Lao was still a painful one, even after all this time. And with thoughts of Ming Lao, came thoughts of Chloe and Jin Jing. She missed them both so much, but Chloe still hadn't faced the death of her mother. She'd set off on her own after she graduated Cliffton Academy. Jin Jing followed her from place to place, trying to catch up with his daughter, but she continually evaded him.

"Come on, Parker. Come on." Emma's soft, patient voice pulled Allie from her reverie and sent all her anger and frustrations to the back of her mind. She broke into a huge smile at the sight of her godson, Alex Parker Loukas. Emma's surprise natural born son was two years old now, and he looked just like his mom with dark hair and crystal clear eyes, but sporting Daniel's Mediterranean coloring and Greek nose.

"Parker!" Allie leaned over as he wobbled across the barn wood floor on unsteady feet. Allie swept him up over her head, spinning him around.

The boy squealed in delight. "Again, Allie."

She twirled him around once more and set him back on his feet, and he darted across the room like a shot.

"Parker, no," Emma groaned, throwing her head back in frustration. "I'm way too old to be chasing a toddler."

"I got him, Emma." Lennox steered him away from the heavy weights and back onto the padded tumbling mats. Seamas and George's seventeen-year-old daughter always watched Parker while Allie and Emma trained together.

"So, on a scale of one to Allie, how much are you freaking

out?" Emma let out a frazzled breath.

"Aw, look who thinks they're funny." Allie gave her mentor a hug.

"Seriously, are you okay? I just talked to Alísun and came right here." Emma shrugged out of her coat, keeping one eye on her son and the other on Allie.

"Grandma made the announcement already?" Allie folded her arms across her chest. She kind of felt like this whole heir business was her news to tell when she was ready to deal with it.

"Just to me and Gregg." She wrapped her arm around Allie's shoulders as they headed up to the old hayloft upstairs for their weekly session. Liam and Darius refinished the cozy little room, so Allie would have a private place to discuss the more terrifying aspects of her gifts, the prophecy, and her uncertain future. No need to give Lennox and Kahlynn nightmares overhearing things they never needed to know.

Emma came into the city once a week to train with Allie, and Allie went home to Kelley's Island frequently. Emma was a stickler for their schedule. It was too easy to get lazy and not put in the work. Allie's training had changed since her days as a high school student. She trained with Darius and Livia daily, focusing on her gifts and the physical aspects of her progression. Her time with her mentor was dedicated to examining her progress and planning for the future as her gifts continued to evolve and become more complex.

"Honestly, I'm trying not to think about it right now," Allie said. "I just can't. Maybe after I graduate, we can have a real conversation about this heir thing, but it's just too much to process."

"No one expects anything you're not willing to give, Allie." Emma settled into the sleek, white leather Barcelona chair Livia insisted was a practical choice for the gym.

"The queen does."

"She doesn't expect anything you're not capable of, and she has no intention of taking this further anytime soon."

"That's something, I guess." Allie took the twin chair opposite her mentor. The black and white cow-hide rug beneath them tickled her bare feet.

"How does it make you feel, the naming?"

"Emma, you know I hate that psychological 'I feel' babble. It makes me *feel* like my dear, frosty grandmother is off her rocker. That's how it makes me feel."

Allie stared through the floor to ceiling glass wall into the gym below. Lennox and her father, Seamas, were chasing Parker across the tumbling matt. Lennox's other father, George, was putting Darius through some level of hell Allie hadn't quite reached yet in her own training. But the quiet little room where she sat with Emma was silent, thanks to Darius and his soundproofing gift. She could feel the evidence of his gift in the room like a part of him was always present with her, even in here.

"Just for fun, what would you see yourself doing as first princess?" Emma asked.

"I don't even know what that means, Emma. Indriell is dead; why do they need a new princess when there hasn't been one in thousands of years?" Logically, Allie understood her grandmother's motivations. Something needed to change. She just didn't see why it needed to be her responsibility.

"The physical nation of Indriell is gone, but its people still thrive. There are many who are unsatisfied with the way the Senate chooses to govern. Many who would remain loyal to the queens if a true heir should make herself known. Myself included."

"So I would be some kind of figurehead? Something to slap a crown on and cut ribbons at ceremonies? That's never going to be me."

"As the named heir, what you do with your birthright would be entirely up to you, Allie."

"If that's really how it works, then let's just let this whole naming business die right here."

"Someday, you may find your title and the authority it commands a useful tool."

"I just want to live my life, Emma. I want to finish school, get a job, and hang out with Darius." *And maybe see Aidan again someday.*

"You want things to keep going the way they have been. You've gotten comfortable in your years at school. Many Immortals your age do. You're young but still not ready to set out on your own. Life at university is better than high school, but it's not quite the real world yet. Don't get too comfortable, Allie. The world is constantly changing, and you've got to change with it. We live forever, but the compromise for that incredible gift is never being able to truly settle down. Nothing ever stays the same. The sooner you learn that lesson the better. Look at me, a natural mom at eight hundred. You know exactly how unprepared I was for Parker. I never wanted or expected to give birth to a child, and here I am chasing a two year old around and loving every minute of it. Change is a natural part of life, Allie."

"I've never liked change." Allie sighed, thinking her clairvoyance wasn't good for much if she was always caught off guard about the big things.

"Tell me something I don't know." A smile tugged at her lips. "How have your visions been?"

Allie sighed again. "Mostly the same. More of a nuisance than anything remotely useful."

"We've been focusing on getting you where you can function for a long time now. You have a certain level of control that is working. But it's never been a permanent solution. I can't pretend to understand this kind of clairvoyance. I fear I am not helping enough."

"You're doing great, Emma." Allie understood her frustration. The way her clairvoyance was evolving just wasn't in the history books. Even her ancient grandparents didn't have a clue. Allie's gift had merged with what Darius called his "CSI gift;" a clairvoyant ability that allowed him to see the reanimation of a crime. The Syntrophos bond had modernized Allie's gift in a way her mentor hadn't expected and still struggled to comprehend. "Can we at least get through my graduation before trying to jump the next hurdle?" Allie knew better than anyone that ignoring her visions was a very bad idea. For so long, the indistinct shapes that followed her everywhere were too nondescript to mean anything, but she was pretty sure they were beginning to evolve again. "I think I'm starting to see faces now." Allie leaned her head back to look at the high wooden beams of the ceiling.

"Then it's time to start discussing a better solution. We need someone who can help you better than I can."

"I don't want someone else, Emma. I just need time to really dig into these visions now that I've finally learned to function with them. I've been so focused on that I haven't had the time to analyze what I'm seeing yet. That needs to come next. Silencing them is still an absolute must. I'm not ready to unlock that closet of horrors again any time soon, but I don't think we need to look for another teacher yet."

"All right, after your graduation, we *will* tackle this. We simply must find a way for you to process the information your visions are bringing to your attention. And then in six months, we'll revisit the idea of bringing in another teacher, deal?"

"Deal." After graduation, she would work her butt off conquering this gift. She couldn't bear the thought of working with anyone other than Emma.

Chapter 6

Allie's arms fell like dead weights at her sides, exhausted from the long day in the gym with her sister. Livia was a brutal trainer, but over the years, she had whipped Allie into prime fighting shape.

Allie lifted her lead sai blade a moment too late. The bite of steel against flesh wasn't a new sensation, but it still hurt like a son of a bitch. "Ow, Livia, that was a cheap shot." She clutched her bleeding forearm against her chest.

"Come on, sister, you can't let a little scratch stop you." Livia raised her dagger, smeared with Allie's blood, as she continued her aggressive attack. "We have to make you into a warrior queen, not a pageant queen."

"You take that back, Liv." Allie sank into a defensive crouch, all exhaustion leaving her at the insult. "You make it sound like I'm not kicking your ass."

"If I really brought it, you'd be on the ground covered in blood," Livia said.

Most of the time, Allie couldn't see the woman her sister used to be. But every now and then, she got a peek of the scary, jaded woman still simmering beneath the surface. It worried her to think of how easy it would be for Livia to fall back into old habits.

"I have never been, nor will I ever be, a pageant queen." Allie and her sister circled the mat, each trying to find an opening for an attack.

"So says the prom queen." Livia's smile held a touch of mockery.

"High school doesn't count. I didn't even know I was up for it." Allie stood from her crouch. "Can we please just strike the word 'queen' from the gym vocabulary?" She slumped her shoulders in defeat.

"You've got to accept this, Allie." Livia stood, pointing her dagger at Allie's chest. "You hear 'queen,' and you think of it in terms of mortal royalty. This isn't Windsor Palace and you are no Kate or Meghan. You will be a ruler, yes, but you will also be a warrior. You have to harden yourself, and at the same time, you must learn to project a queenly persona."

"This is all such crap, Liv."

"Allie, this is going to happen." Livia lowered her weapon, standing with one hand behind her back and her sword arm resting at her side. It was as relaxed as Livia would get with a weapon in her hand. "It might not happen for a hundred years or more, but you have been named. That is not going to go away."

"You take it. You're the epitome of a warrior queen. Not me." She stepped back, as if she could so easily escape the mantle that had been thrust upon her.

"You are too soft, little sister." Livia sighed.

"Soft?" Allie raised her chin in defiance.

"You're an innocent girl. You see a basket of kittens and you smile, eager to play with them. A queen sees a basket of kittens, knowing she must be the one to drown them for the good of her people."

"That is the most screwed up analogy I've ever heard."

"The point is that a royal must make the difficult choices.

She must learn to make sacrifices for her people. And the first thing she must sacrifice is herself. Her future doesn't belong to her. It belongs to her people."

"See, you're so much better at this."

"I will be your second and your champion. I will be the brute force behind you. I will always give you honesty and the kick in the ass you need when you need it. But I do not have the natural, effortless quality that will make people want to follow me."

"But you ruled Soma for years."

"I ruled with fear and I inspired hate. That isn't a leader who earns loyalty. People will want to follow you."

"Have *any* of you met me? My people skills suck. Who's going to want to follow an introvert?"

"Allie." Livia's tone softened. "You still don't see it, do you? There are two Alísuns. You call her the ice queen, and you call her Grandma. She is both. When she projects her queenly mantle, no one questions her. No one ever doubts who she is. And when she drops that harder edge, she is just our grandmother, Alísun. You will need to learn to do the same. The facade you will present to the world doesn't have to be the real you. And we have plenty of time to work on that. Plenty of time for you to decide what kind of queen you want to be. You just need to be damned sure you make the right decisions now while you have the luxury of planning your next move."

"That is not the comforting thought you seem to think it is," Allie muttered.

"You just have to accept it in here." Livia placed a hand over her own heart. "And Grandmother *has* met you, you know." Her lips curved with amusement. "My guess is she brought this all up years before she normally would have because she knows you need time."

"Now, that is a comforting thought." Allie raised her sai,

eager for the distraction of physical activity to put an end to this discussion.

"We're done for the day. Let's go have a chat." Livia sheathed her dagger at her hip.

"That's what we were doing, and I didn't care for the subject."

"I have just the distraction you need." Livia headed for the door. "Come on, we're going to need a drink for this."

Allie followed her sister through the wide barn doors, back to the cottage across the snow swept lawn. But instead of entering the house, she kept going across the street to the home she shared with her husband and daughter.

"Sit." Livia commanded, opening the door to her office.

"Where are Liam and Kahlynn?"

"At some father-daughter dinner thing at her school."

"Aw, that's adorable."

"Yeah, that's all she's been talking about since we got back." Livia cracked a smile as she poured them each a very large glass of red wine. "Drink up, sis. I've been putting this off long enough. You're not going to like what I have to tell you. I'm breaking all the McBrien rules tonight."

Allie almost choked on her wine, watching her sister pace across her office in the dim light of the early evening.

"You have to understand why I'm telling you this."

"Telling me what?" Allie took a larger gulp, bracing herself for something awful.

"I am your sister. I'm not an emotional, hugs and kisses kind of woman, but you mean more to me than you will ever know."

From Livia, it was enough to make Allie tear up. "I love you, too, Liv, but you're scaring me."

"The McBriens are wonderful people. They are my family now, and they've welcomed me with open arms when they probably should have just kept me down in the crypt for the rest of my life."

"But?" Allie leaned forward.

"But my loyalty is to you, and there is something you should know."

Allie held up her finger and drained her glass, sliding it across the ebony desk for a refill.

"Okay, go." Her stomach clenched in anticipation.

"When we were in Europe on our honeymoon, I met Scott McBrien," Livia said softly.

Allie's body tensed. Scott was Aidan's brother everyone affectionately referred to as Fitzy. He was Aidan's guardian while he was in school. If she met Scott, she had to have met Aidan as well. So much of his absence never made sense to Allie, but she'd promised Aidan she would respect his decision to part ways.

"And Aidan?" she whispered. The warmth of her power stirred in her chest as she gripped the edge of Livia's desk. She couldn't remember the last time she'd spoken his name out loud. It sounded strange on her lips.

"I did not meet Aidan. The McBriens have been lying to you, Allie. He hasn't been in school these past four years. Aidan is missing."

CHAPTER 7

Allie shot to her feet. "Missing?" All the color drained from her face, leaving her dizzy and unable to speak.

"Aidan was drafted into the Senate more than three years ago." Livia sipped her wine, like they were just talking about the weather.

Allie sank back down into the chair behind her. "Drafted?" Her mind couldn't make sense of the word. "The Senate? I don't understand. Aidan is an unknown, like me. As far as they know, neither of us exists. They can't ever know we exist."

"I don't know nearly enough to answer your questions, Allie, but this was something you should have known long before now. I've paid attention over the years. I know how you feel about Aidan and how much his bullshit excuses torment you."

For a moment, Allie couldn't find her voice. Her lungs seized, and she trembled with anger. "They've been lying to me," she said in a low voice. "What do you know, Liv? Is he safe?" Allie leaned over Livia's desk, her eyes blazing with fury as the strength of her power flooded her body.

"I don't know, but we will find out." Livia reached for her hand at the same moment something inside Allie snapped.

Allie pulled away, her hands balling into fists at her sides.

Her fingernails biting into the flesh of her palms, she screamed with the rage of her judgment gift and the agony of all the years of separation from Aidan.

Livia rolled her chair back against the wall, fear stark on her face.

"Allie!" Darius charged through the back door. "What's happening?" He stumbled through the kitchen in his rush to reach her. All of Allie's fear, hurt, and rage poured into their Syntrophos bond, scorching them both with the heat of her power.

As he slid into the office, Allie lifted her hand, sending a wave of solar energy against him. Darius slammed into the wall, his feet dangling above the floor. She pressed the weight of her gift against him, her sense of reason gone.

"Allie, no!" Livia stood. "He is your Syntrophos—"

Allie lifted her other hand, flinging Livia back into her chair.

"Did you know?" Her voice sounded like gravel in her throat.

Darius didn't answer.

She balled her hand into a fist, using her gift to release him, only to slam him back against the wall again. Chunks of sheetrock and plaster dust rained down around them. "Did you know?"

"Allie," Livia said calmly as if talking to a cornered beast. "If you expect him to answer, you need to let him breathe."

Allie dropped her hands, letting Darius crash to the floor in a heap, his face red and his eyes wary. "Did I know what?" he rasped. "I'm going to need a little more information, Red."

"Aidan," she hissed. "Did you know he's been some kind of captive for the last *three* years?" She slammed him against the wall again.

"What is she talking about?" Darius shot a glance at Livia, still imprisoned in her chair.

"He didn't know, Allie. Let him go," Livia said.

"He's a McBrien," Allie snarled. "They like their secrets. Of course, he knew. He's been telling me for years Aidan is just off living his life, and I should do the same." She slammed Darius against the wall once more before she let him drop to the floor again. "But he's not, is he?" She balled her hands into fists to keep herself from injuring Darius any further. "It's like Quinn and Sasha all over again." Her voice trembled. "And I've just been here, doing the college thing like an idiot." Gasping to catch her breath, tears blurred her vision.

"Allie, I don't know what you're talking about," Darius said, getting to his feet. "But my brother is a student at the Cologne Conservatory in Germany."

"He's not, Darius," Livia said softly. "He dropped out years ago."

"You really didn't know?" Allie sank to the floor in a boneless heap. All the fight drained from her body. Heat flooded her face when she realized what she'd done, and she covered her eyes in shame. What was she thinking, attacking her Syntrophos like that? "I'm so sorry, Darius," she whispered through her tears.

"It's okay, let's just back up a bit here." Darius slid to the floor beside her. "And maybe let your sister out of that chair?"

Allie pulled the rage back into herself, suppressing the emotion. Her judgment gift sparked and crackled at her fingertips, begging to get out. Darius and Livia obviously didn't deserve her wrath, but the rage of her gift still consumed her sometimes. It was rare she lost it like this. She'd worked so hard to maintain iron control over her deadliest gift.

"Deep breaths, little sister." Livia crouched beside her. "I had no idea she would react so violently." She cast a wary glance at Darius.

"Allie and Aidan ... teenage angst." Darius lifted his hands. "Boom." He shook his head. "They've had a rocky history. You probably should have come to me first."

"I wasn't sure I could trust you."

"I love my family. I would die for them, but my loyalty is with Allie now. We are bonded in a way most people will never understand. If Dad is hiding something, he's hiding it from me, too. She should have known that."

"I can still hear you guys." Allie sniffed. "I'm so sorry. I just lost it."

"You know, when I taught you how to use your solar gift that way, you promised never to use it on me." Darius helped her to her feet and eased her back into the chair.

Allie hands trembled as Livia placed a fresh glass of wine in front of her.

"It won't happen again," she promised. "But you need to be straight with me, Liv, right now. What is going on with Aidan, and why wasn't I informed?"

"I'd like to know that myself," Darius said, sitting on the armrest beside her.

Livia returned to her seat with a sigh. "A few years ago, Aidan was drafted into the Senate. In the beginning, he still lived with Scott, and he continued to attend classes while training with the Senate."

"This sounds a lot like what Sasha has been through before." Allie frowned. "But you said he was missing. I don't understand."

Livia shook her head. "I'm so sorry to be the one to tell you this. But Gregg lost contact with him more than a year ago. Aidan is no longer in communication with his family."

"You haven't spoken to your brother in a year, and you didn't think that was weird?" Allie glared at Darius.

"We haven't spoken much since he left. Things have been a little weird between us since I bonded with his girlfriend."

"So no one knows where he is now? No one knows if he's safe?" The rage swept through her, pulsing like a heartbeat. Her fingertips ached to release her judgment.

"I don't think he is in danger, but no one seems to know where he is," Livia said. "Not even Liam."

"No way. Aidan wouldn't willingly work for the Senate." Darius said, shaking his head. "And if he did, Dad would kill him, unless they took Aidan by force and threatened the family."

"I don't know all the details," Livia said, "but from what I can gather, the Senate hasn't given anyone much of choice where Aidan is concerned."

"Then why hasn't Dad turned the world upside down looking for him?" Darius asked, confused.

"I think it's time we go ask him." Allie stood and crossed the room. "Now," she called over her shoulder. "Greggory McBrien has some questions to answer."

CHAPTER 8

"Pick up the pace, Officer McSlowton." Allie fought the urge to hit the gas pedal with a zap of her solar gift. Darius didn't like it when she did that.

"I am driving the speed limit."

"You two sound like an old married couple," Livia said, snorting from the backseat. "We're almost there, but we're going to miss the last ferry."

"We'll get a boat at the marina," Darius said. "It's just going to be a cold night on the water."

"Take the tunnel," Allie said, chewing her thumbnail.

"You sure about that? You hate the tunnel."

"It's faster."

"Yeah, but do we have to? I hate the tunnel."

"Please, Darius, just get us there."

"Aidan has been missing for a year, Allie, twenty more minutes isn't going to make a difference," Livia said.

"Not funny, Liv." Allie glared at her sister in the rearview mirror. "I can't believe this has been happening right under my nose. I'm clairvoyant." Allie hammered her fist against the dashboard. "How do I keep failing so miserably?"

"You haven't failed, Allie. You're too hard on yourself." Livia leaned over the front seat. "I trained hundreds of kids during my years at Soma, and the biggest frustration everyone experiences at this age is not being able to fully understand their gifts yet. It takes time. You know this."

Allie ran her hands through her hair impatiently. She knew her sister was right. But Allie had dreamed of Aidan so often. *What have I missed?* She chewed on her thumbnail. So many nights she'd spent caught in a labyrinth, looking for the shadow that was always just out of reach. She inevitably woke up calling his name. She'd always thought the dream came when she missed him most. She assumed the fact that she could never catch him had just meant he wasn't a part of her life anymore. The dream was about not having closure. But could it have been a warning he was in trouble all this time? And what important clues had she missed by suppressing her visions? She'd pushed them away for the sake of convenience.

"I'm so stupid," she whispered. "I've dreamed about Aidan for years. I should have seen this coming." She would figure this out. She owed him that much.

"The queen has taught you how difficult dreams are to interpret," Livia said. "They often seem to be about one thing and end up being about something else entirely. It is the nature of foretelling. Nothing is as it seems and more often than not, you figure it out after the fact. You've seen the evidence of that yourself. Many times."

"I know. But this is Aidan. How could I fail him, of all people?"

"If I know my brother, he's the one who doesn't want you to know anything." Darius pulled into the Terminal Tower parking garage. It was late. They would be able to access the tunnel there without notice. "I'd bet my shirt he's the one calling the shots in this mess." Darius pulled onto the train tracks and hopped out of the car to enter the code behind a panel in the wall.

It would be just like Aidan to try to protect me from this. Allie's hands balled into fists in her lap. All of this was bringing up old feelings she thought she'd put to rest years ago. Feelings she didn't want to face again.

As the concrete wall slid aside and Darius pulled forward, leaving the train station behind, Allie stared out the window, the fog of her breath misting the glass. The dark, narrow tunnel brought back bad memories of the night her judgment gift emerged. So much changed that night; she sometimes wished she could go back to the time just before everything fell apart. To the time she'd spent with Aidan, and the moment she'd finally admitted she loved him. She squeezed her eyes shut tight as the darkness of the icy tunnel engulfed them. The memories were painful, yet bittersweet. She still loved Aidan, just as she always had. That had never changed. Yes, she'd built a life for herself without him. She'd found happiness with Darius, and she thrived at school. But she still missed him so much it took her breath away whenever she let herself about him. Allie had dated casually all through college, mostly mortal boys brave enough to ask her out. But nothing serious. She was happy with her life. And all this time, Aidan was in trouble, and, like always, she was the last to know.

"I'm so sick of this," Allie said, brushing her hair away from her face.

"What?" Darius asked.

"I'm twenty-one-years old. I'm about to hold two degrees. I'm the heir of a dead nation, and I'm as independent as a young Immortal can be, but I'm still kept in the dark about the things that matter. I know I'm not officially an adult in terms of my training, but dammit, I'm an adult in every other sense of the word. I am not a child, and I do not need people making decisions for me."

"Especially considering your position," Livia said. "I will

"It's what Aidan wanted," Gregg admitted.

"Is it?" Allie shot to her feet again, folding her arms across her chest in an attempt to keep her temper and her power in check, when what she really wanted to do was slam him around the room a little bit. "And why is that? It has something to do with him protecting me, doesn't it?" It was classic Aidan. If he thought something might affect her negatively, he would take it upon himself to handle the situation for her without ever asking what she thought about it. Once upon a time, it might have been necessary, but it was insulting and infuriating now.

"He was trying to protect all of us," Gregg said, lowering himself wearily into his armchair.

"I'm not that fifteen-year-old girl any more, Gregg. How could you not tell me?"

"He didn't want you burdened with this. He loves you so much, Allie; you have no idea. Please just sit, and I will tell you everything I know."

Some of the fire went out of her as she perched on the edge of the sofa beside Darius.

"When Aidan first went to school in Germany, it was supposed to be temporary." Gregg sighed. "It's one of the reasons we agreed to let him go in the first place. But things changed for him that summer, and he decided to take one more semester abroad."

Her shoulders drooped. "And what, he didn't trust me to understand?"

"I truly think my son found a life for himself at school. I suspect he experienced some of the first stress free days he's ever known, focusing on himself and his music."

"I would have understood," Allie insisted. "I've been doing the same thing here. I would never begrudge him that."

"He knows that, Allie." Gregg voice was soft. "But by that fall, the Senate had already started building a case against him," he continued. "Someone filed an anonymous report, claiming Aidan was a powerful unknown. It would have been a nuisance to deal with the legal matters, but as they observed him, they were no longer concerned with the reasons he was never registered with the Senate. They were only interested in his power."

"Cut to the chase, Gregg. Please?" Allie begged. "Is he okay?" She sat, wringing her hands in her lap, her power buzzing beneath her skin in her desire to *do* something. Anything but sit here helplessly.

"You need to understand that this is not like Quinn's situation. Or even Sasha's. He isn't suffering. That much I do know. But he has been denied his freedom. I believe the Senate thinks he is too powerful to be trusted, and they want him under their thumb so they can use him for their benefit."

"Why the hell haven't you gone in there, guns blazing?" Allie said, voice rising in accusation. "The Gregg I know wouldn't sit here quietly while his son is in trouble."

"You don't think that was my first response?" Gregg's tone matched hers. "I'd like nothing more than to wage war against those who have dared to take my son from his family."

Allie gasped, her hands covering her mouth. "He's agreed to this, hasn't he?"

"Aye." Gregg stood and headed for the bar at the back of his office. "They arrested him at school. They interrogated him for days, refusing to allow Scott to post bail or even act as a representative of the family. The crime was ours." Gregg shook his head in frustration as he busied himself pouring drinks. "Aidan was barely eighteen at the time. By our laws, it still should have been his parents' responsibility to have him and his abilities registered with the Senate. It wasn't his crime, but they charged him with it anyway and escalated the crime to an international felony. I never should have let him go away to school." Gregg leaned against the counter, dropping his head in frustration, the weight of his son's predicament heavy on his shoulders.

"It was just an excuse to take him." Allie sat with her elbows on her knees. The whole situation was beginning to make more sense. Gregg had fought Aidan's entire life to save him from this exact thing. This was killing him. "It wasn't anyone's fault, Gregg."

"I know." He raised his head, placing four cut glass tumblers on a tray. "Things happened fast in the first few days Aidan was in custody. We couldn't get close to him. Our hands were tied. And then one day, he just came home, saying the charges were dropped." Gregg grabbed the tray of drinks along with the matching decanter, serving them each a double shot of his best bourbon.

Allie sat with her drink in her hands and her heart in her throat. "He made a deal."

"Aye." Gregg returned to his seat, tossing back the contents of his glass in one gulp. "I was there when they brought him back. Aidan insisted he hadn't made a deal. That he'd only received a slap on the wrist and some community service. He was supposed to teach a class for young Immortals with gifts for healing."

"I don't buy it." Allie took a sip of her drink, the burn in her throat a welcome distraction.

"Neither did I," Gregg said, pouring himself a refill. "I couldn't fathom why they'd let him go. But things settled back to normal right away. He attended classes and in the afternoons, he trained with a new group of students for his community service. But Aidan wasn't himself. I knew something was wrong, but he refused to talk about it, insisting he had the situation under control. I found out later that things were far worse than I ever anticipated."

"What did he agree to?" Allie sat forward with her arms

around her middle, as if to protect herself from what she was about to hear.

"I always knew it would come to this if they ever found out about Aidan." Gregg scrubbed at the stubble on his face. "When he was arrested and interrogated, the Senate brought charges against me and Naeemah, and all of Aidan's eldest siblings. Even Liam. We were all held responsible for shielding him from notice all his life. They threatened our position as governor, claiming we would all face prison time for the betrayal. We would be ruined, but it was a scare tactic. And it worked."

"We all know Aidan will do anything to save the people he loves," Allie whispered. "Even if it means sacrificing himself."

Gregg nodded. "Aye, they got into his head and found what makes him tick. He's a fixer. Aidan will always do the noble thing." He heaved a big sigh, sitting back in his chair. "In exchange for his full cooperation, Aidan negotiated terms that left his parents and siblings pardoned of all charges brought against us for raising an unknown."

"Who cares? This is your son, Gregg. You never think of yourself when it comes to your children." Allie surged to her feet, unable to keep still. "How could you let him agree to it? What aren't you telling me?"

"I don't know how, but they know about you, Allie," Gregg told her, regret on his face. "Rather, they know *of* you to be more exact. They know you are an orphaned unknown that we have harbored for the last five years. They know you are Aidan's equal in power, and that you mean more to him than his own wellbeing. They do not know about your bond with Darius, or that you are the natural-born child of prophecy and the named heir of Indriell. And they certainly don't know what you can do. They can never know that, Allie."

"How could they possibly have known about me three

years ago?" Allie asked in a panic, not for herself, but for what she knew Aidan would do to protect her.

"I honestly don't know. I haven't been able to identify how they have gathered what little information they have on you."

"So they made threats against me, too, and Aidan caved?" Her voice trembled, and she sat back down. Darius slid closer to her side, letting her rest against his shoulder for support.

"Aidan knew the threats against his family were likely just a ploy. He refused to cooperate at first, but in the end, to keep the Senate from coming for you, to keep you safe, Aidan gave up his freedom. They've agreed to let you live your life, free of their interference in exchange for his full cooperation. To them, Aidan is the prize and you are the sacrifice for that prize. My son has given you the normal life you've always wanted." There was no accusation in his voice. Only resigned acceptance.

"I never wanted this, and you damn well know it," Allie said with deadly calm. "How dare you not tell me? How dare you let him sacrifice himself like this?" Allie's eyes flickered with green fire, and her hands itched to free her power. "And you've lost contact with him now?"

"We've come to realize those first few months after his release were meant to give us a false sense of security. Aidan began to pull away after that. He still attended classes and lived with Scott. We even saw him occasionally when we visited, but he wasn't the same. He'd withdrawn. More like he was before he met you. And then he started traveling a lot. Gone for long periods of time until one day, he just never came back. Little by little, Aidan slipped away from us, Allie. And I've tried everything to bring him home. The last time I spoke to him was more than a year ago." Gregg gave her a haggard look, his eyes pleading with her to understand. "He asked me to stop. Begged me to trust him."

"What about Liam?" Allie set her empty glass back on the tray.

"I take it you two have been working to find him? Doing this the McBrien way, keeping all the little women and children out of it?"

"The very last time I spoke to my son, I promised I would protect you." Gregg's voice shook with anger. "And that is a promise I intend to keep. No matter how much we want to bring him home, you are a far too important to risk."

"I am not a trophy you keep behind a glass case, Gregg. I don't need your protection. I need honesty and the knowledge of what's going on around me so I can protect *myself*. This involves me, and I needed to know about it."

"And her family should have been informed, too," Livia spoke up for the first time. "This affects everything, Gregg. You should know better than to keep something like this from us. Alísun won't be happy we've been kept in the dark."

"I suppose you're the one who told Allie?"

"She is my sister. And she is the heir. She deserves the respect her position demands."

Gregg sank back in his chair, gazing at the stone ceiling. "You're right. But, Allie, you know I love you like my own daughter."

"I know." Her voice softened as her anger wilted. She loved him just as much.

"A parent protects their children. Even when they are children no longer."

"What are you doing to end this?" Allie asked. "I don't understand why Liam can't go find Aidan and just drag him home."

"Liam can't find him," Gregg said. "We believe Aidan is with someone who can mask his location. He pops up every once in a while at different points across Europe." His jaw clenched into a hard line. "But by the time we investigate, he's gone again. This isn't about us failing to rescue him, Allie. My son doesn't want to be found. We've tried everything. Whatever the Senate has him doing, he's in so deep we can't help him. I'm afraid until Aidan shows some sign that he wants our help, there is nothing we can do for him."

"You should have come to me months ago," Allie said. "I'll trade myself for him."

"No, you won't," everyone in the room said at once.

"Not literally," Allie said. "But let's make them an offer they can't refuse. Dangle the redheaded princess like a carrot in their face, and they'll take a nibble. Then we make a move. We all know Aidan is one self-sabotaging, self-sacrificing, broody son of a bitch. If he is evading help, then it's time to stage an intervention and drag him back here kicking and screaming if we have to."

"I'm inclined to agree with you on that, but you can't sacrifice yourself for him, Allie. It is far too dangerous. The queen would never allow it."

"She's not the boss of me," Allie said.

"I won't allow it. Like it or not, you are too important to take such a risk."

"There has to be something we can do."

"The best thing we can do for Aidan right now is trust him. He is safe. Of that I am certain," Gregg said. "I never wanted my son to become a Senate man. We've taken great measures to give him the chance to become his own man on his own terms. I believe in him. Right now, he thinks he is protecting his parents and the girl he loves. But in the end, he will stay true to himself. He will not be swayed by our government. When the time is right, he will reach out to us."

"You've given up?" Allie asked, not believing what she was hearing.

"We are not acting. But we are also not twiddling our

thumbs either. We are waiting and vigilantly watching. For the moment."

"How can you be so sure he's safe?" she asked.

Gregg tipped forward to meet her gaze. She recognized the flicker of passion in his eyes.

"Aidan gave up his freewill to protect us. But somewhere along the way, I believe he has become passionate about his work for the Senate. I don't trust them. But I do trust my son. He's smart. Whatever they have him doing, he has them in his pocket, and they believe him to be an ally. They wouldn't hurt him."

Allie nodded. "Aidan's not an idiot. He would never let anyone influence what he believes to be right. He must—" She inhaled sharply as realization hit her. "They have him working on something important. Something he feels can't be left to anyone else. It's not about protecting us anymore."

"My thoughts exactly," Gregg said.

"I know we need to trust him. Aidan is perfectly capable of taking care of himself, but nothing is worth giving up his freedom."

"I know, sweetheart. But I'm afraid this is one of those times we simply have to wait for a resolution."

"That's not a plan, Gregg." Allie's mind whirled with possibilities. Gregg might not be able to save his son from himself, but there had to be something she could do. Waiting and hoping wasn't an option she could live with.

"We're going to Germany." Allie slid into her car, cranking the ignition of the old Impala.

"Why am I not surprised?" Darius groaned, taking the seat beside her. "What are we going to do there? Knock on doors?"

"I don't know. I need to talk to Scott. He's the one who lived with Aidan through all this. He's the logical place to start."

"You think my brother would know something Gregg doesn't?"

"I don't know, Dare." Allie held a death grip on the steering wheel. "But I can't just go on about my life like nothing's happened. I need to go to Germany, see where he lived. Maybe I can get a read on something the other's have missed."

"I may know someone who can help," Livia said, slipping into the backseat. "We'll go to Germany. It's a good place to start. You will talk to Scott, and I will reach out to my contacts."

"You're on board with this?" Darius asked.

"The Senate has made a threat against Allie. They may not know exactly who she is yet, but it's only a matter of time. And when they do come for her, we must be ready to act. I intend to get ahead of this thing. I am sure Aidan is a strong young man with the greatest of intentions, but I cannot leave my sister's safety in the hands of an Unproven boy I've never met, with an agenda I don't understand."

"All right, then." Allie nodded. "We're leaving tonight."

"Be careful, Allie." Liam's voice crackled over the international call. "I don't like you gallivanting across the world without me."

"Would you relax, you big goober," Allie sighed into the speakerphone. "We hopped a flight to Germany, not Mars. I'm just going to talk to Fitzy. It'll make me feel better."

"Well, when you get back, we're having a family discussion about flying across the world in the middle of the night without giving each other a heads up first."

"You do know you're like, number one on my shit-list, right?" Allie scoffed and Livia's lip curled into a sneer.

"I'm aware," Liam said dryly.

"My dear husband." Livia moved over Allie's phone. "When we get back, we're going to have a long talk about keeping secrets in this family."

"Give me a break. This all happened years ago. And I'm new to this having my own family thing," Liam said. "It's always been my brother's family before you two and Kahlynn came along."

"And?" Livia demanded, tapping her foot against the worn interior of the taxi taking them to a small suburb of Cologne, Germany.

"And I am a Neanderthal who clearly needs to learn how to

deal with ... er ... compromise with the beautiful, yet terrifyingly strong, women of my family."

"That's better," Allie said.

"We need to adopt a son or two," Liam said. "I am outnumbered and out of my depth."

"Stop talking, Liam," Darius said. "Say bye-bye and hang up before you shove that giant foot in a little too deep."

"Just be safe. You two and Kahlynn are my life, so don't do anything stupid."

"Keep an eye on us, Liam. We'll be fine," Livia said gently as she ended the call. "McBrien boys," she said under her breath like a curse.

Allie's stomach plummeted to her toes as the car slowed in front of the house Aidan had shared with his brother, Scott, a.k.a. Fitzy, for at least a portion of the last four years.

"You coming, Livia?" Allie asked as she and Darius stepped onto the curb.

"I'll be back in a few hours," Livia said. "I have a meeting with a contact not too far from here. You do your kind of digging and I'll do mine."

Allie nodded. "Be careful, sis." It worried her to see her sister diving back into her old ways.

"Don't worry about me, Allie. I have a good life now. I'll never do anything to jeopardize that." She closed the door and nodded to the driver.

"You ready to go in there?" Darius asked as they headed up the short walk to the townhouse.

"No." Allie shoved her hands into her coat pockets. "In my head, he's been here for the last four years. Walking into that house and not seeing him..." she choked, her eyes burning with tears.

"We will find him, Allie. And then I'm going kick his ass for doing this to you."

Allie took a deep breath as she stepped into the house, the warmth a welcome respite from the cold German afternoon.

"Darius," Scott McBrien greeted them. "I've missed you." He gave his brother a backslapping bear hug. "I'm so sorry I've kept my distance for so long." He waved them into the living room. "We were trying to spare you both."

"I can't say I agree with your decisions to keep us in the dark, but it's good to see you, brother," Darius said.

Allie shuffled her feet as she glanced around the cozy living room, searching for evidence of Aidan. She gulped back a sob when her eyes landed on his violin, resting in a place of honor in the corner of the room.

"He's-he's not playing?" She could barely get the words out.

Scott came to stand beside her. "I'm afraid the Senate has robbed him of that, too."

Tears rolled down her face as she stared at the intricate vine detail of his Stradivarius. Carefully carved Phoenixes spread their wings along the waist and lower bout of the instrument. Separating him from his violin wasn't just separating the man from his music, it was taking away one of his main lines of communication. Playing the violin wasn't just about the music for Aidan. It was a cathartic release. A way of expressing his emotions in ways he couldn't do with words. Without it, he would be a bottle of feelings ready to explode. Allie doubted if anyone else understood that about him.

"Why is he doing this to himself?" she finally asked, tracing the edges of the priceless instrument. "And please don't say it's to protect me or his family. It may have been about that in the beginning, but I don't think it's just that anymore. We are missing something." She shook her head, cheeks wet with tears, but her voice grew steady. "I will not let him do this. Not for me or anyone else. We have to find him, Scott. I need you to tell me everything you know."

"Like I told you on the phone, Allie, you know what I know." He gestured for them to sit down. "I haven't seen or heard from him in nearly fourteen months. And before that, he was often gone for weeks at a time."

"What was he like then?" she asked, taking a seat next to Scott on the sofa. "I need to understand what he was thinking. I've been in his mind. I know how he thinks, and how he processes information. If I can wrap my mind around his point of view, I might be able to see something you all have overlooked."

Scott nodded. "Fair enough. But you're not going to like it. Aidan was not in a good place the last few times I saw him. He's not the boy you remember."

"We've all changed," Allie said. "You could say the same about me."

"Let me back up a bit," Scott said. "When we first came to Germany, he was reluctant. He wanted to be here but at the same time, he wanted to be back home with you. But this was his dream, and I think he thought if he could live that dream for a few short months, it would be enough for him. He could go back home to finish school at Oberlin Conservatory and never look back. But once he was here, taking classes and immersing himself in this elite world of classical music, he came alive." Scott smiled at the memory. "There is no doubt that you have had a profound impact on him, Allie. Aidan changed when he met you. Having an equal who understands what it's like to be him, it made a huge difference in his life. But coming to school here was like watching him truly spread his wings and fly. He couldn't leave after just a few months. When he decided to take an extra semester, he was so torn. Torn between his love for you and his love for music. But still, he was happier than I've ever seen him."

Allie forced a smile. Of course she wanted Aidan to be

happy, but that was right around the time he'd cut her out of his thoughts. "So all of that changed when the Senate came for him?"

"Yes." Scott sighed. "When they arrested him and refused to let me stand with him, I feared we'd never see him again. He is so powerful." A look of sadness flashed across Scott's face. "I knew they'd never risk losing their hold on him. But when he came home a few days later, I couldn't believe it. And then once he started pulling away, I couldn't get anything out of him."

"You have no idea what kind of work they had him doing?" Allie asked.

"He did let something slip once," Scott said. "He said he wasn't lying about teaching a class, but that he couldn't tell me any more than that. It sounded like he was training with a group of talented students."

"Did he say anything else?" Darius asked.

"He said something about owing everyone to see it through to the end. But he couldn't possibly think that he owes Mom and Dad his freedom just to keep them out of jail for a few years."

"No, that's not it." Allie stood, chewing on her thumbnail as she paced across the living room. "He wasn't talking about the family, Fitzy. Aidan's smart enough to know the Senate can't legally follow through with their threats against his parents and siblings. Naeemah and Gregg are governors; they're public figures, working *for* the Senate." She turned on her heel. "They can't just disappear under the radar the way Aidan has. Everyone would recognize how shady those trumped up charges were."

"Then he must have been talking about you, and by extension, me because of our bond," Darius said with a frown. "Who else would he give up his freedom for?"

stand by your side in this, sister. You are absolutely right. This boy, Aidan, if he is behind this attempt to keep you in the dark as Darius believes, it's high time he stops making decisions for you. You will never become the woman you are destined to be if you aren't taken seriously by those who profess to love you. You need the truth and brutal honesty now, not kid gloves and sugar coated half-truths."

"All of that, yes. Say that to Gregg when we get there," Allie huffed.

"You can tell him yourself. You're a big girl."

"That poor man is going to rue the day he ever met me."

"Greggory McBrien!" Allie stormed up the steps from the crypt, charging across the empty common room. "Where are you, Gregg? I know you can hear me."

"I take it you are displeased with me?" Gregg stepped from the corridor leading to his office. "To what do I owe this late night visit?"

"Aidan. Where is he?" She took a step toward him. "And don't you dare tell me he's at school because I know he's been missing. For a goddamned *year*!"

"I see." Gregg stepped aside. "Why don't we continue this shouting match in my office?"

Allie stalked down the long hallway behind him, her hands itching to wrap around his throat.

"Dad, she's mad as hell, and I can't say I blame her," Darius said. "We need the full story." He steered Allie toward the sofa and pulled her down beside him.

"How can you have a level head with this?" Allie fumed at the way Darius spoke so calmly with his father. "He's lied to us for *years*."

"His students." Allie turned to face them. "Don't you see? He was talking about his class. I know how he thinks, guys. Aidan sees himself as a leader. He's always known that the power he possesses will mark him as either a threat, which the Senate sees when they look at him, or a leader, which his students would clearly see."

"She's right," Darius said. "Dad's always worked hard to prepare him for that eventuality."

"Exactly. And let's say his students are all like him. Powerful young Immortals who haven't been given a choice."

"You might be on to something," Darius said. "Look at what they've done with Sasha? It's not like they ever ask what she wants."

Scott nodded. "Aidan would definitely take it upon himself to protect them."

"This all started with the threats against his family and me, but it's continued because there are others who need his protection. That's why he doesn't want us to find him." Allie sat on the corner of the coffee table, facing Aidan's brothers.

"This could be the reason he's never tried to reach out to us or flip this around and make his own way out," Scott said. "I don't know why we didn't see it before."

"Thank you, Scott." Allie took his hands in hers. "I was hoping to find at least one small piece of the puzzle while we were here."

"We've always suspected the Senate had him working on something he was passionate about. Something he believed in enough to walk away from everyone and everything he ever wanted. This all ads up, but it still doesn't mean we're any closer to finding him than we were before."

"No, but it's something we didn't know yesterday," Darius said.

"If Aidan believes so strongly in what he's doing that he

was willing to ghost his entire family, then he's doing the right thing," Allie said. "We need to trust him. But that doesn't mean we stop digging. I don't want to tear him away from what he believes is right, as long as he is safe. But if there is even the slightest chance that he is hurting or in over his head, we need to be prepared to help him."

"I agree," Scott said. "We've been waiting and watching for so long with no results, and you waltz in here with your knowledge of how his mind works and find something we missed." He rested his elbows on his knees. "You need to keep digging, Allie. Dad doesn't want to let you anywhere near the Senate but it's time. We have to do something, or we're going to lose Aidan forever."

Chapter 10

Allie's feet pounded against the cold marble tile, the walls closing in on her. Black snakes hung from the ceiling and slithered in the shadows, their ruby red eyes stared blankly as she ran.

The labyrinth of corridors seemed endless, never taking her where she wanted to go. Every door stood open, displaying empty rooms.

Tears streaked her face as she darted down the stairs to another floor of endless tiled hallways. Her heart stopped in her chest when she saw him standing by the elevators. *Aidan.*

She could see his face, hard and lean. He stared at her, his dark eyes smoldering with the golden light of his power.

Running faster, Allie knew she was finally going to catch him this time. She stumbled when something cold and scaly fell across her shoulders, slithering around her neck. No. She shrieked, flinging the snake to the floor. It hissed and coiled into the familiar figure eight of the ouroboros.

When she looked up, Aidan stood inside the elevator. The doors closed, leaving her alone in the darkness. Again.

"Get up. We're meeting a contact in twenty minutes." Livia flipped on the lights of the hotel suite Allie shared with Darius.

"Wait..." Allie sat up, bleary-eyed from her dreams. She

was exhausted from traveling across Europe for the last two weeks. "Where are we again?" She ran her hand through her tangled mass of curls. "And what time is it?" She scowled at the late night sky outside the window.

"It's the middle of the night," Darius groaned, throwing a blanket over his head. "Go away, Liv."

"We're in Milan." Livia pulled the blankets off Darius's bed. "It's three in the morning, and we don't have much time." She pulled Allie up from her bed, steering her toward the bathroom. "No time for showers, but do something with that rat's nest on top of your head."

"Didn't we just check in like an hour ago?" Allie fumbled with her hairbrush.

"I let you sleep for two hours. That's enough. Now move it. You, too, Darius. We have an important meeting to get to."

"Who schedules a meeting at three in the morning?" Darius scowled, slipping into his jeans, looking more refreshed than he had a right to after such a short nap.

Allie scrambled around in her duffle bag for her wide comb.

"Someone with a lot to lose and doesn't want to be seen," Livia said. "What are you doing, Allie? Why do you have a brush stuck in your hair?"

Allie glared at her sister.

Livia pressed her lips together, failing to stifle a smile.

"Because I haven't washed it in three days, and I'm probably going to have to shave it all off and start over." Allie raked the comb through her hair with an angry stroke, and several plastic teeth cracked. "Stupid piece of crap." She threw the comb down on the bed and yanked the brush out of her hair.

"Wear a hat," Darius said.

Allie scowled at him and ran her hands through her curls, tugging through the worst of the tangles. With a wince, she shoved it all back into a messy bun and finished dressing in a hurry.

"Let's go." She sighed and followed Darius and her sister into the quiet streets of Milan in the middle of the night. Allie released her visions from her peripheral vision. She checked them frequently now but refused to get her hopes up this time. They'd spent the last few weeks chasing their tails around Europe, reaching out to Livia's less than reputable contacts, and had come up with very little. At this rate, Allie was going to flunk out of her last semester of college, but if they could just find something useful, it would be worth it.

"Who are we meeting this time?" Darius yawned.

"A girl my contact in Paris recommended. She's been difficult to find, but after talking with a few old friends, I managed to get a message to her a few days ago."

"Wait, something's different." Allie paused on the sidewalk. The hazy green light she associated with her clairvoyance lit up the night, illuminating more than a dozen shifting blobs wandering around them. Except these weren't the blobs she was used to. There was more definition. Her visions looked like real people, teenagers maybe. She could even make out a few faces. But nothing familiar.

"What do you see?" Livia asked.

"Nothing useful. But it's different. Different is good. I think we might be on the right track here. What's this girl's story?" Allie asked.

"I didn't tell you what I discovered in Paris because I wasn't sure it would come to anything." Livia slipped into the front seat of their tiny European rental and unlocked the doors.

Allie's heart beat a little faster at this news. "What did you find?" She scrambled into the back, leaning over the front seat.

"My contact in Paris works off the books for several big name Senators. She does undercover work, so she hears things.

There's been a lot of recent talk about a small operative along the Swiss border, a few hours north of Milan up near the Italian Lake District."

"What about it?" Darius asked.

"It's some kind of top secret facility for really powerful kids."

"That sounds promising." Allie sat back, suddenly awake and eager to get wherever they were going.

"It's called the Milan Initiative. The girl we're about to meet might be associated with them, and there's a chance she could know something about Aidan. But she's nervous. She's only here for a few more hours, and she's agreed to meet us at the square near the Colonne di San Lorenzo."

Allie marveled at the way her sister got things accomplished. Since they'd arrived in Europe, Livia had called in every favor she ever earned in her years at Soma. She'd met with some of the most ancient and corrupt Immortals still living in the mainstream world. They were bound to come up with something useful if they kept digging. Allie knew her sister was more concerned with keeping her out of the Senate's hands than with helping Aidan, but she would never be able to thank Livia for all she'd done these last few weeks.

"We're nearly there," Livia said. "You guys need to let me do the talking. This girl is skittish. She might not even show."

Allie fidgeted, twisting her hands in her lap. They needed to find something to go on soon. The thought of going back home empty-handed just wasn't an option.

"Stop worrying, Allie." Livia glanced in the rearview mirror. "You need to focus on keeping that bond of yours concealed. I can't even begin to tell you how much money some people would pay to own the power you two possess as a pair. We cannot allow anyone we meet to know about your Syntrophos bond."

Livia swerved into a street side parking spot near the ancient square. A colonnade of sixteen enormous Corinthian columns cast dark shadows along the empty sidewalk in the early morning darkness. On any other day, Allie would be eager to explore the crumbling Roman relics and the nearby Basilica of San Lorenzo and the Basilica of Saint Eustorgius. But she only had thoughts for Aidan. She felt it in her bones. They were getting closer to an answer.

The spectral figures still roamed freely in her main line of sight. Some had coalesced into more corporeal forms with a green aura. She saw several young faces and studied them carefully, but as much as she tried, she was still missing some vital piece of information.

"Let's go," Allie whispered, heading down the dark sidewalk behind the colonnade. As she stepped aside to avoid walking right through one of her visions, the memory of Aidan's arms around her struck her like a brick wall. The touch of his hand, the warmth of his eyes, it had been so long her memories of him had blended with her memories of high school. They were equals, and they would always be friends, but sometimes she thought she'd built him up in her mind to be something he never really was. They were together once, for a brief time. That was all. *Then why haven't I ever been able to move on?*

"Allie?"

She jumped at the voice she hadn't heard in years. "Who's there?" She stared into the shadows.

"Don't tell me you've forgotten me already?" The girl stepped into the light of the street lamps under the center archway.

"Naomi?" Allie gaped at the young woman she'd never really liked. She hadn't changed at all, still exotically beautiful with her ethnic ambiguity, curly, golden brown hair, and piercing blue eyes. And by the look in those eyes, she still loathed Allie.

"You know each other?" Livia asked.

"She's family," Darius explained.

"Not my family," Allie and Naomi responded in unison.

"This is your contact?" Allie turned to her sister in confusion.

"Yes. I've crawled under every rock in Europe to find her." Livia's tone was sharp with irritation.

"I wouldn't have risked my neck if I'd known it was you." Naomi looked at Allie like she was the last person on earth she ever wanted to see again. The feeling was mutual.

"Naomi, what do you know about Aidan?" Allie asked, not in the mood for her usual petty antics.

Naomi scowled. "It took you long enough to come looking for him. I don't have much time for this, so I suppose you're my only hope." She cast a worried glance over her shoulder. "If he ever finds out I put you in danger, he'll kill me."

"Aidan? You've seen him? Recently?" Allie took a step forward ready to wring her neck if she didn't start talking.

"Every day for the last four years," Naomi said. "We work together."

"Where? Who are you working for?" Allie balled her hands into fists at her side. Livia's hand on her shoulder was a silent reminder to take it easy.

"We live a few hours from here, up near Lake Maggiore. The Milan Initiative is a private project under the direct supervision of the Chief Justice. Most of the International Senate doesn't even know about it. But we agreed to join. Years ago it made sense. And it was what Aidan wanted. But it doesn't make sense anymore. That's why I'm here. I just didn't realize I was coming to you for help, but I suppose you're better than nothing." She didn't try to mask her irritation, but Allie saw the fear behind the girl's bravado. She was terrified and grasping at straws.

"This isn't about me or our mutual dislike for each other, Naomi. This is about Aidan. Why has he pushed us all away? He's evading help on purpose, and it doesn't make sense."

"Don't be stupid, Allie. This is your fault, and we both know it. Aidan will always walk over hot coals for you." Naomi hid among the shadows of the colonnade, shrinking back against the crumbling facade. Her hands trembled and she tried to hide it, shoving them in her coat pockets.

"Aidan has a mind of his own, and he knows I would never ask him to make sacrifices for me." Allie shook her head. "This isn't about me. This is way bigger than high school sweethearts."

"He's still obsessed with you, though I can't imagine why. You've caused him nothing but pain since the day you met." Naomi cast a nervous glance over her shoulder.

"You don't know what you're talking about." Allie glowered. "No one but his equal could ever understand what his life has been like."

Naomi took a menacing step forward. "You're the one who doesn't have a clue."

"Naomi," Darius interjected. "I'm happy to see you, but please keep that sharp tongue in check when you're talking to my Syntrophos." He stepped into the shadows, pulling her into a warm embrace. "And Allie, try to retract the claws. We're not getting anywhere."

Talons of jealousy gripped Allie's chest, threatening to rip her apart. The bond didn't want Darius anywhere near Naomi. She wasn't good enough for him.

"How did you get wrapped up in all of this?" he asked, ignoring the jealous rage he could surely sense coming from Allie. "Dad never mentioned you were involved."

"He doesn't know. Aidan's the main event, anyway. I'm just the side piece that comes with the entree."

"You could walk away. There's no way he would risk your safety and freedom," Allie said. "He wouldn't do that to you." It killed her to admit it, but she knew Aidan cared for Naomi and probably always would. She wasn't entirely surprised to find her mixed up in all of this with him.

"We don't really have a choice, Allie. Surely, you can sense that."

"No." Darius took a step back.

Allie turned at his sharp inhale. "What?"

"They are Syntrophos, Allie."

"What? Who?" She turned back to Naomi. "No. No way." She shook her head stubbornly. "You can't be." Her lip curled in disgust. "It's not possible."

"I love him, Allie. I have for a very long time. And now I know he returns my love. We finally make sense. I go where he goes. No matter what. But I no longer believe in what we're doing. The Initiative is ... I just don't trust them anymore."

"Anyone else." Allie shook her head again. "Literally anyone else." Pure, undiluted jealousy bloomed in her chest. She knew what it meant to have a Syntrophos. She understood the intimacy the bond brought and the unquestionable love she felt for Darius. How she couldn't stand to be away from him. How they moved together, in perfect sync. The thought that Aidan had that with Naomi had her grasping for control.

"Sorry to be the one to break it to you, Allie. Well, not really, I rather enjoy the look on your face. Aidan and I bonded the summer after he left for Germany. It's why he didn't come home when he originally planned."

"You never told anyone?" Darius asked. "You didn't think we'd understand? That we could have helped you?"

"We needed time together." She shrugged. "We weren't ready to tell people yet. And then it was too late."

"I just, I can't." Allie looked to Darius for support.

"We are Syntrophos, Allie. You're going to have to deal with that." Naomi gave her a smug smile.

The rare bond wasn't so rare when it came to those Allie loved. She was the heir. She was gathering her equals as the prophecy said she would, but no one ever dreamed it meant she would build an army of Syntrophos to stand beside her. Quinn and Sasha, she trusted with her life, but she would never have chosen Naomi to stand with her. Not in a million years. They were like oil and water. Allie drew her strength from the sun. Naomi drew hers from the moon. They were natural opposites.

"Aidan is your equal; we know that," Naomi said softly. "But I am his other half."

"A third at best," Allie shot back.

"Enough!" Livia snapped. "We have more important things to discuss than petty jealousy, and boys who apparently can't keep it in their pants. What is this Milan Initiative the Chief Justice has put so much effort into?"

"I think they meant well," Naomi said. "At least it seemed like it in the beginning. The people working for the Initiative have treated us well. For the most part."

"What do they have planned?"

"They mean to strike against Soma and put an end to their slave market. This time next year, Soma will be a government-run institution. It will be a school for young Immortals—the way it's supposed to be now. So they say. But I don't believe them anymore."

"Explain," Livia demanded.

"New management, same old game. Nothing will change. Kids need a place to train. Parents will send them there because they don't have options, and then the Senate will be molding the future of our world, making little Senate babies with blind faith in their government. They're crafting new voters."

"And knocking out the competition at the same time," Livia muttered. "How do they think they'll conquer Soma?"

Allie imagined her sister would take it as a personal insult that anyone other than herself would bring an end to the reign of Soma. She built it from the ground up. It was hers to destroy.

"With an army of Syntrophos," Naomi said.

"An army? How many pairs?" Allie asked.

"There are five of us so far. Another three are being trained separately. I think they realized we were getting too close, so they wanted to create contention among us. The Initiative has scoured the world, hunting for us. They want us young before we've bonded with a Complement. We're more susceptible to the training that way."

Eight Syntrophos pairs? Young ones. Allie turned her focus back to her visions. She counted those with discernable faces. Fourteen in all, always drifting around in pairs. The puzzle piece she was missing. *It seems I was right.* "Aidan is protecting them," Allie said. "It's why he's pulled away from the family. He's taken it upon himself to try to save everyone. Not just himself."

"It's not in his nature to turn his back on them. They're mostly just kids," Naomi said. "Aidan and I were lucky. Some of the others came to the Initiative after losing their families to the Coalition. And most had next to no training with nowhere else to go."

"Sounds exactly like Soma," Livia said, crossing her arms over her chest.

"More of the same, indeed." Allie's fists tightened at her sides. "It's always the same story. Powerful kids taken advantage of by those who should know better."

“We’ve been training for this for years, Allie. In a few months, we’ll be infiltrating Sterling Tower. Once we’re inside, we’ll take over. The new group in training now will see to it we don’t fall down on the job. With eight Syntrophos inside, they won’t stand a chance. Our arsenal of abilities can’t be matched.”

“And you’ve all agreed to this?” Allie asked. Part of her was revolted by the idea that the Senate was exploiting the Syntrophos bond, but another part of her was exhilarated by the new information Naomi brought to light.

“Like we have a choice?” Naomi scoffed. “It was all sunshine and rainbows when they were recruiting us a few years ago. Now that they have us, it’s a different story. We’re a family now. No one understands us more than another Syntrophos. In the beginning, the Initiative was a place where we could learn to be what we are. Now, it feels like we’ve been groomed to be mindless weapons for a cause that’s not ours.”

“Leave with us, Naomi,” Darius begged. “Walk away while you can, and we’ll get Aidan out of there eventually.”

“Surely, you understand by now what this bond means to those like us,” Naomi said. “Would you ever leave Allie behind?” She shook her head. “No. It’s not even an option.

Allie glanced at Darius. She would kill before she would die before she would leave him behind.

“They use our love against us.” Naomi’s tone grew soft. “It happened so slowly, we didn’t notice it for a long time. We’ve been given the freedom to make our own choices. Live where we want and do what we please on our own time. But our freedom is an illusion. We can never leave together without escort or an unwelcome tail. No one followed me tonight because Aidan isn’t with me. They know we will always return for the one who matters most. And they know we will never abandon our Syntrophos family. So, we do what they ask. Their agenda is a good one, at least on the surface. We're going to free the slaves of Soma and never let it happen again." Naomi gave a half hearted fist pump as her voice grew hard and her eyes cold. "But they use the same tricks and mind games Soma does. At the end of the day, they are no better. We'll do all the hard work, and they'll reap all the reward."

"You're right; they will be more of the same under a veil of good intentions," Allie agreed. "We have to put an end to this. The younger generations have been used and abused for too long, and no one does anything about it. It's like it's just the norm."

"We scare them." Naomi jutted her chin out. "We are stronger and more talented than they are. They have the years and experience behind them, but we have a strength and focus they will never understand."

"It's time for a change," Allie said. She just didn't know how to bring about that change when all she wanted was to bring Aidan home. But at the same time, she couldn't stomach the thought of turning her back on others experiencing the same or even worse.

"Can you imagine?" Darius said. "Soma as it is but run by our government. People won't know not to trust them."

"At least Soma knows they're evil bastards," Livia said. "We never tried to hide behind a high horse of morality. We knew we were screwing people over."

"We have to get you all out of there before this thing goes down," Allie said.

Naomi shook her head. "Aidan won't leave. He's changed, Allie. He is not the boy you remember. He's darker ... more dangerous. And he believes in what we're doing. That's why I'm here. We can't let this takeover happen, but I don't know how to stop it."

"Surely, he sees the manipulation going on all around him," Allie said.

Naomi grew pale in the moonlight. "He's so focused on Soma and what happened to Quinn and Santi there. He sees this takeover as a way to get real justice for them. The night Quinn came home, Aidan was attacked and wasn't able to help fight with his family. He carries a lot of guilt for that. He thinks if he can be part of the team bringing Soma down, that he'll be able to walk away feeling like he did his part."

"He's ridiculous if he thinks any of that matters." Darius said. "My brother's a noble idiot."

"Yes." Naomi smiled. "But that's why we love him."

"You've helped a great deal, Naomi," Livia said. "Thank you for taking such a risk to meet with us."

"You two are sisters?" Naomi's brow creased in confusion. "I don't see it. I could like you, Livia. But this one, I don't get what's so special about her.

"They say jealousy breeds blind fools," Livia said darkly. "Maybe that's the problem."

"Be careful, Naomi," Darius interjected. "The next time I see you, I'm taking you home."

"Wait, we're not leaving without a plan," Allie said. "We don't have nearly enough to go on yet."

"I can't stay much longer. I'm taking a huge risk just being here with you two." Naomi glanced over her shoulder. "If the Initiative gets a hint of your bond, they'll hunt you down. And then you will do Aidan no favors."

"We will leave today," Livia said. "We have what we came for."

"Do we?" Allie asked. She came for Aidan and didn't want to think about leaving without him.

"Information, Allie. We've learned a great deal since we

arrived. We might not be able to help him now, but we *will* help him. And we will stop this Soma takeover."

"So it seems we're on the same side?" Naomi managed a grimace of a smile.

"I suppose so." Allie wrinkled her nose. "We both love him. And we both know what he means to you." She shared a look with Darius. "And that he's going to do this his way and be damned if he'll hear otherwise."

"Classic Aidan," Naomi said.

"I suppose we finally have a common goal."

"Protect Aidan and the other Syntrophos, despite his good intentions to take the world onto his shoulders all by himself," Naomi said. "Truce?" She offered her hand to Allie. "For Aidan?"

"For Aidan." Allie grasped her hand. "Take care of him." It killed her to say those words. Almost as much as it killed her to leave without him, knowing he was likely only a few hours away.

Be strong, Aidan. Wherever you are.

CHAPTER 11

Allie reluctantly sat between her sister and her Syntrophos. She thumped her foot against the seat in front of her.

"You do that the whole flight, and I'm going to chop off your foot," Livia said.

"Sorry." Allie wrapped her arms around her middle. "I just can't stand leaving without them."

"Them?" Darius smiled. "Has the hatchet finally been buried?"

"It's not like I could leave Naomi behind. She's his Darius." Allie shrugged. "She'll always be a part of him." *In a way I will never be.* Like it or not, Aidan and Naomi were in it forever now.

"We will get them back, along with the other Syntrophos," Livia said. "I will die before I see Soma fall into the hands of the Chief Justice. If I cannot tear that place down to the foundation with my bare hands, then I will see it become what it always should have been. A safe haven for those like you." She took Allie's hand. "Strong, young, and talented Immortals who need a place to learn. To become what they should be without all of the manipulation, lies, and deceit."

"I don't think I ever realized how lucky I was to have the McBriens to train with," Allie leaned back, buckling her seatbelt. "Navid brought me to them for a reason, but I never really got it 'til now. They carefully integrated me into this world with love and patience. They helped me hone my gifts. Emma has been the mentor and friend I couldn't have survived without. I guess I thought that was something everyone had. I never realized how many young Immortals don't have access to decent training with teachers they can trust."

"Maybe it's time to force a change," Livia said. "It would be nice for me to be on the right side of things for once. Marcus would die of shame."

"How do you even make a change like that on such a big scale?" Allie asked. "We have to start with Aidan and Naomi. And if we can manage it, we'll stop this takeover and help the other Syntrophos, too. Then maybe one day we can do more."

"You're not thinking big enough, sister." Livia shook her head. "Aidan and Naomi are perfectly safe for the moment. But there are so many more who aren't. I have seen into the darkest depths of the Senate and into the lives of those representatives who are hungry for more and more power. The Senate is Soma's best customer, and it seems they've taken enough lessons over the years to start generating their own slaves in the guise of this Milan Initiative."

"What exactly are you suggesting?" Darius asked.

"We take Soma before the Initiative has a chance to, and then we focus on freeing the Syntrophos. We would have a much stronger chance of success with the power of Soma behind us."

"What do you mean, *take* Soma?" Allie frowned. After all her sister had been through under Marcus's rule, she couldn't imagine how she'd ever want to go back, much less take over.

"It's all there, Allie. The facility. Genuine people who care. The kids who need help. It's all just in the wrong hands. I always tried to do little things to defy my father and protect the

Soma kids when I could. In my absence, Jayesh has continued in that endeavor. We've been working together for years to make subtle changes Marcus wouldn't notice, but it's not enough. I'll be damned if I see my life's work fall into the hands of a corrupt government. They'll do more harm than Soma ever did because they'll be doing it from a high moral ground."

"Where would you even begin?" Allie asked.

"We'll discuss it when we get home," Livia said, casting a glance down the aisle at the flight attendants preparing for takeoff.

"It's a long flight, Liv. And I can give us the privacy we need," Darius said. "Let's discuss it now."

Allie could see the physical evidence of Darius's soundproofing gift at work in a way he couldn't. A shimmery golden haze cast them in a warm, glowing bubble. "Pull it in a little tighter." She guided him, watching the bubble shrink closer around them. "That's it."

"No one can hear us now," Darius said. "This talk of saving all the suffering children of the world is all well and good, but Aidan is my *brother*." His fists clenched in his lap. "And Naomi is my oldest friend. We grew up together with Aidan and Sasha following us around like puppies. Naomi presents a hard front, but you have no idea what she's been through. She's not as tough as she'd like you to believe. The Naomi I just saw, something's happened to her. She's heartbroken and terrified, and not just for the obvious reasons. We have to get them out of there as soon as possible. If that means we take over Soma, then let's do it. So long as we're doing something about it."

"All right, what's your plan?" Allie took Darius's hand and turned toward her sister.

"It's simple. We walk in and take it."

"That's easier said than done," Allie said.

"Jayesh has placed people we can trust throughout the

Soma system. Marcus and his loyal lapdogs wouldn't know what happened until it was too late."

"You've been preparing for this?" Darius asked.

"We've just been waiting for the right opportunity, but it will be risky. We need the right people on our side, and we need to plan for every possibility."

"Who do we need?" Allie asked.

Livia gave her a hard stare. "We need you."

"Me? What can I do?"

"We need the heir, Allie. A person the young ones can look to for support. A person who can quickly drive the kind of change we need to see. Someone your generation can get behind. And someone the old ones can respect."

"But how?" There was no way Allie could be all of those things.

"Take your position seriously and use it to help not only Aidan and Naomi, but the countless others who have been used and manipulated for their power. The abuse starts high, and it rolls down hill. I never wanted to be what I became. I never set out to be a ruthless slaver but when I resisted my father's orders, my mother suffered for it. I never had a choice. Soma is what it is because I was too scared to stand up to him. He no longer has me over a barrel. My mother is safe now, and it's time to do something I should have done a long time ago. But I can't do it alone."

"It's a good plan, Allie," Darius said. "It has teeth. It's bold."

"Declaring myself to our world?" The very idea terrified her, but if she were ever going to use her position, it would be for something like this.

"It's not what you say, it's what you do. You walk into Soma like you own the place and you take it. You announce yourself and your agenda. You'll win some over. Some will resist. And some will just want to leave."

"All right, just for argument's sake, let's say I do that, and by some miracle, we pull it off. Then what? How do we keep it? Marcus will blow us off the map. And the Senate will paint us as the bad guys terrorizing innocent children. But more importantly, how would we keep those under Soma's roof from being harmed in the process? This is about ending things like that. Not causing more unnecessary damage."

"I have an idea just crazy enough to work. If Quinn can pull it off, Marcus won't be able to touch us or anyone under our protection," Livia said.

"Quinn?" Allie's mind raced with ideas. Livia was right. Declaring herself would get the attention they needed. And it wouldn't be about Allie agreeing to be some kind of ruler. It would be about using the title to get shit done. And Quinn could definitely help keep them safe while doing it. "You want him to use the dreamworld to protect Sterling Tower?"

"It's been done before. If we can get in the building at the right time when Marcus is away, we can make this as easy as a change in management."

Allie blew out a big breath. She couldn't believe she was even considering this. "We take Soma before the Initiative can. We make it what it's supposed to be, and then we go after Aidan and the others. Give them the same protection we've given the kids at Soma."

"The Chief Justice won't sit back and let it happen. They will come for us," Livia said. "And they'll make us out to be the bad guys."

"Let them," Darius said. "It needs to happen and in time, we'll show the world we're the ones looking out for their kids' best interests."

"It's a stupid-crazy plan. But it could work," Allie said, resisting the tremor of fear at the idea of actually doing what they were discussing.

"We're going to need to visit Jayesh first. We have a layover in New York. We can change our connecting flight to Atlanta and meet with him tomorrow."

"Just to talk about it, right?" Allie eyed her sister. "We're not actually doing this yet?"

"Of course," Livia said, pulling out her phone to text Jayesh before their plane took off.

"What will the ice queen have to say about all this?" Allie asked.

"She will get on board with anything that gets you to consider claiming your title. This is right up her alley. And Grandfather will be all over this."

"And you two? Where will you be?"

"Right beside you," they echoed.

CHAPTER 12

"I still don't think it's safe for you to even be in Atlanta again," Allie said as they stepped onto the MARTA train at the busy Atlanta airport. "You shouldn't go anywhere near Sterling Tower. I'm going to meet with Jayesh alone."

"Not happening," Darius said, clutching the pole with a white-knuckle grip to steady himself as the train took off across the ginormous terminal. "We're all going. I'm not letting you out of my sight, and Livia knows who to trust and who to avoid."

"So does Jayesh," Allie insisted.

"What if you got separated from him? What if you got in and couldn't get back out?" Darius argued.

"It doesn't matter; it's not open for discussion." Livia crossed her arms over her chest as the train slowed to a halt. "You need to get used to the idea that Darius and I will be at your side, always. We each have our roles to play. I am comfortable with mine. It's time you get acquainted with yours."

"My role sucks, want to switch?"

"I was not born to fulfill your role." Livia cocked her head, arching a perfectly sculpted brow. "I was born to fulfill mine. And my role is to be your right hand. While we are in Sterling Tower, you will not leave my side. Understood?"

"Fine, but we're checking into a hotel first," Allie muttered as she followed Darius and Livia from the train car. "My hair has become an emergency situation, and no one's going anywhere until I get a shower."

"No, we can't go anywhere with you looking like that," Livia said, heading for the escalator and down to baggage claim. "You'll never make it past Soma security.

"I told you to wear a hat." Darius winked, but more than anyone, he looked like he could use a good meal, a long nap, and a hot shower.

"Well, at least there's one thing I can count on." Allie sighed as she followed them. "While I might be *thinking* about taking the leap to claim my title as first princess, I'm almost certain you two won't ever be kissing my royal butt.

A sleek, black town car met them at the curb outside their hotel. Feeling refreshed after a long, hot shower and an hour attempting, and failing, to work out all the tangles in her hair, Allie was ready to see Sterling Tower for herself.

"Are you kidding me?" Allie rolled her eyes as she slid into the backseat beside Darius.

"Really, Grandfather, you need some new tricks," Livia said, cracking a smile. "This one is getting old."

"But it's my favorite." Alexander glanced back at them from the driver's seat.

"Grandma, can't you get him on a leash?" Allie asked the queen, sitting in the front passenger seat.

"I've tried. He's become cagey in his old age. I've found it best to go along with his shenanigans. It's usually entertaining. Oh dear, what is going on with your hair?"

“The curls don’t travel well.” Allie sighed. “Why are you guys here?”

"I take it you don't need instructions?" Livia asked as they headed toward Midtown.

“Way ahead of you, sweetheart,” Alexander said.

"You didn’t think we’d let our girls walk into Sterling Tower alone?" Alísun glanced back at them over her sunglasses. "We are here to assist."

“It’s called backup, honey,” Alexander said.

“Ah, well then, we’re here for backup.” Alísun smiled.

“Or take over?” Allie narrowed her eyes at her grandmother.

"My dear, I named you my heir for a reason. Haven't you figured that out yet?"

"Not really, Grandma.”

"We can never return to the days of Indriell, but we need leaders who advocate for their people the way our ancestors did. In the old days, when it came time for a queen to name her heir, it wasn't about strengthening her own rule; it was a symbol of her desire to pass her rule on to the next generation. I named you my heir, not to give our family the power of the royals again, but to give it to you. We are here to support you and give you guidance and protection if you need it. But as they say, the ball is on your side now, dear.”

“The ball is in your court,” Alexander corrected her with a chuckle.

“What he said.” Alísun laughed. “Your grandfather is still trying to teach me all the new slang you kids use these days. We spent all last month on emojis.”

“You still might need to work on that, Grandma. The brown swirly emoji doesn’t mean what you think it means.” Allie laughed at all the times she got a text from Alísun suggesting they go get frozen yogurt.

"Tell us your plan, girls. Your grandfather likes to think he knows it already, but the subtle nuances of intent can escape his omniscient power."

"Hey, I got us here before the party started, didn't I?" Alexander gave his Complement a wink.

Alísun squeezed his shoulder. "Hush, dear."

"We have a meeting with Jayesh. He has been making some changes at Soma," Livia said. "Enough to help us if Allie decides to stage a coup."

"We're—I'm not making any moves," Allie said. "This is just a reconnaissance mission."

"We will be taking over eventually, though?" Alexander asked. "I assume that is your *intent*," he added with an exaggerated eye roll in his wife's direction.

"Just let the girls decide, Alexander. They know what they're doing."

"I'm just asking questions, dear. It's the polite thing to do, rather than *assume* I know it all already."

"Have you two thought about therapy?" Allie smiled, grateful for her grandparent's comic relief. She was so nervous, if she really took the time to think about what she was about to do, she'd chicken out.

"It's just a conversation, Allie," Darius said softly, taking her hand. But he looked even more worried than she felt.

CHAPTER 13

Sterling Tower was a rather unassuming addition to the Atlanta skyline. No one would ever know it was really a prison for innocent children and teens headed for the slave market.

"How will we get past security?" Darius asked. Allie absently took his clammy hand. She eyed him warily, noticing how his hands shook. Everything was moving so fast, she hadn't had the time to ask him how he felt about all of this. He'd seemed all for it on the plane when it was just an idea they were discussing, but everything she did affected him. If she really chose to take on this huge responsibility, Darius would be in it with her, whether he liked it or not. She needed him to know she wouldn't do anything against his wishes. But her forced smile and gentle pressure on his hand was all the encouragement she could muster at the moment.

"Jayesh knows we're coming, and he knows the gist of the plan. He's prepared security for my return," Livia said. "We just walk in like we're home."

"Are you sure about this, Liv?" Allie asked nervously, staring up at the building across the street. "I really don't want you to go in there. This place was bad for you. And you've come so far. I can do this with—"

"I will be fine, little sister." Livia took her free hand and squeezed it tight. "Just ... stay with me and I'll be okay."

"All right, we're all following your lead, then." Allie stepped off the curb, trailing after her sister across the street. She didn't like the way Livia's shoulders stiffened with tension the closer they got to the entrance. Allie took one last deep breath as they stepped through the front doors of Sterling Tower.

"Ms. Livia. It's good to see you," one of the security guards said.

"Thank you, Robert. It's good to be home."

"Mr. Basu is expecting you." The security officer stepped aside to let them through, bypassing the inspection completely.

Allie watched as the other security officers collectively took two steps back from the ancient royals, unconsciously responding to their collective presence.

"May I take your coats? Offer you coffee? Water?" The concierge asked nervously.

Allie gazed around the white marbled lobby. Sunlight streamed in through the windows, setting the crystal chandelier ablaze. She could see her sister's touch in the décor—clean, white, and minimal with small pops of color in the artwork hanging on the walls. Elegant, without much fuss.

"No thank you, Eric," Livia replied. "We will go straight up if you'll call the elevator."

The young man lunged for the elevator bank and inserted a key to call a car down from the top floor.

It was a stressful few moments, waiting in silence for the elevator to arrive. Livia let out a breath as the doors closed behind them, and they began to ascend. Quickly.

"Whoa, that's fast." Allie stumbled, her stomach back on the ground floor with Eric.

"I was an impatient woman back then," Livia muttered.

"This elevator was for my personal use, so I could get in and out of the building quickly and not have to encounter anyone on the way."

"Not impatient, Livia," Alísun said. "You kept yourself as far removed from the children as you could. You had to. To protect yourself."

"This way, quickly," Jayesh said the moment the elevator doors opened. "The fewer people who see you here, the better. I'd rather it be more of a rumor that you're back, than a fact."

Allie had never actually met Jayesh Basu before, but Sasha spoke of him often. The two were close friends after spending years together at the Chola Valley Temple. When they went their separate ways, Jayesh returned to work for Marcus and was put in charge of Soma when Livia went missing. But his time with Sasha had changed him for the better. He was dedicated to making a difference at Soma—as much as one person could do on their own.

"It is an honor to meet you, Allie, Darius." He gave a respectful nod to Alísun and Alexander. "I've heard so much about you all from Sasha. How is she?" Jayesh leaned a hip against the cluttered desk behind him.

Sasha was head over heels for the older man, but Jayesh kept them firmly on the "just friends" track. "She's doing well, thank you," Allie murmured, looking around the disaster of an office. Underneath the mess, the room was once a pristine, white space worthy of Livia's taste for simple elegance.

"What have you done to my office?" Livia cringed.

"I was never a fan of all the cold, hard surfaces in this place. All this white crap needed some color."

"In the form of paper by the looks of it." Livia eyed a stack of brightly colored folders strewn across his desk.

"Have a seat everyone." Jayesh waved Allie, Darius, and

Livia into the seats in front of his desk, offering the couch to Alísun and Alexander. "You were cryptic on the phone, Liv. What's going on?"

"No need to beat around the bush," she said. "The Chief Justice is preparing to make a move on Soma. They intend to hit you with a total takeover. Inside job."

"We've been prepared for that for years. What makes this threat any more vital than the other rumors?"

"It's not a rumor. They are building an army of Syntrophos, called the Milan Initiative," Allie interjected. "They intend to place them all here in the guise of new students. The Syntrophos pairs can work together, using their collective abilities in ways you will never be able to predict. They've been trained as an army. They'll have you over a barrel before you even know they're here."

Jayesh rubbed his chin. "And is the Senate also behind this Initiative?"

"Only the top tier Senators and Chief Justice from what we can tell," Livia said. "They are doing it in the name of ending the Soma slave market and the abuse of the children who come here for help, but when it's all said and done, Soma will be a government run institution."

"So they'll make it even worse." Jayesh sighed. "We can't let that happen."

"Marcus won't let you resign," Livia said. "But you're not working for him anymore. We're going to take Soma before the Milan Initiative has a chance to. You know Allie has been named. She will be able to make a stand."

"I've been ready for this for a long time." Jayesh's face broke into a wide grin. "We need to get our plan in motion, secure the building, and then have Allie address the students."

"Wait a frigging minute." Allie's voice cracked with fear.

"We're just talking here. We can't just wing it. We need to work out a careful plan and then decide if it's even feasible."

"We need to get the ball rolling now, Allie. Before it's too late," Livia said. "I understand if you have reservations about taking your title, but we have to at least thwart this takeover while we have a chance. With or without you."

"I'm with you. I just—it's happening so fast." Allie leaned back in her chair, trying to stop her mind from spinning. She eyed her sister and Jayesh, so eager to move forward with this plan. With a deep breath, she decided to put her big girl pants on and do this thing.

"I won't leave the kids in residence unprotected," Jayesh said, "but we've got a lot of kids in the field we need to think about, too."

"We can't free them all at once," Livia said. "But you can issue a recall on a few select individuals we've placed into slavery. We owe it to them all, but we have to start with those who are essential."

"For what?" Allie frowned. She didn't want to be part of yet another group using young people for their own agendas.

"We will give them a choice, Allie. Complete freedom, no strings attached. Or, if they choose, they can help us end this bullshit once and for all. I imagine most of them will leave us without a backward glance, but a few might stay. One in particular I would like to see stay."

"She will," Jayesh said. "I'll go get her myself. And once she has the full story, I think we can count on her to pick up where she left off."

Livia nodded. "When you return, we will meet again. You will no longer be working for the old Soma. You will be working with us to make a new Soma. It's time we offer these kids a genuine safe haven."

"And it's about time we work together, on the same side," Jayesh said.

"Wait just a minute." Allie stood, throwing her arms out as if to physically restrain them from making plans faster than she could comprehend. "Pause." Her gaze sought Darius. He was pale and far too quiet for one who never hesitated to offer his opinion. The bond between them grew cold, making Allie shiver. "You guys are forgetting one very important thing. If this were just about me taking my birthright and doing some good with it, I wouldn't hesitate. But Darius is my Syntrophos. What we're deciding right now affects his future, too, and I'm not going to make this decision without him."

"We have to do this, Allie," Darius said, his voice weak.

"You say that, but I'm feeling all sorts of things from our bond that say something else. If you don't want to do this, tell me now."

"I'm just a little nervous about what all this means. But you know me. I'm not one to shy away from a fight. You have my full support."

"Okay." Allie sat back on the edge of her seat. "Unpause. We're really doing this?" She gave them each a hard stare.

"Is there really a choice here, Allie?" Livia tilted her head with a pointed look of her own.

"No." Allie focused on her hands in her lap. "Okay." She nodded, sitting up straighter. "I want everyone at Sterling Tower given the opportunity to leave if they want to. From management all the way down to the concierge."

"Agreed," Jayesh said. "Although we will have many more in house who will be willing to stay, but likely, only two recalled from the field will be with us."

"Who?" Livia asked. "Tessa St. James, but who else?"

"Dean McBrien," Jayesh said. "He's with her."

"Dean?" Darius gasped, growing even paler. Dean was

Darius and Aidan's cousin. He was taken the night of Livia's attack on their family.

"You've had him all this time? His parents believe he is in a Coalition prison," Allie said.

"Unfortunately, he is in a prison of sorts, but not with the Coalition. He trusts me. His situation could have been far worse. And Tessa, she's going to be a tough sell. I'm the one who put her there, but I put Dean with her, so she wouldn't be alone."

"We need her," Livia said. "The people here will trust her. If she's on board, she will inspire many others to stay."

"Who is she?" Allie asked.

"She's probably the one we screwed over the most." Livia frowned. "But she might be willing to help."

"Where are they?" Allie asked.

"South America," Jayesh replied. "It will take me a few weeks to arrange their release."

"Meet us back in Cleveland when you've got them," Allie said. "It's time we have something of a summit meeting."

"Are you ready for this, my girl?" Alísun said softly. True to their word, she and Alexander had remained on the sidelines during the entire exchange.

Allie nodded. "Something has to be done. In the last five years, I've seen so many young Immortals suffering at the hands of our very own government. It has to end. If that means I have to be the freaking first princess and heir of the Indriell throne to do something about it, then so be it." Allie stood and faced Jayesh. Livia and Darius rose to stand at her side.

"From this moment forward, Soma is no more. I'm dissolving it, and we're going to work like hell to build it back up into something we can be proud of. But we are going to free the Syntrophos of the Milan initiative, too. Bringing Aidan and Naomi home is a priority. I just need everyone here to understand that I have no idea what I'm doing, and I'm going to need all the help I can get."

"We are right here with you," Alexander said, draping his arm around the queen. "And we are so very proud of you both."

"It is my honor to swear my fealty to the royals of Indriell and to the heir," Jayesh said with respect.

"Oh come on! Are people really going to do that?" Allie groaned.

"You'll get used to it, dear," Alísun said. "You will eventually learn to think of yourself as two individuals. Allie the heir. And Allie the girl. The heir will not flinch when someone pledges their loyalty, but the girl can have a hissy fit about it later." Alísun moved to stand in front of Allie. "You just need to remember that none of us expect you to be perfect." She grabbed Allie's hands and held them tightly in her own. "We simply believe in you, darling girl."

"It's still up to you," Livia said. "Will you be the heir? Will you step forward and use your voice to end this once and for all?"

Allie nodded. "I will." *I have to do this for Aidan.* For Aidan, she would move mountains.

Allie was sitting quietly in the car when the pressure of so much responsibility suddenly hit her. And it wasn't as scary as she'd built it up in her mind to be. She was *excited.*

I can do this.

Livia climbed into the seat beside her, giving a full body shiver the moment she closed the car door. "I'm glad that's over. That place is like stepping into a nightmare of my own making."

"We'll redecorate," Alísun said, sliding into the front seat.

"It'll be beautiful. The place just needs some color and warmth."

"Call George." Darius opened the door and fell into the backseat. "Like right now." He bent over, clutching his head.

"What's wrong?" Allie tugged him closer, running her hands over his back, looking for injury. She felt a tremor of fear and dread wash over her. Fear that wasn't her own. "Darius look at me," Allie said, lifting his chin. His eyes were glazed with pain. "I thought you were just freaked out by the decisions we just made but that wasn't it. What's going on, Dare?"

"I need my mentor." He grasped her hand with his clammy ones. "Call ... George.

"Darius?" Alísun leaned over the seat to check his pulse, forcing him to look at her. "Are you close to your Proving, dear?"

He nodded.

"What?" Allie fumbled for her phone. "That's not possible. It's way too soon! "

"He's not quite there yet, but it's definitely coming. We need to get him back home to George." Alísun helped ease Darius back in his seat, resting his head on Allie's shoulder.

"He'll be fine," Alísun said, smoothing her hand over his forehead. "Don't worry, Darius. We'll get you home as soon as we can."

Darius grasped the queen's hand. "Has it started? I need George. I can't do this without him."

"Relax. It hasn't started. You're a bit young for this, but you still have time. It is important that you stay calm right now."

Allie finally managed to get her phone out of her pocket and hastily dialed George's number. "Hello? George?" she breathed into the phone. "It's Darius. He doesn't look good, what do I do? We're in Atlanta ... yes, our flight leaves soon."

Allie closed her eyes as she listened to George's instructions to keep Darius calm and quiet.

"He'll be okay, won't he?" she asked. She wasn't prepared to help Darius with this. She didn't even understand what was happening.

"Just get him here," George said. "Now."

Chapter 14

"How is he doing?" Sasha watched as Darius made a beeline for the door after class, his phone clutched in hand.

"Freaked out and not talking to me." Allie sighed. "It's weird. We've never had anything come between us like this."

"Entering a Proving at his age, he must be terrified."

"It's killing me that I can't help him." Allie felt caught in a weird timeout. Back home and in class again, nothing felt real. Except the waiting. Waiting to hear from Jayesh about their next move. Waiting and watching Darius with no insight into what he was going through.

"He'll be okay, Allie. He'll talk when he's ready."

"I just stay nearby in case he needs me," Allie murmured. He'd been sick since they got home. "I'm going to go see if he's okay. I'll catch up with you later." She followed her Syntrophos from the building and across the campus quad.

Allie paused, watching Darius pace across the snow-dusted lawn, oblivious of the cold as he spoke to his mentor on the phone. The bond buzzed within her. He was upset. She was jogging to his side before she'd even made a conscious decision to do so. He needed her.

"I'll talk to you later, George," Darius said as she approached.

"Can we please talk?" She took his hand, hot with fever, and headed back inside the humanities building. She had one more class before she was done for the day. An art history lecture she'd been looking forward to all semester. But none of that mattered now.

"Everything okay with George?" she asked. He was Darius's mentor and brother-in-law. They'd trained together since Darius was five years old.

"Fine, just making plans."

He was petrified. And doing a piss poor job of hiding it.

"Let's get a coffee. We have time before my next class." She led him to the coffee cart she was pretty sure she single-handedly kept in business.

After her freshman year, Allie and Naeemah came to terms with the battle over her diet. Naeemah finally relented and promised not to touch Allie's coffee. The trade off was she had to behave in every other aspect of her nutrition. She typically adhered to it—most of the time.

"You're scaring me, Dare. I know this doesn't really concern me. It's something you and your mentor have to get through together, but I want to help," Allie said as they took their seats at a small corner table.

"Everything concerns you." He attempted a smile, but he was so quiet and aloof these days, it scared her. "It's nothing, really. I'm fine." He coughed into a napkin.

Allie suppressed a tremor of terror when she saw spots of blood smeared on it.

"Liar." She tried to return his smile but was equally unsuccessful. "You know I'm not going to give it a rest, so you might as well tell me what's going on. Why are you sick? I don't understand."

"It's nothing. Not in light of the whole Soma takeover." He shrugged, absently shredding a napkin into a thousand pieces.

"Darius." She took his hand. "Nothing that affects you this way is unimportant."

"Ahh, don't give me those Syntrophos eyes, Red. I'll be fine. I promise."

"Our bond goes both ways, Dare. If you hurt, I hurt." She moved closer, lowering her voice. "Now tell me. Why are you sick? We don't get sick."

"George says it's expected with a Proving at my age." He shrugged and took a scalding gulp of coffee.

"In all the years since my Awakening, no one has ever given me a straight answer about what a Proving even is. Like it's an inside secret I'm not privy to yet. All I know is that it's an extension of an Awakening. And it's supposed to happen at a time when you're ready for it. A time when you're a lot older than you are now. This isn't right. You are way too young."

"The time between an Awakening and a Proving is just a reprieve, and it's different for everyone. It happens when it happens, Allie. That's all I can really tell you."

"Bullshit, Darius. You are scared to death. I can feel it in our bond. You're sick. Weak. Terrified. I can't ignore that. Please don't ask me to."

"This is why I didn't tell you," he said, continuing to shred his napkin into little brown paper balls.

"Tell me what?"

"We've been preparing for my Proving for almost a year. George knew it was coming, but we thought I had a lot more time."

"A *year*? Like a whole year and you didn't tell me? Darius we are partners. We don't keep secrets in this relationship." She wanted to hug him and shake him at the same time. "How do I keep missing the important things in my friends' lives? I should be seeing this stuff coming at us."

"You're too close. It's like the way you don't always notice how big Kahlynn's gotten because you see her everyday. Your gift just doesn't notice it."

"I call bullshit. What's the point of seeing the future if you can't help your friends?"

"I thought I had more time, Allie," he said, his eyes huge with the kind of fear he would never let anyone else see.

"This is why you've been so sick?"

He nodded. "The vomiting, coughing up blood, sleeplessness, they're all signs that it's almost here."

"But you're going to be okay, right?" she asked.

"Eventually. But my Proving is coming a good five or ten decades too early." He shook his head. "I'm not okay with that. The symptoms I'm having are because I'm so young. It doesn't happen like this for everyone. My power is ready. My mind is ready, but my body isn't quite there yet."

"What does that mean?"

"We'll have to wait and see, I guess. It's like an Awakening."

"All you can do is get through it and figure out what to do later?"

"Exactly.

"This is because of me, isn't it?" She frowned. "Something about our bond has accelerated your Proving."

"It's not your fault, Allie. You did not cause this, the same way you didn't bring this bond down on us either."

"And if I ask George, what's he going to say?" Allie prodded.

"Well, George is pretty sure our bond has something to do with it."

"I'm so sorry, Darius." She closed her eyes in resignation. She was always hurting the people she loved despite her best efforts to protect them. "You didn't ask for this."

"Neither did you. And if I could go back and undo this bond with you, I wouldn't. It's the best thing that's ever happened to me."

"Me too." She smiled. Darius was her ride or die guy. She couldn't imagine a world where he wasn't by her side. Come hell or high water, they would get through this.

"I don't care what George says, Darius Proving early is not your fault." Emma's eyes flashed with fury. "And if he has implied otherwise, I'll be having a little chat with him."

"Don't be angry with him, Emma." Allie stared out the gym window across the lawn at the little cottage where she and Darius lived. "He's just trying to get Darius through this."

"It's no one's fault, Allie." Emma stepped behind her, placing a comforting hand on her shoulder. "We reach our Proving when it's time. It happens when it happens."

"I expected mine to be early, but not his." She leaned back, resting her head on her mentor's shoulder.

"He will get through it."

"And you will tell me when my Proving is near?" Allie turned to face her. "Like the minute you know?" She pleaded with her eyes. She couldn't be blindsided by this.

"It is my job as your mentor to pay attention to the signs. I will see it and when I am confident it's coming, I will warn you. We've always planned for an early Proving. We will be ready when the time comes."

"Will I be sick like Darius?"

"I don't think so, but I can't guarantee it."

"What does it really mean, Emma?" Allie returned to sit on the ridiculously expensive white leather chair. She leaned forward, resting her arms on her knees. "What am I supposed to Prove?"

"It's a continuation of— "

"I know all that." Allie waved her hand. "But what does that actually mean? What are the consequences?"

"When the Proving comes upon you, it means you have nearly mastered your power. It means you have one last hurdle to jump before you will have complete control over your power and your gifts. It is the last step toward adulthood."

"He's barely thirty years old." She sat back with a sigh. "He's the poster child for Peter Pan syndrome. Darius is not an adult. He is not ready for this. Has my power through our bond pushed him into this way too soon?"

"No, Allie. It doesn't work like that."

"George seems to think I'm to blame. How do you know I'm not? Syntrophos bonds are so rare. A few years ago, we didn't know much about it."

"And you think that when you and Darius bonded, and Sasha and Quinn—my own son—bonded, that we didn't look into it? That we haven't spent the last four years uncovering every detail we could about the Syntrophos bond?"

"Fair point. What have you discovered?"

"Nothing that would indicate what you suspect. There is simply no way you have brought this down on Darius."

"So you're saying if Darius had never met me, he'd still be facing an early Proving right now?"

Emma's brow furrowed in frustration. "Not ... necessarily," she admitted.

"Exactly." Allie twisted her hands in her lap.

"You and your bond are a contributing factor, but that doesn't change the fact that he *is* ready. The circumstances of his life have played out in a way that makes him naturally ready for his Proving. Had you never met, those circumstances would be different, and he might not be ready. But the bottom line is it's not your fault."

Allie nodded, still not convinced. The concept of the Proving still evaded her. There was something about it she failed to wrap her mind around. Something important.

Chapter 15

"Feeling better?" Allie grasped Darius's hand as they headed into their favorite restaurant near school.

"Yes." He smiled, looking more like himself again. Some of his color had returned in the last few days. "I think I'm actually hungry."

"That's a good sign, right?" She was desperate for him to pull through this. She hated feeling so useless, and she knew her constant hovering was driving him insane.

"As long as I don't throw it all back up after." He waved at George across the restaurant, heading to join him and his family.

"Hey, Lennox." Allie slid into the booth beside Seamas and George's daughter. Dressed in her Cliffton Academy uniform, she reminded Allie of a version of herself from another lifetime. Cynical and a bit of a wild child, Lennox and Allie were good friends, despite the years between them. A product of Soma, Lennox had grown up without the benefit of family and friends. When Quinn and Santi made their daring escape from Soma, they refused to leave Lennox behind and arranged for her escape as well.

"We've already ordered," George said, "but we haven't been here long." He waved the waitress over.

"Hi there, handsome, what can I get you?" The waitress immediately gave her full attention to Darius, practically sitting in his lap.

Allie and Lennox shared a silent fit of giggles. Women were always throwing themselves at Darius. Most of the time he was eager to catch them, but he so wasn't feeling it today.

"He looks like he's going to puke again," Lennox whispered behind her menu.

"Poor guy." Allie stifled her laughter. "I think he might actually be embarrassed."

The waitress was absolutely besotted with him. She was a sweet, innocent girl, just looking for love anywhere she could find it. Allie's clairvoyant gift allowed her to see those kinds of things in the people she encountered. She could see right down to the root of a person's true character and know who they were at their core. Darius had recently learned that their bond allowed him to see some of the same details, but on a much smaller scale.

"I'll just have the soup of the day and some bread, please," Darius said, his ears turning bright red at her blatant attention.

Allie kicked him under the table.

"Oh, and a dozen hot wings with blue cheese, a basket of cheese sticks, and a coke," Darius added.

Allie cleared her throat.

"And a slice of cheesecake, too."

"And you?" The waitress turned her nose up at Allie.

"Caesar salad with extra chicken and a bowl of vegetable soup," Allie said, staring at the menu. "And a lemonade, please. I'll probably need a to-go box, too."

"To-go box?" Lennox wrinkled her nose after the waitress left to get their drinks. "I feel so sorry for you, Allie. Dads, I don't ever have to eat like that, do I?" She turned to George and Seamas for confirmation.

"It wouldn't hurt when you're a little older if you put some effort into a clean diet," George said. "It will make you stronger."

"It sucks, Len. Don't listen to him." Allie loaded up a dinner roll with copious amounts of butter.

"It's all about moderation, sweetheart." Seamas eyed Allie with raised brows. "We've worked hard these last few years to get you where you are now. Your diet is fine. You've made a lot of sacrifices in your recovery. Food shouldn't be one of them."

"We could talk about a not-so-strict clean diet, Seamas," George said. "Our daughter is seventeen now; it would help—"

"I finally have my power under control for the first time since I was thirteen," Lennox said. "I'm more than good with that."

After suffering an early Awakening, Lennox had to work hard to maintain control of her power. She'd worked with Seamas for hours every day since she joined their family. She flourished under Seamas's experience and after nearly four years, she was progressing normally.

"The effort now will save you a lot of worry later," Darius said.

Everyone looked at him like he had three heads. "Coming from you, I don't quite know how to take that," George said.

"I'm just saying, a little more discipline now would go a long way in preparing her for things later in life."

"Uncle D?" Lennox frowned at him. "Are you sure you're feeling all right?"

"He's fine." Allie assured the girl. "He's just having a tough time lately." Allie didn't want to worry her. Lennox had been through enough in her short life to last her an eternity. She didn't need gloomy talk of unexpected Provings wearing her down. After her escape from Soma, Lennox fell head over heels for her new dads. She'd bonded with Seamas on sight and with

George not long after. But she'd struggled to acclimate to the kind of idyllic childhood her new fathers tried to give her. To look at her now, you'd never know she'd spent her early years training for a life in slavery.

"Seriously, what's the point in salad?" Lennox wrinkled her nose as the waitress placed a bowl of greens in front of Allie. "How can you get through a day eating rabbit food? I think I'm too much of a carnivore for clean diets." She dove into her bloody steak.

"Salad is the devil." Allie shoved her plate aside. She'd take it home for lunch tomorrow. "Naeemah makes it hard to enjoy a night of splurging. She's hit every restaurant in town so no matter what I order, this is what they bring me. So we have a system." She met Darius's high five without looking. She nodded at him. "We split his food and take mine to go."

"I'm sure Mom knows exactly what we're doing," Darius said, "but Allie sticks to her clean diet most of the time because it does help."

"But when I don't, I do so with great gusto." Allie dipped her spicy wings into the cool blue cheese, her stomach rumbling in anticipation.

"You guys are adorable." Lennox smirked. "You should totally hook up."

"Hey, now, what do you know about hooking up?" George grumbled.

"Aw, Dad, you're so cute. I know things. And these two should totally be together," Lennox insisted.

"We are together as Syntrophos," Darius said, picking at his breadsticks and leaving his soup untouched. "Any more togetherness between us would be way too much togetherness for anyone."

"Damn straight," Allie agreed. But her heart sank at the

sight of him barely touching his food. He might be feeling better, but he was still scared.

Idiot. She wanted to clap herself on the forehead. The fact that his symptoms were fading wasn't a good sign. It meant he was out of time.

Chapter 16

Allie walked beside Seamas on the way out of the restaurant. "You think he's okay?" she whispered, watching Darius walk ahead of them. His feet shuffled across the parking lot, like he wasn't quite in control of his steps.

"It's getting close," Seamas said, "but we're watching him for the signs. Try not to worry so much. Honestly, that's the best way you'll be able to help him." He laid a comforting hand on her shoulder.

"Uncle D?" Lennox rushed across the parking lot. "Dads, something's wrong!" She took several steps away form Darius who was standing in the middle of the drive, blocking cars from entering the restaurant.

George and Allie were at his side in a heartbeat.

"Darius?" Allie snapped her fingers in front of his face, but his eyes were glazed over, unseeing and smoldering with the golden light of his power.

"We're out of time," George said, moving into action. "Seamas, can you take Lennox and Allie home?" He guided Darius toward his SUV and away from the honking drivers waiting to park.

"Of course." Seamas stood with Lennox beside Allie's car.

"Like hell. I'm coming with you." Allie tossed Seamas the keys to her car and scrambled to help George with Darius.

"I don't have time to argue," George said. "Just stay out of the way."

"Darius?" His face was ashen and his mouth twisted in agony, like he wanted to scream but there was no sound. Allie cried out in alarm when he collapsed beside the car in a boneless heap. "What's happening?" She bent over him, helping George get him to his feet. His head lolled back as they laid him across the backseat.

"It's starting, Allie. We need to get him to the underground. Now!" George raced to the driver's side, his long dreadlocks a blur behind him.

Allie hopped into the backseat, crouching beside Darius as George flew out of the parking lot.

"It's going to be okay, Dare." Allie brushed her hand across his brow, burning hot with fever. *Please, God, let him be okay.*

"Hurry, George." Allie clutched Darius's hand as he thrashed from side to side on the backseat. He'd gotten worse on the longest ferryboat ride of her life.

"Almost there. Hold on." He took a fast turn down the back road behind Gregg and Naeemah's property. "Gregg and your grandparents are waiting for us in the garage." He clicked a remote on his dashboard, quickly entering a code.

Darkness cast Darius's pale face in shadows as George pulled into the tunnel leading to the underground garage.

Allie was out of the car before George had it in park. "Quick, we need to get him upstairs." She flung open the side door. "He was fine at the restaurant, and then he just collapsed on the way to the car."

"Come on, son, we've got you," Gregg said, easing Darius out of the backseat. "He's coming around. Let's get him settled in the yard."

"Come with us, Allie." Alísun gently held her back, so Gregg and George could get Darius up stairs.

"Careful," Allie blustered as they carried Darius between them up the stairs to the common room. She broke away from her grandmother and rushed up behind them, but she nearly tumbled back down the steps when Darius screamed.

"Oh, my God." She hunched over at the waist, her knees giving out. The bond writhed and churned with his agony. "I think I'm going to be sick." She felt it. Just a fraction of what Darius was experiencing. The fear causing him to scream was like a knife, hacking away at their bond. She was about to lose her shit. Seeing Darius so terrified, she didn't know what to do. She was utterly useless.

"This isn't going to be easy for you either, I'm afraid." Alexander lifted her back onto her feet. "We're going to need you to trust us, Allie-girl."

"Let's get you some tea." Alísun wrapped her arm around Allie's waist, and her grandparents led her up the steps.

"This is ridiculous. I'm fine; I don't need any tea." Her voice shook and her hands trembled. Allie tried to break away from Alexander's hold, but the ground swayed under her feet, and she couldn't take a step forward. Panic held her rooted to the spot. "What is this? Like sympathy pains?"

"Something like that," Alísun muttered, steering her toward the nearest sofa in the common room.

"No, I'm going with Darius." She tried to stand.

"I'm sorry, you can't, Allie." Alísun pushed her back down onto the sofa.

"Where are they taking him?" Allie darted under her grandfather's arm and stumbled across the room like a drunken sailor. She followed Darius's screams down the long corridor to the yard. "Wait!" she called, rushing to catch up, but her wooden legs wouldn't let her.

Gregg turned back toward her, leaving Darius with George. "Allie, you can't be here for this. You have to go." He pointed in the direction of the common room. "Get her out of here, Alísun."

"Like hell." She reached out to the stone wall, steadying herself. "You'll have to shoot me in the face first."

"Allie." Emma charged up the hall behind her, Naeemah in tow. "You are not yet Proven. You cannot witness this."

"You think I care about tradition?" She whirled on her mentor. "I'm staying with him, and you can't stop me."

"This isn't about tradition, Allie." Emma grabbed her by her shirt collar and slammed her against the wall. "It is not your place to be with him. You will do him no favors interfering in this. I need you to trust me."

"He's so scared, Emma." Allie's eyes filled with tears as she watched them disappear with Darius into the yard.

"He is going to be fine, but you have to let him do this without you."

"You don't know what you're asking, separating us at a time like this. Please, Emma. Don't make me leave him." Allie reached for Emma's hands, shaking her head. "Please?" Tears streamed down her face. The echo of Darius's cries bounced off the stone ceiling. Each one like a razor cut to their bond. "Darius!" she screamed, trying to break Emma's hold on her.

"I know, sweetheart. I know. Hate me if you need to, but you have to come with us now." Emma nodded to Naeemah as both women wrapped their arms around her, pulling her back down the hall.

"Darius!" Allie screamed again, fighting their hold on her. Her heart lay in a thousand pieces at their feet, and still they wouldn't allow her to stand beside the most important person in her life during the most difficult thing he would ever have to do. "No. Please," she sobbed. "Please don't do this."

She was frantic; the only lucid thought in her mind was getting to Darius no matter who she had to go through to reach him. Rage bloomed in her chest as the little blood vessels in her eyes burst. Her judgment gift crackled at her fingertips, seeking an outlet.

"Get off me." Allie stood up straight as a burst of her solar gift blasted through the hallway. Emma and Naeemah tumbled to the ground, and Allie turned to charge down the hallway. But they were faster and had her by the shoulders before she could even reach the entrance to the yard. Allie grasped both of them by the wrist. Throwing her head back, she screamed, letting the rage rush from her body.

"Take your hands off my daughter." Navid's voice seethed with venom. Livia and their grandparents stood behind him with grave faces.

Allie fell to the floor, sobbing in frustration. She'd wanted to hurt them for stopping her. She was so caught up in her desperation to get to Darius; she'd used her judgment gift on two people she loved more than they could ever know. But her power didn't touch them. She couldn't take their immortality just because she was mad. It didn't work that way. The person on the receiving end of her judgment had to deserve it, and neither Emma nor Naeemah would ever deserve that kind of punishment.

"I'm so sorry," Allie cried. "I didn't mean it."

"It's okay, sweetheart." Navid crouched down beside her. "We know you are hurting in a way we can't understand." He wrapped his arm around Allie and helped her to her feet.

"We will be taking care of Alexis," Alísun said.

"Allie-girl." Alexander took her hand in his. "It is important that you stay calm." He leaned down to look her in the eyes. "Can you do that?"

Allie shook her head. "No ... I can't do this, Grandpa." She burrowed her head against his shoulder. "Will you go be with him?" Allie begged. "Tell him I'm trying to get to him, please? He'll think I've abandoned him."

"Shhh, my girl." Alexander hugged her close. "He'll think no such thing. Darius knows you would fight your way through hellfire to be with him. But I'll go check on him for you."

Allie nodded. "Thank you."

"Let's get you back home, dear," Alísun said, turning to leave.

"No, I'm staying right here." Allie backed away.

"Don't you want to rest in your own bed?"

"She is going to need her mentor," Emma said. "I know you all are her family, but this is going to be a difficult experience for Allie. She needs to stay with me."

"We will all stay with her," Navid said.

Livia looked skeptical. "Surely, you all know this is not how you help Allie through a difficult situation. You cannot force her into anything without an explanation she can understand. She will just rebel."

"She isn't Proven," Naeemah said. "There are no terms she will understand."

"You cannot be with him, Allie." Livia turned, carefully placing her hands on Allie's shoulders. "As much as your bond tells you he needs you, there is little you can do. This isn't about you and what you are feeling."

"I know that," Allie said. "I'm not thinking of myself. This is about Darius and what I know he needs. He is feeling the pain of our separation, Liv. On top of everything else, he doesn't need that, too. The separation is physically painful. Do any of you know what that's like?"

"We do not know what the Syntrophos bond feels like, but the Complement bond is similar in that way. It pains me to leave Gregg. Even after all this time," Naeemah said.

"It's not the same." Allie shook her head. "You make it sound like we're just love-sick teenagers who can't stand to be more than three feet apart. That's not it. The bond. It's like a living, breathing thing connecting us. When you drag us apart, the bond reacts like a wounded animal. Darius is terrified, Naeemah. He doesn't think he's ready. And separating us now is like pouring salt on the wound."

"It is normal for him to feel unprepared," Emma said. "But he is ready for this, Allie. I promise."

"Please, let us take her to my garden," Naeemah said. "You are all welcome. Please, Allie, come with me and we will—"

"I swear if you say let's go sit vigil for him, I will lose it, Naeemah. Do I look calm enough for that? Have I *ever* been able to sit vigil for anything?"

"We will go sit in my garden and discuss what's about to happen. And we will be here to help you get through this. My son has the biggest hurdle of his life staring him down right now. Decades before he should be faced with this. I do not have it in me to sit vigil either. Perhaps you can also help me get through this?" Naeemah held out her hand, her eyes filling with the same fear Allie felt for Darius.

Allie nodded and took her hand.

"Are you okay?" Navid asked, a worried frown wrinkling his brow.

"No, but I will be if someone can please give me an actual reason why I can't stay with him. And I don't want to hear 'because I am not Proven.'"

Allie followed Naeemah, her mentor, and her family into the small underground garden.

"Lay down," Emma instructed, pointing at the grassy lawn

cast in moonlight where silken white pillows and cushions waited for her. Candles lay scattered everywhere, their flames flickering in the breeze. Incense burned in braziers and crickets chirped in a rhythmic chorus. It was such a serene setting. Like they prepared it just for this occasion.

She lowered herself onto the cushions, her body shaking with the anxiety coursing through the bond she shared with Darius.

Emma knelt in the grass beside her, taking her hands. "Darius must face his Proving with the guidance of his mentor. He cannot have any other outside help. That is how it works."

"That's still not an answer."

"George and I have been working together for months, trying to find a precedent for a Syntrophos pair who have yet to experience a Proving. There are none. This is going to be difficult for you both, but you will get through it. And I will guide you every step of the way."

"You make it sound like I'm the one about to face a Proving."

"In a manner of speaking, I believe you are about to go through your own version of Darius's Proving, and *that* is why you cannot be with him now."

CHAPTER 17

Allie lay with her head cushioned in her grandmother's lap. The serenity of Naeemah's garden did very little to dispel her tension.

"Take deep, calming breaths," Alísun murmured. Candlelight sparkled around them as the women Allie called family did everything they could to create a relaxing environment.

The tinkling sound of running water splashed in one of the many stone fountains. A cool breeze swept the hair from her face, and the spicy scent of incense lulled her into a false sense of peace.

Navid stood by, ready to meditate with her when she was ready.

Yet, she felt like climbing out of her own skin just to escape the madness happening inside her body.

"Relax, Allie. You must stay focused. Darius needs you to be his rock right now," Emma said. "Remember, everything you are feeling is just a shadow of what he is feeling. We cannot let your own anxiety for him trickle down through the bond to exacerbate his emotions right now. He needs to sense nothing from you but strength and moral support. That is how you are going to help him through this."

"Right, he has enough to deal with on his own." Allie

sighed, willing herself to ignore his fear. His gut-wrenching fear that made her want to chase down all his demons and slay them. In her mind, he was just a scared little boy, caught up in the terror of his worst nightmares, and there was nothing she could do for him but step aside, allowing him to sink or swim.

"Are we sure this is enough?" Naeemah asked as she massaged Allie's hands with lavender and coconut oil. "Should we try to help her sleep?

"We aren't sure about anything, Nae." Emma wiped Allie's brow with a cool cloth. "And Allie's dreams are too unpredictable. She needs to stay right here with us."

"How has this become about me?" Allie took Naeemah's hand, waving away the scented oils. "You should be focused on your son, not pampering me with spa treatments."

"Caring for you *is* me focusing on my son. I promised him I would be with you during his Proving. He made me swear I would stay with you."

A tremor of a smile touched Allie's lips. "Of course he did."

"Are you sure that helping her slip into a peaceful rest wouldn't be the best course of action? At least at first? I have some potent teas that would do the trick." Naeemah's hands twisted nervously in her lap.

"Maybe if Allie wasn't linked so strongly to the dreamworld," Alísun said. "But I doubt she'd follow the flow of her natural dreams."

"What if Navid and Livia were there, waiting for her," Naeemah suggested.

"No, I don't want Navid to risk being there longer than he should. If I go to the dreamworld, I'm finding a way to get to Darius. I don't think I could stop myself."

"She knows how to navigate her dreamscape as well as any dream walker," Navid said. "She could evade me. It's too much of a risk."

"And we know from experience the dreamworld is no place to experiment," Livia added. "The things that happen there can influence reality."

"The things Darius will be facing will likely happen in some remote corner of the dreamworld," Alísun said. "She cannot go there."

Naeemah nodded. "Then we will have to keep her awake the whole time."

"I'm not remotely tired. There is no way I'm sleeping through this." Allie clenched her fists, grasping at the ground beneath her to keep from running straight to Darius's side.

"We might be here for quite some time," Emma said.

"How long does a Proving last?"

"We will likely be here for a few days. Maybe longer," Navid said. "Darius is so young. It will be harder for him."

"Shit." Allie covered her face with her hands, willing herself not to cry. It would just make Darius crazy. He couldn't stand her tears. "You know it really sucks being an Immortal. Eternal life sounds great, but no one in their right mind would sign up for this. Karma played us all for fools."

"In these moments, I would tend to agree with you." Emma smiled. "But there is another side of this abyss for you and Darius. Keep your mind focused on that, and we will all do our part to get you both through this."

It wasn't like an Awakening. At least not for Allie. She was lucid and in control—mostly. But experiencing Darius's Proving was a dark and twisted pit of an emotional hell for her. Allie's only job was to keep a level head and squash her own emotions. This was not a time for Allie to feel her feelings.

The garden had grown quiet after three days of forced

serenity. Allie sat quietly across from Navid, meditating. It took her several hours to find a place where all thought was driven from her mind. Focusing on the bond she shared with Darius, she imagined it as an invisible life force connecting them, body and soul, and she sent him as much positive energy as she could muster.

More than anything, it felt like Darius was fighting for his life. For the past twenty-four hours, there were moments when their bond weakened and faded, sending her into a wild panic she had to suppress for his sake.

Warmth stirred in her chest as he rallied, desperately clinging to his end of the bond. Allie willed her strength to him. She could see their bond in her mind, visualizing her strength coursing along that bond to bolster him using her gift to lend vitality. She imagined her strength leaving her body in search of his. It wasn't possible. She had to be touching him to do it, but she pretended for a moment that she could feel herself growing weaker.

"Allie, stop," Navid said sharply. "What are you doing?" He pulled her out of her meditative state.

Allie blinked, coming back to the present. Her eyes widened with the realization of what she'd done. "I didn't think it would actually work." She wasn't supposed to help him. Darius had to do this on his own. She reigned in her power, pulling away from Darius in her mind. She'd always needed physical contact to use her ability before. She'd never realized she didn't need it with Darius. "It was only for a minute," she said, her heart hammering in her chest. She didn't want to be the reason this went on any longer for him.

"It's okay," Navid assured her. "Just don't let it happen again."

"Will you go check on him? Just to be sure? We haven't had a report from Grandpa in hours. I'm worried."

"Of course, Livia and I will go and come right back."

Navid left her in Naeemah's care.

"How are you feeling?" Naeemah asked.

"Sore. I think I need to lie down again." The tension and lack of rest was its own kind of torture, but Darius was experiencing a level of pain she couldn't fathom. Allie only felt a shadow of his physical pain, but it was enough to wreak havoc on her body.

"Come, let's go rest by the fountains." Naeemah guided her across the soft green lawn to the bed of pillows they'd made for her there. She loved them for trying so hard to make this easier on her, but all the spa music in the world wouldn't help after days of this endless waiting. She really just wanted to curl up in a dark corner by herself and pray for daylight.

"Was this what it was like for Aidan when he sat with me through my Awakening?" Allie asked. It felt odd saying his name. She rarely talked about him with his family anymore.

"In a way, yes, but on a much smaller scale," Naeemah said. "There is no doubt Awakenings are painful, especially for those like you and Aidan, but there is something particularly awful about an adult's Proving."

"I miss him, Naeemah." Her voice sounded like sandpaper against wood.

"You and me both." She smoothed Allie's hair back. "But Aidan will come home to all of us one day."

Allie shook her head. "He left me. I don't think he's ever coming back. Not to me."

"Leaving you broke something inside him, Allie. It was the hardest thing he's ever done, and he didn't do it without good reason. Trust in that. Trust in the boy you fell in love with, because deep down inside, he is still that same boy. He has *never* stopped loving you."

"So many years." Allie shook her head. "He sacrificed

himself when he didn't need to. I don't know if I can forgive him for that."

"You're both still so young," Naeemah said. "Love makes us do stupid things when we're young. He was only eighteen, Allie. I think Aidan made the best choice he could in an impossible situation."

"You're probably right. But I still want to scratch his face off for being so stupid."

"You and me both." Naeemah smiled.

"He is coming out of it!" Navid jogged across the lawn to her side.

"It's over?" Allie scrambled to sit up; a spike of pain shot up her back like liquid fire. Her bones creaked and popped as she moved to stand. She couldn't imagine how Darius would feel.

"Not yet, but he is lucid. He should be through the worst soon."

"Thank you, Navid." Allie breathed a sigh of relief. She took a step toward Naeemah's office. "I have to see him."

"You can't, Allie. Not yet," Alísun said.

"I've had enough of this." Allie made a run for the door, but she slammed into her sister. "Out of my way, Livia." The surge of strength evaporated at the look on her face.

"He isn't done with his fight yet, Allie," Livia said gently.

"But he's lucid now. He's asking for me."

"No, he isn't." Livia's tone was hard, and her silvery stare grew icy.

"What are you saying?" Allie tried to shove past her sister, but she was like an immovable mountain. It wasn't like Livia to be evasive. She never sugar coated anything.

Livia stood ramrod straight, the image of the woman she used to be. "Darius doesn't want to see you."

He doesn't want to see you. The painful words had swept the rug out from under Allie. As hard as she tried, she couldn't keep her emotions in check.

"How is he?" Allie grabbed Navid's hand as he stepped into the yard. Her body ached with the exhaustion of five days without sleep. Five of the worst days of her life, separated from her Syntrophos. The last day was worse than all the previous days combined when he hadn't wanted to see her.

Allie had retreated to the farthest corner of the garden to sit in a swing by herself. She'd spoken little and ate nothing as she waited helplessly while Darius fought his way through the final stages of his Proving. But he'd done it. And then he'd shut her out. The whole thing was such a foreign concept for them, Allie didn't know how to react. She was just numb.

"He's had a difficult time, sweetheart." Navid wrapped his arm around her waist, helping her walk. "I know it hurt when he refused you, but that had nothing to do with you. One of the most difficult things about a Proving is coming face to face with who we really are, and that is never an easy thing to accept."

"But he's okay now?"

"He will be once he sees you. He started asking for you about an hour ago, and he's been anxious ever since."

Early morning fog drifted across the grassy fields of the yard. She wanted to run, but her body just wouldn't cooperate.

"The separation is painful," Allie said. "How did Kassandre and Gregg do it?"

"They had so many years together." Navid set a careful pace across the yard. "But separation was never easy for them. It's something you two will always have to take one day at a time."

"Hurry, Navid." Allie's bloodshot eyes filled with tears. "Where is he?" She quickened her step, forcing her legs to move.

"He is with George at my cabin. He is comfortable now." Navid led them around to the back of his cabin, facing the small underground lake that hadn't always been there.

Years ago, when Ming Lao died, the yard had flooded when her gift no longer existed to keep the underground intact. Jin Jing and Chloe had taken measures to reduce the flooding and shifting of the structures above them, but Chloe decided to leave the small lake at the far corner of the yard, in memory of her mother. Allie thought of Ming Lao every time she came here, but this morning, her thoughts were only of Darius.

"He will not seem quite himself yet, Allie. You will need to give him time to find himself again."

Allie nodded, but then she saw him. Darius was sitting in a rocking chair on the back porch, gazing across the tranquil waters. Bundled in a white blanket, he shivered, caught up in the torment of his mind. George sat beside him, offering his silent support. George looked as haggard as Allie felt, but Darius looked strong and healthy. His color was good, and his eyes were clear. Allie was comforted that he seemed physically fine, but he'd retreated so far into himself, she couldn't sense much from their bond. She wondered if it would ever be the same again. He stared down at the steaming cup of tea in his hand. He moved to place it on the table beside him, his hands shaking like an elderly man's.

"I've got it," George said, taking the cup from him.

"Allie?" Darius stood, turning to face her. She stumbled away from Navid, taking the porch steps on her own. She didn't say anything. Just flung her arms around him, holding him tight. Strength surged back into their bond, and they both sighed with relief.

"I'm so sorry, Allie." His voice was barely more than a hoarse whisper.

"Shhh," she hushed him. "It's okay, you don't have to talk."

He just stood there, holding her, shaking like a leaf. He didn't cry, but his eyes were red rimmed.

Allie slid her hands down from around his neck to cup his face. "It's okay, Darius. It's behind you now."

"The worst part was being away from you," he whispered. "Let's not do that again."

"Deal." She pressed her face against his chest, feeling like they'd just completed the world's worst marathon.

CHAPTER 18

"I know this is the last thing you want to hear, but Jayesh will be back with Tessa and Dean tomorrow," Livia said. "We should start making plans for our meeting."

Allie sat on the porch of her little cottage, watching Darius and Navid sparring with Kahlynn and Lennox in the back yard. Her niece loved being outdoors so at the first sign of spring, they moved their training outside and flung open the barn doors and windows of the gym. They didn't have nearby neighbors to worry about anyone snooping around.

"He's so good with them." Allie smiled. It had only been a few days since his Proving, but Darius wasn't quite himself yet. He laughed and joked, but his eyes still held a haunted look. She was beginning to think she would never have her Syntrophos back as he was before.

"Focus, Allie," Livia said.

"What?" Allie glanced at her sister.

"You have to get your head back into this."

"Into what?"

"Soma. Taking over. Doing something about the mess Marcus and the Senate have made of our world. Ring any bells?" Livia frowned.

"Right." Allie sighed. "What is it about this Tessa girl that we need so badly?"

"She was a talented girl, but she was gullible. We turned her into the poster child of Soma. Made her think she was a shining star with a bright future. She dedicated her life to training with us. We charged her and her mother a fortune to train her, and then we sold her for fourteen million dollars to Vivian Dyson of Valkyrie Enterprise. She's one of many." Livia's jaw set in a hard line. "That was Father's favorite scheme. Make them think you're helping them. Teach them how to use their gifts, gain their loyalty, and then they'll never see it coming. It makes the transfer to the new owners easy. They don't usually realize they're a slave until long after Soma is out of the picture."

"That wasn't your scheme, Livia," Allie said. "You did what you had to do."

"I know, but I've always felt really bad about Tessa St. James. We screwed her over more than anyone. She was a star at Soma and at Amrita. She was a sweet girl, but she was completely oblivious. Everyone knew who she was, and they all aspired to be her. Her gifts are environmental. Tessa has the power to clean damaged ecosystems and return them to their former glory. And we sold her to someone who uses her to generate cheap, clean energy for those who can pay for it. Vivian Dyson has made billions off Tessa's back. She spends her days locked in a laboratory, doing something she hates when she should be outside, thriving in her natural environment."

"That's awful," Allie said. "But if she's willing, we could definitely use her help." Some of Allie's initial excitement for the takeover had deflated after recent events. But Livia was right; she needed to get her head on straight.

"If we can get her on our side, others like her will respond to her story and listen to her opinions about what we're doing," Livia continued.

Allie nodded. "We will have to win her over."

"I'm afraid that will be your job, sister. She's not going to want to hear anything I have to say."

"You will have to try, Livia. She needs to hear your story, too, you know? I've been lucky. I don't have a story like Tessa's, so I have no way to relate to her. You do. She needs to know that." Allie turned her attention back to her niece. She hated the thought of leaving her again, even for a short while. But if they were really going to do this, they needed to do it soon.

"You know, for someone so young, you're a wise person, Allie Carmichael." Livia draped her arm over Allie's shoulders. "Don't let me forget that."

"Let's call this meeting, Liv. Before I change my mind."

"Who do you want to invite?"

"Everyone we trust. The whole family. All the McBriens and the Loukases, Liam and Darius, of course. Let's ask Gregg to bring in a few of his most trusted lieutenants, too. We're going to need the manpower. And then Quinn, Sasha and Santi, Grandma, and Grandpa. And Navid."

"Dad shouldn't take such a risk. He needs to stay here," Livia insisted.

"I won't be sitting this one out." Navid withdrew from the sparring match, leaving his practice sword sticking in the ground. "Sorry to eavesdrop," he said as he came to join them on the porch. "But there is simply no way I'm staying behind. I've lived the last eighteen years in hiding for only one reason." He sat down on the top step between his daughters. "And that was so I could be here for you both. Your mother and I made so many plans for you girls. So many decisions to give you each the chance to become the women you needed to be to face what you must. I'm done hiding. If someone recognizes me, then they recognize me. I'm with you both from here on out."

"We need you, Navid." Allie reached for his hand. "We need your guidance. And Quinn will be needing you, too."

"I don't like it," Livia said. "I don't want you taking risks anymore. You've been doing that for years. I want you to be safe."

"None of us are ever safe, Livia," Navid said softly. "You know that better than anyone."

Livia nodded, her shoulders stiffening in the way they did when she was trying to keep her emotions in check. "All right, I'll get everyone to this meeting. Allie, all you need to do is figure out what you're going to say."

"Yeah, that's going to be breeze." Public speaking was not Allie's forte. There was an extremely high possibility she was going to fall flat on her face.

Chapter 19

"How did I not know Liam's bar was this fancy?" Allie wandered around the huge, marble-tiled room, flooded with afternoon light. "I've only ever seen his crap bars with dirty floors and sketchy looking patrons."

"He built this place a few years before we met," Livia said. "It was supposed to be a nice place for local Senate gatherings but turns out my husband has no patience for champagne fountains and black tie events."

Allie snorted. "I could have told him that."

"Maybe we could use it as your headquarters, now that I get a good look at it." Livia elbowed her.

"I do not need an office." Allie scowled, eyeing the growing crowd. "I know I called this meeting, but it seems like the guest list has grown." The circle of black and chrome chairs surrounding the conference table and lining the back of the room would house more people than she expected.

"Relax, Allie. We're all on your side. You just need to breathe."

Allie was so nervous; she could hardly sit still. Gazing out the floor to ceiling windows, she took a few moments to catch her breath, hoping she wouldn't screw this up.

"Allie." Emma approached her. "How are you doing?" She hugged her close. "I know this is not your thing at all."

"Freaking out. I'm really glad you're here." Allie placed her hand over Emma's. "I couldn't do this without you."

"I'm so proud of you." Emma said. "You've come a long way from that snarky little girl you used to be."

"Used to be?"

"Well, you're a snarky little woman now." Emma smiled. "You've got this. We're all behind you."

"Thank you, Emma." Allie turned to the growing group of people waiting for her to speak. They were all familiar, friendly faces. But it was a make or break moment. If she succeeded today, she would be taking a huge step toward staking her claim. If she failed, then she wasn't living up to the prophecy.

Allie glanced at the maps strewn across the huge conference table. Gregg and Daniel already had plans in the works. She wouldn't be doing this alone. If she were honest with herself, she was just the mouthpiece for this movement. Other people would be doing the hard work, making things happen in her name.

"You're stressing," Sasha said, coming to stand beside her with Quinn and Santi in tow.

"She's Allie, of course, she's stressing," Quinn said.

"You know you couldn't have any stronger supporters than the three of us," Santi added. "Quinn and I lived the nightmare of Soma, and Sasha's been through her own kind of hell. We're behind you all the way."

"Thank you, guys." The three were a walking miracle in Allie's opinion. Sasha and Quinn were Syntrophos with an even closer bond that came from a lifetime of growing up together. Allie always expected their romantic past would be a huge obstacle for Quinn and Santi's relationship, but they all managed to make it work. Sasha said the Syntrophos bond helped put her feelings for Quinn into perspective, allowing her to be happy for him and Santi. But they still had their jealous moments when Quinn struggled to divide his attention between the two most important people in his life.

Allie couldn't imagine making it work with Aidan and Naomi. Even if she and Aidan could patch things up, having Naomi become such a huge part of her life, there was no way it would work. It would tear Aidan apart.

"We're going to need your help. Especially you, Quinn."

"The dreamworld and my walkers are at your service. What do you guys need from us?"

"When the time comes, Sterling Tower is going to need protection."

Quinn nodded. "We'll handle it."

"Navid will be there to help," Allie said.

She turned to Sasha. "When this all goes down, I'm going to need you to remind me why we're doing this. But I also need you to be a liaison between us and Jayesh."

"We've been talking," Sasha said. "He has a lot of plans, but his special ops background is going to be a problem. He moves too fast sometimes. I'll keep him on your pace, so we're not overwhelmed."

"Thank you." Allie smiled nervously as the time drew near for her to address the group.

"You've got this." Santi squeezed her hand, giving Allie a moment of peace. Allie closed her eyes, allowing Santi to touch her soul in her special way.

Calm and in control of her nerves again, Allie thanked her. "You have no idea how much I needed that." She closed her hand over Santi's. "We're really going to need you to work with the Soma kids. You have a unique understanding of what some of them have been through."

"It will be my pleasure to see that place become something good."

"Thank you, guys." She forced a smile. They were so supportive, but they didn't know the full story yet. They all thought this meeting was about a group endeavor to take down Soma and ultimately bring Aidan and Naomi home.

"They're on their way." Alísun came to her side. "It's time, Allie."

Allie closed her eyes, steeling herself for what she was about to commit them all to.

Aidan, I wish you were here for this. Wherever you are... You have to know I'm doing this for you.

She opened her eyes to find Alísun staring at her. There was no doubt Alísun loved her granddaughters, but the queen needed an heir. This was big moment for her, too. She was more than ready to pass the torch. Allie frowned, realizing how much stress her elderly grandmother was under, carrying the weight of their world on her shoulders. She needed a break. She deserved a break. Allie's resistance was selfish. She was young and motivated to make a change. She could take that burden from the queen. It was time. "I've got this, Grandma," Allie whispered.

With a gentle squeeze of her hand, the queen drifted into the crowd. As Allie turned her back to the windows, she found herself alone at the front of the beautiful room. She recognized all the faces. This was her family and a few friends she trusted. She shouldn't be this nervous, but only a handful of them knew she was the named heir of Indriell. She hadn't even told Sasha yet. But they were all about to find out.

"Thank you for being here today," she finally spoke. "I know some of you aren't sure what this is about." She glanced at Quinn, standing with Sasha to his left and Santi to his right. She wondered what they would think about the naming.

"I've asked you all here today because I need your help. We are still waiting for a few others to join us, so I will tell you all right now, if anyone wants to leave at any point, you are always free to do so. If you've had enough struggle in your life..." She gave Sasha a hard look. "Please understand that I will *never* make you feel like you can't walk away."

"If you are here, we are here with you," Sasha said. "No matter what."

Quinn nodded.

The sound of an opening door sent a hush across the room.

"This way," Liam said.

Allie watched as her brother led a petite young woman into the room, Dean right behind her.

“Livia?” Tessa took a menacing step toward Allie's sister. Allie lifted her hand, her solar power sparking at her fingertips —an involuntary reaction to the threat.

"Don't you dare zap her," Livia muttered.

“That's far enough.” Liam stepped in front of the girl. “My wife is not the person you remember.”

“Your *wife*?” The girl sneered, her blond hair falling over her shoulder.

“Much has happened since we last saw each other.” Livia moved to stand beside her Complement. “I don't deserve it, but I hope you will give me a chance. As trapped as you've been for most of your life, I have been as well. Soma was my prison, too.”

Allie heard the pleading in her voice. Livia thought she would never be able to atone for the things she'd done. But if Allie could forgive her for what she’d done to their family, then she hoped Tessa could find it in her heart to forgive Livia, too.

“We have a lot to discuss, and I’m a nervous wreck.” Allie managed a tight smile. So, let’s get to it. Please everyone, take your seats.”

Allie felt Darius's eyes on her. They'd discussed this part. If they wanted to foster a sense of honor and honesty, this was the moment they needed to do it. It went against the grain, but with a shudder, Allie dropped the pretense shielding their Syntrophos bond. The bond was something they protected with their every breath. But it was also something everyone in this room needed to witness. The family knew, of course, but she especially wanted Tessa and Dean to understand.

"My name is Allie Carmichael, and this is my Syntrophos, Darius McBrien." She gestured for him to come join her.

"Most of you know me well enough to know it would take an act of God to get me in front of a room full of people. And some of you know how much I've battled accepting this Immortal life. I never wanted this ... any of it." Allie gave a bitter laugh. Five years ago, she didn't even know Immortals existed, and now she sat poised to lead them into a questionable future. Who did she think she was?

Aidan. You're doing this nonsense for Aidan.

"But our world is changing, and our generation is suffering." Allie lifted her chin. "My maternal grandmother, Queen Alísun, the last queen of Indriell, has named me her heir." Allie chanced a glance at her grandmother. She stood at the back of the room, a look of fierce pride on her face. "A position I've resisted for years," Allie admitted. Alísun may have just named her the heir, but Allie had been resisting her connection to Indriell since the moment she found out about it. "But I have finally learned to accept it," she finished. "By the right of my birth, I am the first princess of Indriell. That knowledge cannot leave this room. We need to keep it within the family and our most trusted friends."

Allie chanced a glance at her friends, but they stood with approving smiles on their faces as if they'd known all along. Their silent encouragement gave her the strength to go on.

"I am the second natural daughter of the ancients,

Kassandre and Ashar. My mother, Kassandre, was the natural daughter of Queen Alísun. My elder sister is Livia. She was once my enemy and is now my strength and my ally." Allie wasn't sure those simple words were enough to convey what she felt for her sister. After all they'd been through—together and apart—Livia meant more to her than she'd ever thought possible. "Together, we are going after Soma, and we are asking you all to join us."

Allie took her seat at the head of the table, not sure her legs would hold her upright much longer. "The ancient, Lord Teigan, known today as Marcus Servius, is behind Soma. He isn't the only one using and abusing our generation, but he is the worst. He claims that Soma is a safe place that we all desperately need, but it is a guise used to lure unsuspecting young Immortals into the web of Sterling Tower. Too many have realized the trap only after they've been sold into slavery. It has to end." Allie took a deep breath, listening to the conviction in her own voice.

"Livia and I are going to return to Soma to bring it down from the inside and build it back up into the institution it claims to be. And then we're going after the others—all of those who've been sold into slavery. Most of you have already agreed to help. But we still need you, Tessa. And Dean." She gave them a pointed look. "You both have a unique experience with the enemy. Others will look to you for the truth. Tessa? Are you with us?" Allie wouldn't blame her if she ran shrieking from the room. But she saw defiance in the woman's eyes. She was a fighter.

"I'm in." Tessa nodded firmly and for one horrifying second, Allie thought she was going to bow. A fire of determination lit Tessa's eyes. Allie gave her a nod, grateful for her support.

With a glance around the room at all the approving nods,

Allie let out the breath she'd been holding. "Good because someone I love is in trouble, and I need your help. All of you."

Allie stood, too nervous about this next part to remain in her seat. "The Chief Justice is building an army of Syntrophos with the intent to overtake Soma and make it a government run institution. We have to stop them."

A collective gasp swept the room as the realization of what she was asking hit them all at once.

"I know I'm asking you to defy your government. A government most of you work for, but we cannot allow the Senate to take that much power for themselves. We cannot allow a Chief Justice to wield the power of a Syntrophos army—an army taken by force. They have Aidan and Naomi. We owe it to them to bring them home. It might mean war against our leaders, but for the good of our children, we simply must provide a safe place for those who do not have a family like ours. We are lucky to have you all." Allie met her mentor's gaze. "To have teachers with the wisdom and experience to provide the training we desperately need.

"We will be taking Soma before the Chief Justice has a chance to, and then we will find a way to free the Syntrophos under their control."

"Excuse me," Tessa said softly. "What is a Syntrophos?" She glanced from Allie to Darius. And then to Sasha and Quinn. "I can sense it in this room, but I don't understand."

"It is a bond," Quinn said. "Much like the Complement bond, but it links you with your ..."

"Your best friend," Sasha supplied. "But that's not a strong enough word for what Quinn is to me. It's far more than that."

"It's an ancient bond that dates back to my ancestors," Allie said. "The Queens of Indriell surrounded themselves with their Syntrophos armies—the strongest of our kind. When linked as we are, what wouldn't we fight for to protect the two most important people in our lives? Our Complement and our Syntrophos. We were unstoppable. No one dared come against the queens and their most fierce protectors."

Tessa nodded. "And you say our government is now developing this army?"

"Yes. And you should all know exactly what that means. When a pair of Syntrophos bond, they form a unique connection allowing them to have access to the other's power. We influence each other's gifts. There are so many things I can do now that I couldn't do before Darius and I bonded. Together, our arsenal of abilities has tripled over the last four years. We continue to discover new ways our bond has allowed us to use the power."

"May I?" Gregg stood to address the room.

"Please."

"I was Syntrophos to Allie's mother, Kassandre. I have been able to teach these young pairs uniting as they did in the days of Indriell. Yet, I have neglected to teach them one last crucial detail. I didn't want to burden them with the knowledge until it was time. It is time they know now. The way Allie describes their use of the power is telling. Some of you ancients have likely already guessed. A Syntrophos pair uses the pure, untainted power as it was before the Great War nearly destroyed it."

"What?" Sasha gasped.

Allie's mind reeled, and she had to sit down.

"That's impossible," one of Gregg's lieutenants said. "The power was almost destroyed, so how could they?"

"It is the nature of the Syntrophos bond. It's stated in prophecy. 'The Power is corrupted and will remain so *until* a new generation is born with the strength of their ancestors, led by one with an unsullied, *natural* connection with the power. Her heart will guide her, giving her the restraint to wield her power wisely. She will *gather her equals* and together they will stand against those who persist in the corruption of the natural order. She will be strong and fierce in her beliefs and steadfast in her love. Born the second child of the seventh daughter of her line, she alone will possess the skills and the knowledge *to heal what has been broken*.'"

Allie breathed a silent thanks when he left out the last part about how she would have the courage to judge unbiased and mete out the ultimate punishment. They didn't need to know that aspect of her abilities.

"The Chief Justice is currently training *eight* Syntrophos pairs," Allie said. "Looking around the room, I can see the fear in your eyes, just knowing that there are two Syntrophos pairs in this room. Can you imagine what the leader of our world could do with an army of sixteen well-trained warriors, each with a partner that allows them access to the pure power?"

"We are with you, Allie," Gregg said. "What will be our first move?"

"You are with me on this?" she asked. She'd fully expected him to resist on the grounds that she was too young to attempt something so dangerous.

"I stand behind my queen." He nodded to Alísun. "And with the heir. I know my son would do the same, if given the choice. I'd like to offer it to him."

It bolstered her confidence to have Gregg behind her. "Then we will be making a move against Soma immediately. Before Marcus or the Chief Justice suspect anything."

"You believe we can stand against Livia's father?" Tessa asked. All color drained from her face. "He is Soma. He's ancient, and his forces are impenetrable."

"He is not my father. Marcus raised me," Livia said. "And once, when I was a child, I wanted nothing more than his approval. I have not loved him as a child loves a father in a very long time. Navid is my father. The only true father I have ever known." Livia took Navid's hand. "Marcus is confident in his position, and he is confident that I would never betray him."

"He believes we still hold her captive," Liam added. "If we strike now, he will not see it coming."

"I want this to be a peaceful takeover," Allie said. "As peaceful as we can manage. Right now, Marcus is away from Sterling Tower with several of his closest companions. Livia, Darius, and I will walk into Soma tomorrow and take the helm along with Jayesh Basu."

"And how will you keep it?" Tessa asked. "Marcus will return and he will retaliate. He would sooner blow Sterling Tower up than to see it stolen from under his nose."

"Leave that to me and a few of my dream walkers," Quinn said.

"Dream walkers?" Dean spoke for the first time.

"It's been a while, nephew." Quinn smiled. "But yes, I am a dream walker now."

"Then you know Brecken?" Dean cast a worried glance at Tessa.

"We've met." Quinn's eyes narrowed to slits. "How do you know him?"

"We've spent the last four years as slaves to Vivian Dyson," Tessa said. "Brecken was our jailor."

"We became cursory friends over time. But I still wouldn't trust him," Dean said.

"You leave Brecken to me," Quinn said.

"You're going to do what he did?" Tessa asked. "We were free to come and go as we wanted on Vivian's vast property, but we could never leave its borders. We were surrounded by the dreamworld. There was no way out."

"Or in," Quinn said. "Once I create a rift between the waking world and the dreamworld, I will surround Sterling

Tower with a barrier none can cross without my permission. Anyone inside the building will be free to leave under escort, but no one enters. Including Marcus, the Senate, and anyone else who opposes us."

Tessa nodded, her eyes bright. "But we ... we aren't going to be stuck in there?"

"I will not ask you to give up one prison for another," Allie said. "We desperately need you inside Sterling Tower to help us convince those in residence we have their best interests at heart. But you can leave at any time."

"I remember you, Tessa," Quinn said softly. "That day in the warehouse. You showed me kindness in a place where I thought none existed."

"You were running like your life depended on it," she said.

"It did in a way." Quinn smiled. "If I had failed my task, Santi would have suffered greatly for it. You helped me succeed that day. I give you my vow, if you ever need to cross my barrier, I will personally escort you and Dean to the other side."

CHAPTER 20

"You sure about this?" Navid asked. "This is the point of no return."

Allie stared across Monroe Drive and up at Sterling Tower, certain she was doing the right thing. The shifting spectral figures of her visions swarmed the park and the city block. There were more here than she'd ever seen anywhere else, and she struggled to keep them confined. But her visions shone with the green light of her power, and that was always a good sign.

"I'm sure." Allie nodded. "Just scared."

"It's a good plan, Allie," Navid said. "And we are all with you."

"Are you sure you're ready to go back in there?" she asked Navid. The dreamworld was a dangerous place for him. He'd spent too much time there in recent years, and it had left him struggling with the addiction to his power like he hadn't experienced in a thousand years.

"I can manage this. We won't be there longer than my threshold allows, and Quinn knows how to pull me back if I linger too long. Don't worry about me, sweetheart."

"What about you, Quinn? Are you ready to go back to Soma?"

"No. But this will be different. I'm not a captive anymore."

"Let's do this." She took Quinn and Navid's hands, Livia stepping up to clasp Navid's free hand. Quinn and Navid would guide them into the dreamworld; something they'd done an awful lot of in recent years. As the daughters of one of the most ancient dream walkers, she and Livia both had an affinity for the place. They could do things other dreamers couldn't, but they needed the assistance of a walker.

Allie took a deep breath. She needed to clear her mind to reach a meditative state. Entering the dreamworld this way was never easy for her. She gripped their hands tightly, resisting the urge to fight the force pulling her from the waking world. It felt like drowning. All the air was sucked from her lungs until she thought she would pass out.

The park dissolved in a swirling mass of green as they collectively fell into the world of dreams. Allie and Livia stumbled with the wrongness of the entry. For them, it was unnatural to arrive this way. They could only do it because they shared their lineage with Navid, but it didn't come without consequences.

It always took Allie a moment to remember how to breathe. With a great gasp, she finally inhaled and then promptly spewed the contents of her stomach behind the wooden Piedmont Park sign.

Livia closed her eyes, swaying on her feet, the only indication she'd experienced the same discomfort as Allie.

"Ugh. Haven't done that in a while." She wiped her mouth, freezing in the eerie silence of the dreamworld as a dozen heavy footsteps sounded in the distance.

"Relax." Quinn clapped her on the shoulder, beaming with the vibrant health and vitality the dreamworld gave those like him. "My walkers are here to help." He jogged across the lawn to meet them on the sidewalk across the street from Sterling Tower. Rather, the shadow of Sterling Tower in the dreamworld. It was and was not the real building.

Allie eyed the twelve men and women who followed Quinn in this world. Some of them were ancient, bearing the physical signs of spending far too much time in the dreamworld. Some were haggard, tattooed, and aged more than any Immortals she'd ever seen—a consequence of staying here too long. The others were young, like Quinn. As a whole, they were a rough looking bunch, but they were loyal to Quinn and that was good enough for Allie.

"Spread out," he instructed, sending his walkers to take up their positions around the building. "We will have to be quick about this before Brecken suspects what we're doing. He's the only one who could stop us. Allie and Liv, Navid will be helping you patrol the perimeter. This place needs to be empty before we're done sealing the border."

"Got it." Allie and Livia watched as Quinn and his walkers set to work, creating the barrier that would encompass Sterling Tower like a thin soap bubble. They moved slowly around the building in a clockwise pattern, arms spread wide.

"Will anyone inside the building realize what we're doing?" Allie asked.

"Probably not, and if they do, it's already too late for them to stop us," Navid said. "There are no dreamwalkers inside Sterling Tower."

The screams began as the walkers moved. It took a little while, but they always came. The dreamers. The whispered words and frightened voices of those caught up in nightmares echoed all around them. The voices were the only sounds here. No wind or rain. Thunder or lightening. The utter stillness of this world was disturbing.

With his walkers in place, Quinn spread his arms wide.

The air above him seemed to ripple like fabric on a breeze, until a horrible ripping sound echoed like cannon fire. The tear across the sky was clean and edged in golden light. As the rip widened and stretched to the ground, Allie stumbled back. The edges of the tear began to rise, folding in opposite directions.

"Time to go, girls," Navid said. "You two will circle the property, and I will go straight down the middle between the tower and parking garage. If you need me, just whisper my name and I'll hear you."

Allie turned and raced east along Monroe Drive to make her first sweep of the perimeter. They would meet back at the entrance to Piedmont Park, but she had a job to do before the building was completely enveloped in the world of dreams. As she took a right down Cooledge Avenue, she shoved innocent dreamers outside the growing bubble and back into their own dreamscapes. It was her responsibility to make sure no one was trapped inside the barrier once it was sealed. She heard the voices, dreamers calling for help in the throes of their nightmares. Others laughed, urging her to join them in their blissful dreams. She ignored them. Allie had learned to resist the lure of the voices a long time ago. She was unaffected by them now.

Livia was busy hunting for any enemies who might try to stop them. Allie could sense them, too. There were precious few dream walkers left. Most of them were loyal to Quinn, but there were still some who opposed him. Those who'd given into their addictions long ago and never left the world of dreams. They were the terrifying stuff of nightmares.

Allie passed four of Quinn's walkers along Cooledge Avenue, moving counter clockwise now. They were nearly done. She had to hurry.

Livia's scream of fury came from just around the corner on Park Drive. Allie ran faster, sai blades at the ready. Nearing the rear of the building, Allie saw Livia locked in battle with an ancient walker. He lunged at her, weaponless and more beast than human; she shoved him back toward the edge of the new barrier. Allie raced to help her. Whirling into a high, round house kick, she struck the walker's jaw. He stumbled and turned his attention on Allie.

"That's right, ugly, come get the redhead." Allie lured him away from the sidewalk and into the empty street, allowing Livia to sneak up behind him.

"You're here with him," the pale man hissed, lunging for Allie like a wild dog. These guys didn't like Quinn and Navid very much.

Livia aimed a swift kick to his backside, sending him staggering across the street and through the barrier to haunt someone else.

"Navid." Allie pointed at the end of the street where their father battled two ancient dream walkers by himself. They ran to help him, but by the time they got there, he shoved the last one through the barrier, sheathing his sword at his side.

"We better hurry." Navid glanced up at the sky. The barrier was almost complete.

"You don't have much longer before you'll be in trouble," Livia said to Navid.

He nodded. "I'm still okay, but the clock is ticking."

If he stayed here too long, it would become harder and harder for him to leave willingly. At that point, he would start losing the battle with his addiction and begin the slow transformation into the things they just fought.

"Let's go." Allie ran with her sister and their father down Virginia Avenue, making quick work of the dreamers wandering aimlessly down the street. They arrived back at the park entrance just in time.

"We're clear," Navid said, looking healthier than she'd seen him in months. It was good for him to be here—but bad for him to stay much longer. He was at the tipping point.

Quinn's hands fell limply at his sides as his walkers stopped their slow progression around the building. "It's almost done. Allie and Liv, check the perimeter one more time before we seal it." He dropped to his knees in exhaustion.

Allie and Livia ran in opposite directions again, making one last sweep. The barrier had to be a no man's land for it to work. A wasteland of the dreamworld cut off from all sides—once the barrier was sealed. She searched long and hard, hunting for stragglers. She still heard the voices. That was just part of the dreamworld, but the barrier was eerily still.

Allie walked along Virginia Avenue, doing a careful sweep of the area. It was strange; she couldn't actually see the barrier so much as feel it. A replica of the city streets stretched in a grid pattern in all directions across Midtown, but Allie could sense the way the barrier followed the area enclosed by the city block where Sterling Tower stood. If she crossed the street to the opposite sidewalk, she would wander into the huge world of dreams and be lost forever without a guide to lead her. Once the barrier was sealed, she could walk across the street and keep walking forever in circles, trapped like a goldfish in a bowl.

"All clear," Allie called when she arrived back at the park entrance. "We need to wrap this up soon." She glanced at Navid. His eyes were glassy, and his face was flushed from the adrenaline coursing through his veins. He was past the tipping point.

"Navid, take Allie and Livia back," Quinn said. "We'll be right behind you after we seal the rift. I'll be leaving four of my walkers to patrol the barrier."

Navid nodded and reluctantly took his daughters' hands. His natural instincts told him to stay in the dreamworld where he was most powerful, but Allie knew he had enough experience with his gift to realize that was the road to ruin.

Allie took one last look at the narrowing rift, still glowing with a golden light. It was done. She felt an immense sense of relief. Now, no matter what happened next, the people inside Sterling Tower were safe.

CHAPTER 21

"You okay?" Darius asked, a doubtful look on his face.

Allie nodded, trying to remember how to breathe in the waking world. With a lurch, she bent over, dry heaving with her head between her knees. It always took her a minute to leave the dreamworld behind. "You'd think I'd get used to that after all this time." She stood, wiping her clammy hands down the front of her jeans.

"You'd think," Livia agreed.

"You sure you're okay." Darius took her hand. "You look a little green."

"I'll be okay. Where is everyone?"

"They're gathered on the other side of the park." Liam came to join them. "We need to move quickly before someone raises the alarm when they realize they can't get in or out of the building."

"Jayesh has issued a lockdown inside," Livia said, returning her phone to her back pocket. "The kids will all be in their rooms within ten minutes."

Allie nodded at Liam. "Send them over." She stepped back and stared up at Sterling Tower. It was a beautiful building. And after today, if the takeover went as planned, it would be hers.

"It is done, sister," Livia said. "We've nothing left to do but step inside."

"I'm not ready," Allie said. "I'll never be ready for this ... crushing reality of what my life will be. That my life was decided long before I was even born."

"Prophecy be damned." Livia took her hand. "You have a mind of your own, Allie. Use it. This doesn't have to play out as some preordained sequence of events our parents planned for us. It is for you to decide how it will play out. You mold the future as you see it. Not anyone else."

"Your sister is right, Allie." Navid said, giving them a strange look, as if he was finally seeing them clearly for the first time. "Everything your mother and I have done—all the manipulation and deceit was to get you both here. Possibly to this very moment. We've seen a thousand different futures for you both, but right now, I see two young women ready to take on the world and make their own futures. My work is done."

"We will always need your guidance," Allie said.

"We can't do any of this without you, Dad," Livia agreed, holding her hand out to their father.

Liam approached with an army of McBriens and Loukases in tow. Armed and dressed in fatigues, they were prepared for anything once inside. Allie wanted a peaceful takeover, but she wasn't naive enough to think they could do it without a display of force, even with Jayesh on their side.

Allie crossed the grassy lawn of Piedmont Park to the stone entrance. The dreamworld pulsed around Sterling Tower. The busy city sidewalks filled with mortals, coming and going about their day. None passed in front of Sterling Tower. Their natural instincts led them around the barrier. Any Immortals nearby would sense the danger, but even if they wanted to cross the barrier, they couldn't without a dream walker.

Once Marcus learned of the takeover, he wouldn't be able

to retaliate. Those inside were safely out of his grasp now. She just needed to get inside and let them know they were free of his influence. Those who wanted to leave would be escorted by one of Quinn's team.

"Is it safe?" Tessa asked as she approached. Her eyes were glued to the building where she grew up. For her this was a homecoming in a bizarre, twisted sort of way.

"It won't be like it was in South America," Dean replied, coming to stand beside her.

"It's safe," Allie said. "Soma is no longer a prison. No one will keep you here if you don't want to stay." She could see the fear and distrust in the girl's eyes.

"But they need you in there," Allie said, nodding at the building. "I can't imagine how difficult it is for you to come back here after all you've experienced. After all they have done to you."

Tessa wrapped her arms around her middle like a child afraid of the dark.

"I need you to tell your story, Tessa," Allie said. "These people trust you. They remember you and admire you. They will listen."

"They are the only reason I'm even here right now. Them and you. You'd better not let me down, Allie."

Allie nodded, feeling the true weight of her new responsibilities. "Let's go." Allie and Darius followed Quinn and Navid to a secluded corner of the park, just across the street from Sterling Tower.

With everything they'd done to make a move against Soma, Allie couldn't contain her visions. There were so many of them swarming the park, seeking her attention. She saw faces and settings all around her; things she should study but there wasn't time. There was never time. She would have to focus despite them.

With Allie and her team guarding Quinn from curious eyes, he stood at the barrier entrance, his eyes glowing with the presence of his power. Holding his arms aloft, a tiny fissure in the thin veneer of the dreamworld began to spread. Edged in smoldering golden embers, the rift grew wider as Quinn created a narrow tunnel through the dreamworld to the front door of Sterling Tower. It was like walking through an aquarium. They weren't actually in the dreamworld this time.

"We go one at a time," Navid said. "Follow me and do not wander off. Don't listen to the voices urging you to leave the tunnel. Stay close." Navid entered first, using his gift to extend the tunnel, pressing against the walls of the dreamworld and creating a safe pathway through. Allie and Darius followed with Livia, Liam, and the others bringing up the rear. They were few in number, but they didn't need numbers. Sterling Tower was already theirs.

Chapter 22

"Livia?" Eric jumped to his feet the second they entered the tower. "We didn't expect you back so soon. I will call Jayesh at once and let him know you're here." The concierge lifted the white phone from its cradle.

"No need, Eric. I'm already here." Jayesh stepped off the elevator. "Make our guests feel at home," he added.

"Would anyone like coffee or wat—Tessa?" Eric stammered.

"Still here?" She offered a watery smile.

"Same old, same old." Eric frowned, eyeing her from head to toe.

Allie could imagine after four years as a slave, Tessa wasn't the same girl Eric remembered.

"I think all that's going to change now," Tessa said softly.

Allie turned at the ding of the elevator and a slow smile spread across her face.

"Lucien? Imogen?" Sasha's voice broke on a sob as she rushed to throw her arms around her sister and brother-in-law. Four years ago they were taken captive the night Livia's people attacked Imogen's home. "You've been here all this time?" Sasha asked through her tears.

"We've been helping Jayesh." Imogen smiled. "But we had to stay under the radar until now."

"You couldn't have told me?" Sasha turned on Jayesh, her eyes flickering with anger.

"No. It wouldn't have changed anything and you know it," Jayesh said.

"You could have—"

"Can you read him the riot act later?" Allie leaned in with a whisper. "We're kind of in the middle of something here."

"Right." Sasha blew out an angry breath. "I'm not done with you." She pointed at Jayesh.

"I'm not surprised." He gave her an arrogant smile.

Allie shared a last look with her grandmother before she stepped forward with a confidence she didn't feel. "There will be time for catching up later, I promise. Right now, I need Eric to call the entire security staff to the front lobby to speak with my team." For this to work, she needed Jayesh to coerce the security team to follow her orders. They wouldn't question his leadership.

Eric shook his head. "On whose authority?" He eyed Allie like she was a child in way over her head. "We cannot pull all of security away from their posts. What exactly do you think is going on here?"

Alísun stepped up beside her, placing a hand on her shoulder.

Allie's shoulder smoldered with heat, radiating from the queen's hand and down through her arm into her fingertips.

She lifted her chin, aiming for one of her grandmother's most regal looks. "On my authority as the named heir of Indriell, Sterling Tower belongs to me now." Allie closed her eyes. There was no turning back now.

The scalding heat of the queen's power swirled inside Allie's chest as the ancient mantle of the Indriell queens settled around her shoulders. The room grew thick with tension and the resounding presence of the queen's authority.

From the gaping looks of those gathered around her, there was no doubt everyone in the room felt the heavy burden of the power exchange.

"Oh—" Eric sputtered. "Oh." His eyes grew wide as the enormity of what he just witnessed registered. He lowered his head in reverence.

"You heard the heir," Jayesh said with a hint of awe in his voice. "Call security."

"Yes sir—er, yes, yes, ma'am." Eric fumbled for the phone and gave the order to the head of security. The dozen or so guards manning the front doors craned their necks to get a good look at the heir. Their eyes glazed in confusion as Quinn and Navid outlined the rules for anyone leaving the building.

"Thank you, Grandma," Allie whispered, grasping her grandmother's hand. Passing the torch to her granddaughter must have been bittersweet as well as an enormous relief.

"Grandpa?" Allie turned around, looking for Alexander.

"I'm here, Allie-girl." He stepped forward. "You need me?" He seemed surprised she would ask for his help first.

"You're probably already doing it." She smiled, taking his hand. "I need you to be the Scholar. Watch and record everything that happens inside and around this building. Alert me to anything that might need my attention."

"Of course, darling. I'm already on it." He shuffled back to sit on a bench along one of the lobby windows, clutching one of his leather journals in hand. His eyes clouded, growing opaque as he entered an omniscient trance that allowed him to see everything happening at once.

"What now?" Jayesh asked, looking to Allie for direction. He was always on board with them, but even he had a new tone of respect for the heir.

Allie fished a folded piece of paper from her pocket. She scanned the list of names one more time. Ryan and Selena, she knew, but Jayesh had added twelve names to the list of people they needed to round up immediately. "Gregg, take three groups and send one of Jayesh's guards with each group to collect these people." She handed Gregg the list. "Nothing is secure until they are all are escorted from the building."

"You want them free to return to Marcus?" Gregg asked.

"Yes." Allie gave him a hard stare. "I mean it when I say we will never keep anyone against their will. Although, I'd like these people gone before they learn anything of importance. Except Ryan. We will need to detain him long enough to deal with the question of the Soma brands he controls. Find out if he can pass them off to you."

"I'll report back when we're done." Gregg gave her a curt nod and selected his three groups from their small number.

Allie's mind whirled with everything that needed to be done, but a new sense of calm settled around her. *I can do this. I am doing this.*

"Liam, can you, Emma, and Daniel take Imogen and Lucien with a large group of Soma security when they arrive and do a sweep of the building while it is still on lockdown? I need you to make sure there aren't any surprises lying in wait."

"You will keep Livia and Darius with you at all times?" Liam asked. "I don't want to leave you unprotected."

"We're not leaving her side no matter what she says." Livia stood ramrod straight beside Allie. Like barnacles on a boat, as long as they were inside Sterling Tower, Allie wouldn't be able to shake her sister or Darius even if she tried.

"I'll stay with them, Liam. Promise." She gave him a wink to break whatever spell Alísun had cast over them. Allie might be the official heir now, but they all needed to get over this googlie-eyed sense of awe they had when they looked at her. She was still Allie.

"Quinn, assign one of your men to guard the lobby and then take the rest of your walkers and have a Soma security guard show them where all the exits are. We need to make sure that anyone requesting to leave will have access to an escort. And rotate your dream walkers as often as you need. I don't want anyone out there too long. Navid will stay with me, but call me if you need his assistance."

"Will do," Quinn said. "And thank you for thinking of my team's wellbeing," he added for good measure.

Allie rolled her eyes at his formality.

"What about the warehouse?" Santi asked. "Lots of people train out there, so they might not know we're on lockdown."

"Jayesh, do we need to send someone out there?" Allie asked.

"We've closed the warehouse for the past few days, so there shouldn't be anyone inside other than the man who created it, but it wouldn't hurt to check."

"Santi, take Sasha and Tessa with you," Allie said. "Try to talk to the man who lives there and find out if he's going to cooperate."

"Do we need a guide?" Sasha asked.

"I'm your guide," Santi said. "I know that place like the back of my hand. We won't be gone long."

"It seems you have everything well under control," Jayesh said, observing all of the activity around them.

"You and Livia have done so much to prepare for this," Allie said. "I can hardly take credit."

"I'll be talking to the security team in a moment. Is there anything else you need from me?"

"Um. I need to speak with everyone here as soon as the building is secure from the inside." Allie shook her head to clear the visions from her sight. There were even more inside the building than there were outside. She couldn't spare the effort to keep them locked away.

"Eric, please call each floor manager and tell them we are on lockdown for at least two more hours. Have them standby for further instructions. Once you have the go-ahead from Ms. Carmichael here, make an announcement for everyone to convene in the gym on the seventeenth floor. No one is to leave their rooms until then. Do not, under any circumstances, tell anyone about anything you've seen."

"Yes sir," Eric said. "Although, I have no idea what's happening anyway," he added under his breath.

Allie turned to her sister, panic in her eyes. She didn't know if she could sit here for two hours with everyone looking at her in expectation. Not with the visions plaguing her as they were. She needed a quiet moment to get them under control.

"We will wait in my old office," Livia murmured, leading Allie to the elevator bank.

Allie stepped onto the elevator with Navid, Darius, Livia, and Dean. Alísun followed, guiding Alexander, still in the throes of his Scholar trance. As the doors slid shut in front of her, Allie's knees refused to work and she sank to the floor. Taking deep breaths, she refused help.

"I just need a minute on the floor, thanks."

What have I just done? She didn't want this. She never wanted the limelight.

Aidan. It always circled back to him. She had to do this for him and everyone like him. As the elevator came to a halt, Allie got to her feet. "I'm fine," she whispered, clutching her grandmother's hand.

"We'll wait here until it is time," Navid said, steering Allie into the office that once belonged to Livia.

Allie glanced around the messy room with Jayesh's files and

papers stacked in piles on every surface. Half dead plants stood in large pots in front of the widows.

"We'll get this all cleaned up for you, Allie," Alísun said.

Allie nodded, as a cold chill swept through her body and her hands shook.

"It's the shock," Alísun said, guiding her to the chair behind Jayesh's desk. "It will pass as you become accustomed to the mantle of Indriell."

"You know, I always thought you meant that metaphorically." Allie managed a tight smile.

"I couldn't prepare you for the passing of the torch. I had to wait until you'd stepped forward and accepted your birthright publically and willingly."

Allie nodded. "I understand so much now." She patted her grandmother's hand. "It's just ... overwhelming."

"Now that it's done, we have much to discuss. At a later time, of course. I won't bother you with the details in the middle of staging a coup."

"Am I the queen now?" Allie's brow furrowed in confusion.

"No, my darling-girl. You are my official heir. You will train under me for many years before I name you queen."

"Okay, good. That gives me time to get used to one insane thing at a time."

The white phone buzzed on her desk. Allie glanced around the room as everyone looked to her to answer it.

"Hel-hello?" she said awkwardly.

"It's Jayesh, ma'am. We've secured Michael's dungeon. The entire staff there has opted to leave."

"I've heard of Quinn's experiences down there. Was it really still functioning?" She would have thought Jayesh had put an end to it long before now.

"Not quite as it was when Quinn was there. Michael disappeared the night of the attack on your family," Jayesh said. "No one has seen him since then. But his department was still operating. I have done my best to discourage the things that have gone on down there, but I haven't had the authority to shut it down completely."

"Now you do," Allie said. "Shut it down and seal the rooms. We will find a much better use for that space in the future."

"Yes, ma'am."

"Jayesh, don't call me ma'am." She hung up the phone.

The mention of Michael's disappearance struck a nerve. She'd never had a name to go with the face. Gregg had always taken great measures to keep her from the man she'd ruined that night. Now she knew. Michael was the one who had dared to attack Aidan and take his gift of healing. It had ignited a fury inside Allie like nothing she'd ever experienced before. That night a dark power emerged from within. She'd taken Michael's Immortality. An act she'd never repeated since. He was still safely locked away, deep in the crypt below Kelley's Island. For now. Eventually, they would have to deal with him.

Gregg always said he'd deserved what he got. Logically she knew that. Her gift wouldn't have worked otherwise, but at least now she knew the extent of his crimes. It did a lot to alleviate her guilt.

"I need a minute." Allie stood. "My visions are out of control, and I just need a quiet corner to collect myself."

"There's a private bathroom through that door," Livia said. "Take all the time you need."

Allie stepped inside the cool bathroom. It was beautiful, like all the places that bore Livia's touch. Black marble veined with gold topped the vanity and huge white marble tiles covered the floor. She pressed her palms against the cold stone surface of the counter, closing her eyes. The silence was exactly what she needed.

With a deep breath, Allie splashed water on her face, clearing her mind of all thought. The visions swarmed around her like bees around a hive. She lay down on the cool marble floor. Closing her eyes, Allie focused on her clairvoyant gift. Slowly, the spectral forms drifted back where they belonged. When she opened her eyes, she was in control again.

She allowed herself five more minutes on the floor, taking slow, deep breaths. When she stood, she was ready to join the others.

"There is one thing I'm not sure how to handle yet," Allie said when she entered the office to find Jayesh had joined them. "We need to know for certain who we can trust. I'm able to do that when in close contact, but when I go out there and talk to these people as a whole, we need to know how they are responding."

"I can help you there." Dean stepped forward. "I'll be able to tell if the crowd is with you or against you. And which ones can't be trusted."

"How close do you need to be to do that?" Allie could always get a sense of a person's true character, but she had to be in close proximity to do it. The more isolated, the better.

"I just need to be in the same room." Dean shrugged.

"And you can pick out the assholes?"

Dean grinned. "One by one."

"I knew I wanted you on my side." She returned his smile. "Anyone Dean says needs to go gets escorted out immediately. We aren't here to gather huge numbers. We are here to protect the ones who need this place to be what it claims to be."

"About time too," Jayesh said. "Good luck out there, Princess."

"Nope," Allie said. "I have only one rule; do not call me princess, ma'am, or anything like it, please. I am Allie. Plain and simple. If you must call me something formal, call me the heir. I can deal with that one."

"Allie, dear. The people will want to refer to your title. You're going to need to get used to it," Alísun said.

"Can't I be like the CEO? Do I have to be a princess?"

"It's what you are, Allie." Livia sat on the desk beside her.

"I don't see anyone calling you Princess Livia."

"I'd shoot them." Livia gave her a wry smile.

"I've got a gun," Allie said.

"Girls," Alísun said. "Titles don't mean anything to the people who have them. Not in any way that really matters. I have been a queen nearly all my life, but I don't think of myself that way. It's a persona I put on from time to time. It's not who I am. You both will need to adapt to your new stations, but you can't let a thing as simple as a word define you."

"Granny's right." Allie sighed. "It's just a word."

"Granny?" Alísun frowned. "I don't recall approving that title."

"You call me princess, I call you granny."

CHAPTER 23

"I'm going to vomit," Allie whispered. Public speaking was a huge source of anxiety for her, adding to the stress she was already under. She could hear the sheer number of people waiting in the gymnasium beyond the room where she and Darius waited. She would stand on the observation deck and address them all in just a few moments, but she was struggling to keep her visions locked away. Since arriving at Sterling Tower, her visions were overwhelming. She had to find the time to learn to cope with this aspect of her gift, or it would drive her insane.

"You'll be fine, Red. I'll be right beside you," Darius said.

"I took public speaking as an online course, so I'd never actually have to do this."

"I told you that was a bad idea."

"How are you doing? You just came out of your Proving a few days ago. You shouldn't even be here."

"Well, that's not an option and you know it. You fight, I fight." Darius took her hands in his. "I'm fine, I promise. Physically, I feel better and stronger than I ever have before."

"What about up here?" She tapped his forehead.

"That's another matter. But it can wait. I'm fully committed to this, Allie." He gave her hands a gentle squeeze.

"Don't worry about me. You've got enough to handle at the moment."

"How am I going to convince them?" Allie gave him a desperate look. She knew what she was going to say, but she didn't know if that would be enough to convince the residents of Soma to trust her.

"We can see it, you know." He brushed the hair from her face.

"See what?"

"Whatever Alísun did ... passing you the torch. It's plain as day when I look at you now. I can see it in your eyes and feel it in my bones."

"What is it?" Allie's voice wavered at the look of respect in his eyes.

"I always wondered how the ancient queens inspired such loyalty. For thousands of years, their rule was never questioned. I get it now. You're the real deal, Allie. They will see it too."

"See *what*?" She lifted her arms and glanced down at herself, trying to see what he saw.

"I can't describe it." He chuckled at her frustration. "It's just there, plain as a crown on your head. You're our ... hope. You are Indriell."

Livia stepped into the room after knocking at the door. "It's done, the building is secure."

"And those on the list?" Allie asked, staring at Darius to make sure he wasn't just messing with her.

"Thirteen have been escorted through the barrier, and Ryan has been detained for the moment."

"Are we forgetting anything? I feel like we're overlooking something important." Allie swept a nervous hand through her hair.

"Breathing, maybe?" Livia cocked her head with a smile. "Relax. Soma is yours now."

"I just have to go in there and tell them." Allie shook her sweaty hands, trying to dry them

"You ready for that?"

Allie took a deep breath and nodded as the others filed into the room. She'd asked Navid, Emma, and her grandparents to be there with her and Darius. Along with Livia and Jayesh, Sasha, Santi, Quinn and Tessa. Gregg and the rest of the McBriens and Loukases were down below with the crowd just in case things got out of hand.

"Allie?" Tessa stepped up beside her. "I know you're nervous, but just say what you said to me when we met. You said all the right things then. Just be honest and more than anything, let them see how much you care."

"Thank you, Tessa." Allie gave her a hug. "I'm so glad you're here with us."

Allie cared. That wasn't a question. Her emotions were definitely driving this bus. With a last look at Darius, she stepped through the door to the observation deck and approached the railing. She sensed the others following. Darius and Livia stood just behind her.

She stared down at the mass of unfamiliar faces scattered across the gym. A hushed silence fell upon them as they looked at Allie. The ancient mantle of Indriell burned bright within her, causing some to stare in awe, recognizing her for what she was just the way Darius had. Others displayed their skepticism or thinly veiled hostility. Sterling Tower was a large building, more than twenty floors. Each floor served a purpose. Some were dedicated to the very young children of the Fold and others to the older students of Soma itself. Many agents, counselors, and trainers were in residence. Some worked directly for Soma, others were waiting for an "assignment" as Tessa had done for so many years. All together, more than two thousand

her brother has been missing after the Senate arrested and interrogated him for reasons we've only just begun to discover.

"I've seen others experience much worse. Many of you know Quinn and Santi." Allie nodded in their direction. "They trained here, but neither was ever given a choice. I know because my sister, Livia, was the one to take Quinn from us." Allie turned to face her sister. "I hated her at first. But when she was finally free of this place, I grew to understand that she was a victim as much, if not more, than any of us. Raised by a cruel man, Livia was forced into the role she played here at Soma. I am proud to say she is not the woman you all remember. And I hope you will give her a chance to show just how much she has changed."

Allie scanned the crowd, looking for Dean. He stood in the middle of the gym, taking a reading of the crowd. He gave a subtle thumbs up to keep going.

"It ends now. From this day forward, Soma *will* be a place of refuge for those of our generation who need it. I claim Sterling Tower as the new headquarters of Indriell, in the name of the ancient queens whose blood runs in my veins. I am the first princess, granddaughter to Queen Alísun and Alexander the Scholar." Allie gestured at her grandparents as they came to stand with her.

The crowd murmured anxiously, casting wary glances at each other.

"First and foremost, you are all free to leave whenever you like. Soma is not a prison anymore. But for those who would like to train with us as we build a new Soma, you are welcome to stay. We have taken measures to ensure your safety. The building is protected. No one can enter without our permission. Not even Marcus Servius himself. But that means no one can leave without escort, either. So if you want to leave, please ask. Do not try to leave the building on your own. You won't be able to."

"Just like that?" A girl in the crowd asked. "We can leave?"

Allie nodded. "Just like that. If you're ready to go now, line up at the exit and someone will escort you from the building." A few of the older students made a beeline for the exit, but Allie still held the crowd's attention.

"And if we want to stay, just to see what you're about?" the girl asked.

"Stay as long as you like and leave whenever you're ready."

"How can we know you're for real?" a boy called from a group of younger students. "All this stuff you say about how bad Soma is; how do we know you're not just making it up?"

"She's not making it up," the first girl said. "I've wanted to leave for years and I've never been allowed." She pushed up her sleeve. "The Soma mark won't let me. I guarantee if you'd ever shown an interest in leaving, they'd have stopped you."

"She won't be any better," a young girl about Lennox's age stepped forward. "First princess or not, this is Livia's sister we're talking about."

"She is the first princess, though," another said. "That's obvious." A few others nodded, leaving Allie wondering how they could be so certain when she still doubted it.

"May I?" Tessa stepped forward.

"By all means." Allie and her grandparents moved away from the railing.

Tessa addressed the crowd calmly. "Allie is the real deal. You all can feel it. I can see it in your faces, but I know you're guarded. It's not easy to trust people here. You only have to hear the passion in her voice to know Allie cares deeply for all of us. If you need more proof, look no further. I grew up here. I'm literally the poster child for what Soma professes to be." She pointed at a banner on the wall. A much younger, naive version of Tessa smiled back at them. The caption read 'be a shooting star like Tessa St. James.' "All my life, I was told how Soma would provide the kind of future I wouldn't otherwise be able to attain on my own. I did everything right, and I waited patiently to receive a summons for my first assignment as a Soma agent. It would be the pinnacle of my education and the final feather in my cap. After my first assignment, I could go anywhere in the world and Immortals would be lining up to offer me jobs I could only dream about if it weren't for the education I received here. It was all a lie.

"The day I was finally summoned was the happiest day of my life. I couldn't wait for the opportunity to use my gifts to do great things. Only the work I had waiting for me wasn't what I'd been led to believe. That wasn't what I was purchased for. Yes, I said purchased. Vivian Dyson paid Soma fourteen million dollars for the rights to own my gifts. She bought me at an auction run through the Amrita events." Tessa gave a mirthless laugh, casting her eyes down at her captive audience. "It still took me weeks to figure it out. My first assignment was nothing like I dreamed it would be. I can do the most beautiful things with my gifts." She shook her head.

"When I finally realized I was a slave and that this *assignment* would never end, I fell into a deep depression. I thrive in the natural world, but for nearly four years I was locked in a cold and lifeless laboratory for sixteen hours a day. I was forced to use my gift in the most profane ways until I dropped from exhaustion and could no longer walk out on my own. My health suffered and I grew weak. But I produced what the master wanted." She gave a caustic smile. "Vivian made billions off my back.

"I am only standing here today because Jayesh, Livia, and Allie have given me my life back. But I couldn't go home. My work here is not done. I stand behind the new first princess, ready to fight."

Tessa turned toward Allie, taking her hand. "You have my loyalty, my respect, and my fealty. Never again." She turned back to the crowd below. "Never again will a child of Soma experience what I and countless others have."

The crowed cheered for Tessa. Another thumbs up from Dean told Allie they were, indeed, swaying the crowd to their side. Gregg and his team had only removed a few individuals Dean had flagged throughout her speech.

But Allie wanted them to know everything before they decided to stay or go.

"It's not just Soma," Allie said, raising her hands to take the crowd's attention once more. "Our own government has stood by and let this happen to us. The Senate is one of Soma's best customers, buying and selling us like cattle. And now, they want to take Soma for themselves. That is why I am here today." She took a deep breath, feeling the tension ease from her shoulders. "I will not allow that to happen. I am making a vow to you all right now that I will be the advocate our generation needs. I will protect you all with the might of Indriell behind me."

For a horrifying moment, she thought the crowd was going to laugh at her audacity to think she could lead them. Silence so loud she could hear her heart beating in her chest threatened to send her running from the spotlight.

The thunderous applause caught her by surprise, leaving her stunned and humbled by their acceptance. Allie waited for them to settle back down before she continued.

"I will not lie. Someone very important to me is being exploited by the Senate. I am here today, claiming my birthright in a way I never thought I would because I can't sit back and allow this to happen to him or anyone else. If you are with me, you are welcome here. We need you. If you don't want to be involved, but you want a safe place to train, you are welcome. If you want to leave, we will not stop you. You have tonight to decide. Tomorrow, we will be changing the ways of Soma forever."

Chapter 24

"What do you mean, you're leaving?" Livia snarled. "We just got started with this takeover."

"I have to go check on my parents, Liv." Allie folded a t-shirt and slipped it into her carry on bag. "I'll only be gone a few days."

"Gregg left Lily and Carson with ample security," Livia said. "Besides, it's not safe for you to go without me."

"Emma, Daniel, and Darius are going with me. I just need to see for myself that my parents are being guarded day and night, and Darius needs a little down time after all he's been through. While I'm there, I'm going to see if I can salvage my college career. I'm hoping my professors will let me submit my work from here, so I can still graduate on time."

"I can't be in charge." Livia sat down on the edge of Allie's bed. "I don't even want to be here."

"It's not permanent. And you have Liam, Navid, and the grandparents here to help you. The students see you as an authority figure—"

"They're afraid of me, Allie. I don't want to slip back into the woman I was."

Allie grabbed her sister's hands and sat down beside her. "You have your husband and family with you now. We will not let that happen. Just think of what a great place this could be to train Kahlynn."

"No." Livia pulled her hands away. "I will never bring my daughter here. I don't want her to ever step foot inside this place."

"You're thinking of the old Soma. This isn't the same place it once was. It might take a while for the old demons to leave but they will. And we'll make new memories here. It's just a building, Liv. Concrete and steel beams. We get to decide what happens now."

"Don't be naive, Allie. The Senate is going to retaliate. They might not be able to blow the building off the map, but they will respond. And when they do, you need to be here."

"Marcus might beat them to the punch." Allie crossed the room to gather her last few things. "Right now he only knows we've taken over. It's only a matter of time before he realizes I'm the child of prophecy. That I'm the one with the gift he believes belongs to him." Allie shut the dresser drawer with a sigh. "That's why I need to go home now. While I can. I need to tie up some lose ends so I can put my full focus here. If I wait too long, I won't have that chance."

"I should go with you." Livia insisted.

"I'll be quick. I promise. Would you feel better about staying here if I left Jayesh in charge?"

"Yes." Livia let out a breath.

"Fine. It's done." Allie hugged her sister.

"Thank you. I do understand your need to protect Lily and Carson. I would never have left my mother unless I knew she was safely out of Marcus's reach." Porcia had spent a lot of time with the McBriens and the royals over the years, but Livia and her mother ultimately decided she needed to be somewhere Marcus could never find her. Sasha and Jayesh had helped with that. Porcia was with Mother Raghavan in the Chola Valley.

Her time there would be a peaceful respite until it was safe for her to return to her daughter.

"Perhaps it's time you and your little family go for a nice long visit with your mother. Once things settle down here. You could use the break."

"That would be wonderful." Livia's eyes brightened at the idea. "A few days there would feel like months. That's exactly what we need."

"We should go." Allie tossed her bag over her shoulder. "We have a meeting with the trainers in the dining hall before I leave. I'll be back this weekend, so we can discuss having a meeting with the parents of all the younger children in residence here. They need to be informed of the takeover and what we intend."

Allie and Livia left the suite they'd used for the last few days and headed down the hall to the stairwell.

"Allie, hey." Jayesh hopped off the elevator as they passed. "Just the person I was looking for. Do you have time to talk to the onsite staff before you go? I'm hearing some grumblings about job security with the new regime."

"Job security?" Allie frowned as she took the stairs down to the dining hall with Jayesh and Livia behind her.

"The support staff. Cooks, housekeepers, concierge staff, all the people who make this place run smoothly. They just need to know where they stand."

"Of course, they are welcome to stay in their jobs. I will talk to them this evening if they can all be gathered in the gym?" She took a left down a side hall to catch a shortcut across the building.

"Can you stay until tomorrow? Not everyone is here today."

"I'm leaving tonight. I can do a letter or something to address their concerns, so they have it in writing."

"Okay, that'll work."

"Thank you, Jayesh. I appreciate all you've done for Soma since you've taken the leadership role. You've done a great deal to make this takeover easier. I'd like you to continue to be in charge while I'm away."

"Me?" He sighed. "I hate this job, Allie. It was supposed to be temporary, but that was almost four years ago." He glanced at Livia, frowning. "I was hoping with your return that you would take your old job back."

"I don't want it," Livia growled.

"Someone has to stay in Marcus's pocket," Jayesh said. "I kinda thought that would fall to me since you're married with a kid now."

"Enough." Allie blew out a breath as she stopped in front of the dining hall doors. "We will deal with Marcus eventually. Right now, he can't reach us here, and he doesn't know anything about me yet. We have some time before we have to deal with that confrontation. Neither of you are going back to Marcus. Ever. We're done with that."

Jayesh and Livia shared a look that said neither could believe that part of their lives was really over. She was so tired of seeing that skeptical look on so many faces. She could see it in Sasha and Santi. Quinn and Dean. Everyone she loved was so used to being used, they couldn't see a different way of life even when it was staring them in the face.

"Jayesh, I need you here just a little longer to keep this place running smoothly. And Livia, I need you to help establish the new rules and get these kids on the right path. And I need you two to work together. You're on the same side now." She turned, catching the scowls passing between the two. They were like siblings in their rivalry. It would be amusing if it weren't keeping them from moving forward.

"Now, we have some trainers to talk to. I want them to

understand what we expect. They need to know certain practices are no longer acceptable. I'm asking Gregg and Naeemah to come teach a class on how to train young Immortals. And then Emma and Daniel can teach them how to properly mentor."

Allie reached for the double doors and paused.

"Allie?" Livia frowned. "How did you know how to get here? You get lost every five seconds without a guide."

Allie stared at her hand, wrapped around the door handle. "I don't know." But she did. These halls were familiar to her. She'd walked them in her dreams for years.

Chapter 25

"I'm very proud of you, you know," Alísun said as she drove Allie and Darius from the airport back to Sterling Tower. Emma and Daniel stayed behind with their son, Parker, but planned to return with Graham once he graduated from MIT in a few weeks.

"I can't say I'm not still completely terrified," Allie admitted, "but I'm also excited by the prospects for the future."

"I would worry if you weren't scared shitless," Alísun said with a wry grin. "If you're afraid of making the wrong decisions, then you're on the right track. No just ruler has ever not been weighed down by the responsibility to their people. I know I chose well." She patted Allie's knee as they approached Midtown.

"Darius, I trust you are recovering from your Proving?" Alísun asked.

"Spending a few quiet days at home was good for me. I feel more like myself."

"Bouncing back from a Proving can be startling." Alísun glanced at him over her shoulder. "You suffered through this monumental change, and you expect your physical recovery to be just as arduous as recovering from an Awakening, but with a Proving, recovery happens up here." She tapped her temple.

"It's certainly confusing," Darius said.

"Slow down, Grandma," Allie said. "I need a minute before we go in there." Her newly clarified visions were running amok, and she couldn't seem to silence their babble.

"The visions are strong with you." Alísun parked on the street in front of Piedmont Park. "And they manifest in such a strange way."

"How could you tell that's what I'm struggling with?"

"Who are you talking to, dear? I know because I've been there myself, and I raised a clairvoyant daughter."

"Most of the time, it's like walking into a swarm of bees no one else can see. I just have to ignore them. In the last week, the most persistent have been making themselves known. They were silent before, but it's like they want my attention more than ever now. It's so loud." Allie rubbed a hand across her face where eyelid twitched with tension.

"Take a few deep breaths, and we'll go in when you're ready," Alísun said.

"Thank you." Allie closed her eyes, focusing on clearing her vision. Sasha called earlier to warn her that the kids had been hanging out in the lobby all day, hoping to get a moment with Allie when she returned. She just needed to get inside the building and on to the elevator. Then she could go up to her room and rest for a little while.

"Grandma?" Allie played with the zipper on her purse.

"Yes, dear?"

"I think I screwed up." She stared up at Sterling Tower. "I've been dreaming about Soma for years and I never realized what it meant. I thought the dreams were about Aidan. Now I'm not so sure."

"It happens to the best of us, Allie." Alísun reached for her hand. "Looking into the future is so often a confused, snarled mess of information. Our gifts aren't infallible. We just have to do the best we can with the tools we have. You are so young. No one expects you to fully understand everything you see. It would be a miracle if you could. These years are meant for you to practice and learn what your gift is capable of."

"I'm still having the dream." She'd chased Aidan in her dreams again, but this time she recognized the labyrinth of corridors as Sterling Tower. "But I don't know what it means."

"It's a warning, dear. Your dream is telling you to be on your toes. When it comes to fruition, you will realize it and you'll be prepared."

"It's her."

"She's so pretty."

"You think she will take students?"

"Let's kill her."

"Are we supposed to call her your majesty or your grace?"

"We have to take her unharmed."

"I don't think she likes that."

"She so powerful."

"She's dangerous."

"She's coming inside, hurry. Let's get a good view of the new queen."

"She's not a queen yet."

"We answer to no queen."

"She's a princess. The first, first princess in thousands of years."

"I love her highlights."

"She's an imposter."

"He is looking for her."

"Those aren't just highlights. The old queens had gold and

silver hair just like hers. Between that, her power, and that freaky aura she has, there's no denying her right to the throne."

"But there isn't a throne, is there?"

"Take her."

Allie shook her head, trying to separate what was real from what was phantom. The voices weren't even the difficult part. Everywhere she looked, she saw eager faces swarming the Sterling Tower lobby, but she also saw faces that weren't actually there. Hundreds of them. Some spectral, which she was used to seeing, and others were more defined, moving stealthily toward her. But some were so real, she couldn't decide if they were actually there or not. And the snakes. The floor was covered in writhing black snakes with ruby red eyes. She'd seen those snakes often enough in her dreams. She didn't need them invading her reality.

"Allie." A young girl rushed to greet her. "We're so happy to have you back," she said breathlessly. Allie pushed the girl behind her, putting herself between the girl and the man with the assault rifle aimed right at her.

"I'm sorry," Allie said, shaking her head, desperately trying to get a grip on her gift.

"You'll have to excuse the princess," Alísun said. "She's had a hard few days." She draped her arm around Allie, moving her through the crowd of students gathered to greet her return.

"Wait." Allie pulled back. This was how bad rumors would start. She looked certifiably cray-cray, and these kids would be quick to talk. "Can everyone settle down?" she called loudly across the nearly silent room—silent for everyone but Allie. A sea of blinking eyes watched her in surprise when she climbed onto a white lacquered bench against the windows.

"I'm so sorry." Allie rubbed her hands across her face, trying to ignore the black-clothed men and women who raced through the front door wielding guns. "We're all young here," faces stared up at her, wondering what this crazy redhead had to say.

"Thank you all for coming." Her voice rang out, clear and full of confidence she didn't feel.

Darius and Livia stepped up beside her. A quiet murmur of interest buzzed through the crowd at the sight of Livia. Allie needed to give off that same vibe of authority Livia seemed to be able to do in her sleep.

"Soma is no more." Allie lifted her chin high. "Today, we offer a true safe haven for you and all those of our generation who need it." She felt like an absolute ass.

"Introduce yourself," Livia hissed.

"My name is Alexis Carmichael. I'm—I'm..." She dropped the formal tone. If she was going to do this, it had to be as her and not some queenly persona she adopted for special occasions. "I'm just a girl. A young Immortal just like all of you." Her voice began to sound like her own again. "So many of us have been exploited for our gifts. Used and manipulated for the power we possess. I see some of you nodding in agreement. You've been there. You know what I'm talking about." She placed her hands on the cool stainless steel railing in front of her. "And some of you have yet to experience it. You come as young children to the Fold, hoping to one day work your way into Soma to train and hone your gifts, believing that those in charge have your best interests at heart. But they don't."

"You're doing well. You've got this," Livia whispered.

"Three years ago, I was betrayed when someone I trusted thought to use me and my power as a bargaining chip. My friend, Sasha, was taken from her home when she was just seventeen when the Senate decided she needed a special kind of training. They called it an investment in her future. No one ever asked Sasha what she wanted. And for the last three years, she said to the crowd. "Every one of you knows what it's like to have an evolving gift send you straight into crazytown, right?"

Heads nodded as they began to understand.

"I'm clairvoyant. Just like my mother and grandmother. All the women of our family have the sight. It manifests differently for each of us. Right now, my visions are swarming all around you guys like bears looking for honey, and I'm the honey. I'm not crazy. I'm just seeing a lot of activity I'm not used to seeing."

Allie stood taller, focusing on the here and now, ignoring what was likely not there. It just made her so nervous to think of how easily she could dismiss something as a vision that could be happening right under her nose.

"We are making big changes here. Everything we're doing right now will shape the future before us. Not just for those of us standing here today, but for our entire world. Sterling Tower is a difficult place for me to be in right now, but I won't be leaving again anytime soon. This is where I belong. With all of you. So if you see me acting like a total nut-job, just remember, I'm still learning, too."

"I remember when I first started understanding languages I didn't know I could speak," a young man said with a dimpled smile. "People are drawn to me, like they instinctively know I can understand them. When I was twenty-three, it escalated to this constant tidal wave of people talking in dozens of languages. It was an awful year until I finally learned how to mask my gift."

"Growing pains, am I right?" Allie smiled at the crowd. "I'm eager to meet with all of you, but for the foreseeable future, can you come at me in smaller groups?" She laughed. "Just so I can give my full focus to you and not the snakes crawling around on the floor?" Pointing down at the floor, she grimaced. "Why do you think I'm way up here on this bench?" She gave another smile as laughter spread across the room.

"Let's go, dear," Alísun said. "You should rest this afternoon." She offered her hand for Allie to climb down.

"Thanks, Grandma." Allie waved at all the kids beaming at her as she took an exaggerated step toward the elevators. *Why is it always snakes?* Her enemies always seemed to manifest in her visions as ugly, writhing, black snakes with creepy red eyes.

Allie flashed one last smile as the elevator doors slid shut.

"You are a natural with them," Alísun said, hitting the button for the basement.

"Where are we going?" Allie asked.

"The warehouse. I hear it's ten times the size of the yard back home. We're going to go have a chat about your clairvoyance and that little freak out back there."

"I haven't had a chance to come down to the warehouse yet. It's so beautiful. And quiet." Allie threw her head back, letting the sun warm her face. Acres of rolling meadow spread out before her with wildflowers painting the world in vivid colors. A tall, rocky mountain rose in the distance with thick forests surrounding its base. Allie caught a glimpse of a sparkling lake and waterfall in the distance, with cabins and trails winding in every direction.

"Jayesh has kept the warehouse closed to the students and staff for now," Alísun said. "Once we establish the new regime, we'll open it back up. Before, this lovely place was used as both punishment and reward."

"Quinn and Santi had to run up this mountain every day for weeks," Allie said. "Just to keep each other safe for one night."

"For reward, the young children of the Fold got to come here for an hour's recess once a week." Alísun shook her head in dismay. "They earned extra *minutes* here for good behavior. Can you believe that? Minutes."

"Once a week? That's not a reward, that's a tease. We should allow everyone to come here whenever they need to get outside and stretch their legs."

"You see the cabins over by the lake?" Alísun pointed as they walked in that direction. "That's where Tessa used to train. She brought me down here a few days ago when she gave me a tour of the whole facility. She said there used to be rows of small ponds over by the cabins, but when she left, the man who lives here transformed the ponds into one big lake."

"Is he someone we can trust?" Allie asked.

"Yes, Harold's an old hermit who doesn't want to be bothered. As long as he can continue to create this beautiful oasis as he sees fit, he doesn't care who is in charge."

"This would make a great summer camp for the kids."

"They would love it. I think that's a grand idea and a good way to illustrate to the kids and the parents the kinds of changes we intend to make."

"Just about everything we would need is already here. I'm sure we could set up a team and give them a budget to make it happen for this summer." Allie walked ahead of her grandmother, inspecting the cabins and the fishing dock. Canoes stood in rows along the shoreline and an area near the waterfall was dedicated for swimming. It already looked like a camp.

"You seem better here than back in the lobby," Alísun said, following her out onto the dock.

"It's quieter here. It's easier to think when there's not so much going on around me."

"Your visions are so unlike mine." Her grandmother came to her side, staring out across the crystal clear water. "I want to help you make sense of it, but I cannot fathom what it is like for you."

"They're everywhere these days." Allie swept her hand across the lake. "Like ghosts demanding my attention at once. But they are so much stronger now. Not really ghosts anymore, but real people with defined faces and strong voices. They want to be heard."

"You've always kept them silent before," Alísun said. "What's changed?"

"At first I thought it was Soma. It's like walking into a field of angry vipers whenever I walk into a crowded room here. Sometimes literally. So much of the immediate future is entangled with everything going on now, it makes sense that Soma would intensify my visions."

"But?" Alísun prodded.

"But it didn't really change when I went home." Allie turned to face her grandmother. "I think Darius's Proving is the real culprit. We affect each other in so many ways; I guess I should have expected this, too."

"You're right. I expected this, but I didn't think it would happen so soon. Darius will be experiencing a lot of progress over the next year. It usually takes about that long for the dust to settle, so to speak. When he progresses, you progress. But you always do things faster than we expect."

"It's terrible timing." Allie squinted in the bright sunlight, trying to decide if the person she saw walking the trail between cabins was real or a vision.

"I know we've been over this before, but tell me what you see," Alísun said. "Help me understand the way your sight works."

"Well, it's kind of like seeing into another dimension. Before, I just saw people and places as indistinct shapes. Like I was looking through an infrared lens, seeing the heat signature of the people around me. Blobs of yellow, red, green, and blue.

"You've lost your grandma, dear. Infrared?" Alísun's brow furrowed in confusion.

"Uh, it's a science thing I don't really know much about, but you see it in movies a lot. It's kind of a device that detects living things based on the levels of heat they give off."

"I see." Her grandmother nodded uncertainly.

"Anyway, not important since they've evolved. Before I was able to keep them locked in my peripheral vision, and I've always kept them silent, so I could function in my daily life. But all that is gone now. In the last few days, I've had very little control. It takes more effort to keep these visions locked away, and they just don't stay there like they used to. There are too many of them, and they're so real. But the information I should be getting from them is a snarled mess in all the chaos."

"You young Immortals are so impressive with your modern gifts. But it's so difficult for the older generations to teach you. I am a powerful clairvoyant and prophetess. It's absurd that I don't have the skills to help my granddaughter." Alísun's voice took on an angry, frustrated tone.

"Okay." Allie kicked off her shoes and pulled her grandmother down to sit on the dock beside her. "There has to be a way for the old and young to bridge these gaps in knowledge. We can communicate better than this." They let their feet dangle in the cool water lapping at the dock.

"You're right, let's take a few steps back," Alísun agreed.

"When you see a vision, it's prophetic. It comes to you in words, right?"

"Yes, but there is a strong visual element to what I see, too. It can sometimes be more metaphorical than literal. Kassandre's visions were always literal in the sense that she saw events unfold in a way she could understand, but for much of her life, she was powerless to influence what she saw. Until she bonded with your father." Alísun smiled.

"Really? Dad doesn't talk about her much." Allie leaned in closer, eager for more information about the mother she knew so little about.

"Your father gave her balance. He is a dream walker, so he could observe her visions right along with her. He had a unique understanding with his own interpretation. Together, they were able to influence the things they saw. He is the reason why your parents were able to plan so much of your lives. Without Navid, I shudder to think of what might have happened to my girls."

Allie held her grandmother's hand, breathing the fresh mountain air. Being here was good for her soul. She needed to make an effort to come here whenever the stress of her responsibilities got to be too much.

"Did Kassandre's visions always come to her as dreams?"

"Yes and no. She experienced waking visions as often as she dreamed them at rest."

"That's how my visions manifested at first," Allie said. "Except I *never* know what they mean. So, imagine a typical waking vision. When I have those, it takes me out of my surroundings and places me into the vision. I don't have a strong sense about what is happening in the present. If I was seeing my fiftieth birthday in Paris right now, I wouldn't be aware of this dock or the cool breeze whistling through the trees. I would be *in* Paris."

"I'm with you." Alísun nodded.

"With the way my gift is evolving now, it would be like I am here having this conversation with you, fully aware of the beauty around us, but I'd also see a thin veneer of Paris and my birthday cake over there by the cabins. And my friends would there by the rows of canoes. But at the same time, I'm still sitting here with you, fully immersed in *both* moments. Now imagine that same scenario, times a hundred. There are all these moments demanding my attention at the same time. I can't possibly process everything I'm seeing. So, I've learned to ignore it simply so I can function, but that system seems to be failing. Fast."

"I see." Alísun frowned. "You poor thing. You must be losing your mind."

"Exactly." Allie breathed a sigh of relief. "And now I have to go back up there and be the first princess, giving all those kids the attention they deserve. But right now, my gift wants me to see everything, and I don't know how to do that at the same time I'm supposed to be running Soma. Suddenly, the visions are so real, Grandma. If it gets any more real, I'm never going to be able to distinguish reality from a vision. And with everything going on, I'm terrified I'm going to miss something vital. I have to get a handle on this."

"You're absolutely right. We will keep working until we find an answer. This isn't a question of understanding your clairvoyance. You can't begin to face that until you've learned to ... to process an incredible amount of information quickly."

"That's what Graham thinks. I Skyped with him while I was home. It turns out he's struggling with a very similar progression with his gift as well. He sees the world through tech lenses, kind of like augmented reality in the movies. It's a lot for him to process, too, and it's made his last year at MIT even more difficult. He's going to come here to Soma after his graduation to focus on finding a solution."

"Well, then. I haven't the slightest clue what augmented reality is, but we will just have to find you and Graham the techiest tech person out there and get them here to help you."

Chapter 26

"You're never going to convince me to keep running Soma on blood money." Allie glared across the conference room table at Jayesh and Gregg. "We are not keeping the hundreds of millions of dollars sitting in our accounts right now. There is more money there than we could ever spend."

They were lucky to have it. Gregg discovered a young man among the Soma trainers who had a gift much like Graham's. Gabe was able to hack the Soma accounts within hours after the takeover, moving the money to newly secured accounts Marcus wouldn't be able to access. But that money belonged to the Soma slaves.

"Allie, we have to think long term. We cannot afford to pay that kind of restitution to the freed slaves," Gregg argued. "I agree, we should offer them something, but if we return their purchase price to them in full, we'll be bankrupt in a decade. It's going to take an enormous amount of money to keep this place running the way we want to."

"You can't tell me that Tessa doesn't deserve every penny of the fourteen million dollars Soma made when they *sold* her to Vivian Dyson!" Allie leaned on her elbows against the cool surface of the conference table inlaid with a map of the world in black onyx against a sea of white marble. She traced the golden borders of New Zealand with her fingertip, wondering how she could have come so far in just a handful of years.

"Of course, she does," Jayesh said. "They all deserve it, but it just can't be done. It isn't feasible."

"Then let's make it feas—"

"I don't want it." Tessa stood, slamming her fist down on the table. "It's not going to buy back the last four years of my life." Taking a deep breath, she sat back down. "Keep` it for the new Soma and make this place better. Use it to keep what happened to me from happening to anyone else. I guarantee the other freed slaves will feel the same way. Some will take whatever you offer, but others won't want anything to do with it. Allie's right; it's blood money, and I never want to see it."

"You will be getting some form of restitution," Livia said. "It's only fair."

Allie massaged the tight spot of tension at the back her neck, trying to pay attention, but she was struggling to divide her focus enough to keep her visions in check.

"How about this?" Tessa leaned back, crossing her arms over her chest. "Vivian paid us for our work. She treated us well to make us complacent, so we'd never want to leave. Never mind that we *couldn't* leave—the perks were there to make us happy enough not to try. I made nearly a million dollars during my time with Vivian, but because we escaped, we didn't get to take that with us. Pay us a fair wage for our time in captivity, and keep the rest to take care of these kids."

Gregg nodded. "That's a good solution. A fair one. We could come up with an average dollar amount for each year in captivity and pay everyone based on that. That way we can control expenses, pay a universal restitution, and keep our doors open."

"I can live with that," Allie said. "Thank you, Tessa."

"Fifty thousand dollars per year?" Jayesh suggested. "Maybe seventy-five. We could easily afford that."

"No, it should be much more than that," Livia countered.

"Double it." Allie tried to keep the pain out of her voice. Her head throbbed like a vice tightened around her skull. She had to get out of this room. "It needs to be at least a hundred and fifty thousand dollars per year served. We pay them the total for all their years in service, unless that total exceeds their original purchase price, in which case, we would offer that amount instead."

"It's still way too much, Allie," Gregg insisted.

"You're not thinking far enough in the future, Gregg. We've freed how many slaves so far?"

"Twelve," Livia said, checking her reports. "Including Tessa and Dean."

"And even that was a struggle. It's going to take years of digging and searching until we've released them all. So, we pay restitution as they are freed, in small amounts here and there. In the meantime, we keep the bulk of the money earning interest. We invest, making that money work for us. We restructure salaries from mine all the way down to the janitors. No one will be low-balled, but we shouldn't be paying some trainers a ridiculously high wage and not paying others at all. Then we streamline every position. We don't need college advisors and accountants for the students in residence because they're just ripping them off, and we're paying them to do it."

"I used to pay my college tuition to Soma directly, and my advisors took care of everything for me," Tessa offered. "I just found out I was paying triple for my classes and books. My mother paid my tuition here when I was a child. But when I started paying it myself, they still charged her as they always had, double dipping us without our knowledge. Everything here was a scheme to fleece the students and their families of as much money as they possibly could. All that money went into Soma's pockets."

"I'm so sorry, Tessa," Livia said. "I never knew that was happening, or I would have stopped it. It's no secret that my father paid me a fortune to run this place, but I had blinders up. I refused to see so much." Livia's hands twisted in her lap. "I'd like to pay twenty percent of each person's restitution myself. It's the least I can do. That should help counter some of the cost."

"I'll split it with you," Jayesh said. "We each pay ten percent. I did my fair share of looking the other way for more years than I care to admit."

Allie could tell by the look on her sister's face that there was no arguing with her on this. "I appreciate that. It will go a long way in helping these people pick up their lives again and move on. And, as we build the new Soma," Allie continued, "we will find ways to earn an *honest* income. We'll run out of blood money eventually, but by then, if we're smart, we'll be making what we need to keep our doors open in the years to come."

"A hundred thousand per year," Gregg countered, his notebook a scribble of sums and annual projections. "That's as much as we can reasonably afford. With Jayesh and Livia contributing twenty thousand of their own money, it should be more than enough compensation for their time."

"Agreed," Allie said. "Is there any other business to discuss?" She needed to find a quiet, dark place so she could breathe. Her head was pounding from the effort of controlling her gift.

"Tuition for the summer camp," Jayesh said. "We should be able to run with it this year, but we need to send letters to the families with pricing information as soon as possible."

"It's going to be free this year," Allie said, sighing. She wasn't getting out of here any time soon.

"Come on, Allie." Gregg ran his hands through his hair in frustration. "That's just not smart business."

"We owe it to the families of the Fold. If we expect them to trust us with their youngest children, then we need to show them the changes we're making. The summer camp is the best way we can do that. The kids will get to have a fun summer, while still keeping up with their training, and we invite the parents to come check it out. Let them stay a night or two to see what we're all about. It's a chance to suck up to our existing clientele, so they keep coming back when the Senate starts their smear campaign. But we'll tell them what the tuition will be for next summer, making it clear that this is the only free service we are offering. They will all likely take advantage of it, giving us the golden opportunity to win them all over."

"I can't even argue with that." Jayesh threw his pen down. "Didn't you go to art school?"

"I minored in business with a special focus in business ethics." Allie shrugged.

"Let's set up a team of volunteers to help counter some of the costs," Gregg suggested. "And let's work on ironing out the big changes for Soma, so we can give the parents a presentation on what to expect over the next year, like lower tuition rates and more visitation days for the older students."

"I'll volunteer some time for that," Livia said. "I think we should all pledge a certain amount of hours to help with the camp."

"Both excellent ideas, let's do it." Allie added the items to her growing to-do list. Her chest tightened with worry over how she would ever accomplish it all. "I think we're done for the day. Good work everyone." She was the first one out of her seat and across the room.

"Allie-girl?" Alexander called from her office through the open double doors of the conference room.

"Hi Grandpa." Allie smiled with relief. "Let me grab my bag and we'll head out." Allie tossed her notebooks and endless reports on her desk, snatched her messenger bag, and followed her grandfather out of the office before anyone could stop her.

Alísun and Alexander had developed a habit of tag teaming her. Whenever Allie found herself in a stressful situation with people vying for her attention, one of them would show up and sweep her off to the warehouse for a little break away from the madness.

She took his hand and practically ran for the elevators. "Thanks for the rescue," she whispered.

"Ms. Carmichael?" A slender woman with slightly graying hair called to get her attention.

"Dammit."

"Should we run?" Alexander murmured.

"I wish." Allie sighed. "Hi there, Elizabeth. What can I do for you?"

"We really need to talk about the curriculum changes to the training program. I sent you a proposal a few days ago."

"I received it, and it's very high on my to-do list. I have some ideas I'd like to discuss with you. Can you call my office to schedule the next available appointment? I'll text my assistant to let her know to expect your call," Allie said as the elevator arrived.

"Thank you, Ms. Carmichael. I can't tell you how happy we are to have you here."

Elizabeth was among many of the staff eager to stay on board after the takeover. She managed the training programs before, and that made Allie hesitant to keep her in her role. But her proposal was strong. She had a lot of ideas and a lot of heart for her students.

"I'm so proud of you," Alexander said as the elevator doors closed.

"Thank you." Allie leaned her head on her grandfather's shoulder. "I'm so exhausted."

"I can imagine. You've taken on an enormous responsibility for someone so young."

"I love what we're doing here. I just hope it slows down soon. I can't keep up this pace." The work was rewarding, but the stress of waiting and wondering who would retaliate first, the Senate or Marcus, was eating her alive.

"It's all about delegation. You'll find the right pace once you have the right people on your team. People you trust to make good decisions. You're so involved with everything that goes on here; you need to hire several assistants, so you can delegate more."

"You're my favorite assistant." Allie walked with him toward the warehouse entrance in the basement. "You and grandma are saving my life with your little ninja sneak attacks, forcing me to take a break."

"We're almost afraid you'd forget to eat and sleep if we didn't make you." He chuckled. "You're so much like your father in that way."

The warehouse was open again, so there were a few students coming and going, but they kept their distance as Allie and her grandfather walked along the trail around the lake and up to the waterfall. Allie moaned in relief as she released her tenuous hold on her visions, letting them out to wander in their haphazard way, no rhyme or reason to their movement.

They walked along in silence, her grandfather content to let her relax in the stillness of the sunny afternoon.

"Who is that following us, Grandpa?" Allie glanced behind them. "He seems familiar."

"Who?" Alexander frowned. "The boys at the dock?"

"No, the guy with the beard, just over there." She pointed by the cabins. "I know I've seen him around here before."

"There's no one behind us." Alexander looked over his shoulder. "Describe what you're seeing. Maybe your old grandpa can help you figure this one out."

"It's so frustrating seeing people who aren't there. I don't know how I'm ever going to distinguish real people from fake people. Maybe I should just run around and poke everyone with a stick."

"You're young. It's supposed to be hard." Alexander smiled. "It was different in my day. Most young people were not as talented as your generation, even though their access to the power was not as limited. It was a different time, and gifts manifested more slowly. I was the exception of my generation, too, you know. I can still remember how isolating that was. To be head and shoulders above the rest."

"Sometimes I think I'm getting a grip on it again, and then I fumble and have to start back at square one."

"You've hit a rough patch. You'll get through it."

"I must have seen a vision of this guy before." Allie frowned at the bearded man, wondering how on earth she was ever supposed to understand what he represented for the future.

"This spectral man follows you often?" Alexander asked. "That could be a sign that you need to give him more attention than the others."

"I don't know; he has the kind of face that blends in with his surroundings. He's very forgettable, but I get the feeling he's always there and I just don't notice."

"Hmmm. Describe him for me." Alexander frowned.

"I can draw him." Allie headed for a grassy patch in the sunlight, pulling a sketchpad out of her bag.

Alexander hung over her shoulder as she quickly sketched

the man lingering along the trail near the waterfall. As she filled in the details of his unremarkable face, she could feel Alexander's tension mounting behind her.

"This man follows you, watching your every move?" he asked, taking a seat beside her in the grass.

"He's just a vision, but yes."

"This is Marcus Servius."

Allie turned toward the man who was responsible for nearly every bad thing going on in their world. The man responsible for all the years her sister had suffered under his thumb.

Her face flushed with anger as she scrambled to her feet to get a closer look. He was bland and boring, the beard his most distinguishing characteristic. Brown eyes and hair. Brown tweed jacket, tan pants, and brown shoes. Average height and build. He would blend in with any crowd with his ordinary face and common features.

"How did I miss this?"

"Marcus is a chameleon, but that is part of his gift. He appears so ordinary that he can blend in wherever he goes, become whoever he needs to become. Without Livia's mother, Porcia, beside him, few would place him as one of the most ancient Immortals still living in the mainstream world. The question is, why is he following you, even if it is just a ghost of him?"

"He's watching me," Allie said as she began to put bits and pieces of the puzzle together in her mind. It was all a giant jumble of information, but once she found a key piece, the others started coming together with ease. "Not this replica of him. But the real Marcus is out there, watching. He surely knows what we've done here by now, but he knows who I am, Grandpa." Allie turned wide eyes on him.

"Keep going, Allie-girl. Talk it out. I can see the clairvoyance sparkling in your eyes," Alexander whispered.

"Livia always said Marcus was so focused on the prophecy that speaks of me as a male that he never stopped to consider he might be looking for a girl instead." Allie whirled around to face her grandfather, her chest warm with the use of her power. "He was convinced Aidan was the child of prophecy, but that was just grandma's way of protecting me from him. Now, he knows it's not Aidan he's been looking for. He hasn't retaliated against us because he doesn't care about Soma anymore. It's me he wants now. More than anything."

Allie turned back to Marcus, taking a moment to examine each of the other figures that wandered aimlessly around him. But they weren't aimless. Not all of them. Sixteen young Immortals stood around him in a wide circle. She wouldn't have noticed if not for the open spaces here in the warehouse. As she turned slowly around, she recognized Aidan and Naomi standing in the distance. The other fourteen moved in pairs—the Syntrophos army of the Milan Initiative.

"Oh, my God, he is using Aidan to get to me." She sank to the ground, too stunned to stay on her feet. Marcus stared right through her, illuminated with a green aura now. "He's the one behind the Milan Initiative. The Chief Justice is building an army of the most powerful young Immortals they can find, but they're doing it for Marcus. Not for the Senate or even themselves. It's him they serve. And somehow, Marcus knows what Aidan means to me. He wants to pit us against each other. He's a lunatic if he thinks that will ever work." Fire smoldered in her core. Her hands itched with the urge to release her rage on the one man who deserved it more than anyone.

The aura around Marcus grew brighter. He turned to her, a thin smile spread across his unremarkable face. And then he was gone. One by one, the Syntrophos pairs disappeared, too.

"What just happened?" Allie lurched to her feet, whirling around, looking for the visions. "He vanished. They all vanished."

"Who?" Alexander asked.

"Marcus and the Syntrophos. They're just gone."

"That's your solution, Allie-girl."

"What?" She frowned, throwing her hands up in frustration.

"You figured out what his vision meant," Alexander said. "Your gift knows you don't need him or the Syntrophos visions anymore, so they're gone. You figure out all the rest, and you'll be able to function."

"I—you're right." Allie sat back on the ground, wrapping her arms around her knees. "Do you have any idea how many visions I've let pile up around me?"

"It'll take a while, but you'll thin the herd, so to speak. And then you won't be under this much pressure. You'll be able to function *and* keep on top of what you see."

"I need to figure out what I'm going to do about Marcus first. How can I deal with him if I don't know where he is or what he's planning?"

"You let your old grandpa do some digging," Alexander said. "I'll find out what he's up to."

Chapter 27

"Do we even have a plan?" Darius asked as they headed down to the lobby.

"I have no idea." Allie slouched against the wall, wishing the elevator would get stuck so someone else would have to deal with the Senate forces surrounding the building. "I'm relying on Gregg and Liam to handle this kind of thing, but I still have to go out there and talk to them."

"Livia and I will be right there with you."

"Thank God for that."

The Senate forces had arrived at dawn. Nearly a hundred black clad soldiers surrounded the building. They couldn't get inside the barrier, but they were clearly not leaving until they spoke with her.

"How are the visions?" Darius asked.

"Quiet and in control for the moment," she said. Eliminating the visions of Marcus and the Syntrophos had helped her gain the upper hand on her gift. But she needed time to deal with the others. Time she didn't have.

"What are you going to do?"

"I don't have a clue, Darius. I'm terrified! I don't know how to negotiate with an army.

As the doors of the elevator slid open, the lobby erupted in chaos. Her own black-clad forces were gearing up to escort her through the barrier to talk to the Senate's representative.

"Put these on," Livia shoved a set of protective gear into her hands, instructing her to put them on over her clothes. Allie already had her own weapons tucked at her waist.

"What's the plan?" she whispered. She didn't want anyone to think she wasn't fully in control of the situation.

"We've been expecting this," Livia hovered at her side. "Our numbers nearly match theirs. We have the advantage because they cannot breach the barrier, and since we will not be leaving it, this will come to nothing. They're just trying to intimidate us."

"They're going to expect us to negotiate." Allie strapped on a protective vest and buckled a weapon's belt around her waist, sheathing her sai blades in the holster. "But that's not going to happen. Not today anyway."

"They think they can frighten you into a surrender with a show of force."

"Oh, I'm frightened all right. But let's go show them how good we are at bluffing." Allie slipped her hands into fingerless gloves and turned to face the waiting group. With a wave of her hand, the doors to Sterling Tower were thrown open, and the dream walkers took position.

Navid led the way through the barrier with Sasha, Quinn, and Santi spreading out behind them. Allie followed with Darius and Livia at her side and her grandparents right behind her. Her soldiers brought up the rear, working with the walkers to widen the tunnel and surround Allie in a protective cocoon. She was proud of them and all they had done to begin the transformation of Soma, but they weren't nearly done yet.

Seriously, how did I get here? Just weeks ago, she was an art major, waiting for the day she would graduate and move into the next phase of her boring, normal life. Now, she was about to start a war with the Senate.

As they approached the edge of the barrier, Allie's nerves went into overdrive.

"Relax, daughter," Navid whispered, coming to stand directly in front of her. "You are in control of this situation. Just be confident in your desire to protect everyone behind you. Remember that is your single motivation in doing this." He paused. "This is a big step; are you ready, or do you need a minute?"

Allie nodded. "I'm as ready as I'll ever be."

Navid and Quinn took the last step forward, breaching the barrier to allow this meeting. They refused to open the barrier more than a few feet, but that was all she needed.

Allie took a confident step up to the mouth of the tunnel to await the arrival of the Senate's representative.

As her people gathered protectively around her, Allie marveled at the way they stood so firmly with her, conviction on their hopeful faces—both her family and the people of Soma. Gregg and Liam marched down the lines of soldiers, giving instructions. She trusted them to handle the military aspect of this face off and prayed that's all it would be.

A large party began to approach across Piedmont Park. Their numbers were equal to hers. Dressed in black fatigues and armed to the teeth, they came for a battle and they meant business.

With one look at the representative they'd sent, Allie almost lost her will. He was so *angry*. She saw it written all over his face. A face she knew almost better than her own. *Aidan?* How had this happened? After all of this time, after staking her claim as the heir in a bid to help him escape the Senate's grasp, how had they ended up on opposite sides?

"Alexis." Aidan's voice was like broken glass. His real

emotions hidden behind a calm facade she didn't trust. He stood tall, his eyes burning with the force of his power. He was furious with her. "Or should I say, *princess*?" He gave a mockery of a bow.

Allie couldn't have been more surprised if he'd slapped her.

"Aidan, don't be a dick." Sasha took a step forward, but Quinn held her back.

Aidan ignored his sister and raised his hand in a gesture to stop those behind him. They lined up like experienced troops on a battlefield. Against her ragtag team of forces in mismatched battle gear, they were intimidating to say the least.

"Aidan." Gregg came to stand beside Allie. His arms were crossed behind him as if standing at attention.

"Dad." Aidan nodded at his father.

Neither said anything further, but the tension between father and son was palpable.

Naomi warned her that he'd changed. She was right; the last years had made Aidan darker and more deadly. Allie closed her eyes for a brief moment. *Not like this.* She'd never imagined it would go down like this with them on opposite sides.

"You know me better than this." Her voice came out strong and steady.

"Do I? You've made some serious claims against the Senate," he said. "The Chief Justice calls you an imposter, and I'm inclined to agree. The Allie I knew would never reach for this kind of power."

She saw the disappointment spread like a shadow across his face. He thought she was power hungry? "I am no imposter." She lifted her chin in defiance. "I am the named heir of Alísun, the last queen of Indriell and you damn well know it."

"How can we know your claim is anything more than words?" he asked. "The queens died ages ago without naming an heir. Indriell carries no weight with the Senate or the

Immortal population. How can an unknown girl expect to take the name of Indriell without any proof?"

"I see my idiot brother has reached an entirely new level of stupid." Darius gave Aidan a hostile glare. "You know who she is, Aidan."

"I thought I did." Aidan stood with his hand on the hilt of his sword.

She wanted to throttle him. He knew very well she was who she claimed to be. He'd been among the first to know of her connection to the prophecy and the ancient queens. But if he wanted proof, she would give it to him.

"We are her proof." Alísun and Alexander stepped forward. "She has been named." The aura the queen gave off at will was firmly in place. There was no mistaking Alísun for the queen she was, but she wasn't the only one who could do that now.

"I've got this, Grandmother," Allie said respectfully. She summoned thoughts of Indriell and its people until the weight of the mantle fell heavy on her shoulders once more. Her power stirred like lava in her chest, her heart beating steady, and filled with an awe-inspiring love for those who stood behind her. It nearly took her breath away.

"Indriell carries no weight with the people?" Allie tilted her head. "I'm sure the Senate would like to think so. Yet look at all the Immortals standing behind me." She gestured over her shoulder.

"I see," Aidan said in his flat, heartless tone. But his eyes widened as he took in her newly acquired aura. "You are supposed to be dead, Alísun." He turned to face the queen. "The history books tell us you died thousands of years ago."

What have they done to you? She wanted to scream at him to answer her thoughts the way he used to do.

"I am the Scholar. I wrote the history books, son," Alexander said. "To protect our family, I recorded our death."

"Now that we're here face to face, I can sense you are who you claim to be," Aidan said with a hint of regret in his voice. "But the Chief Justice would ask you, what right have you to return, seeking power after all this time? Why use this girl to make such a claim?" He leveled an accusing glare at Allie.

"We have not—" Alísun began, but Allie held her hand up to silence her grandmother. This was her battle to fight.

"Use?" Allie arched a brow at Aidan. "I'm no puppet. The queen has named me her heir, and it is my place to decide what's to be done in my name."

He knows me better than this. He'd changed a great deal in the intervening years, physically. He'd always been tall, but he was bulkier now with a five o'clock shadow and a menacing presence. But could he have changed so much on the inside that she truly couldn't recognize him anymore? She had changed and grown in his absence. But surely he could still see the girl he once professed to love?

"Our lineage gives Alexis the right to stake a claim in the leadership of this world," Alísun said. "The people here today have chosen to follow her. And more will come in time. Alexis has the authority of the ancient queens coursing through her blood. The people recognize that and they will follow her. She will be heard. She will be respected. But she will *never* be controlled."

"What do you expect to accomplish by standing in the way of the Senate, Allie?" Aidan asked, returning his gaze to her. His voice wavered as he spoke her name, holding the barest hint of what he might be feeling at seeing her again. He wasn't immune to his feelings any more than she was, though he tried to hide it.

"Soma belongs to the royal family," Allie said in a firm

voice. "I do not wish to rule anyone, and I have no thirst for power. You know that better than anyone, Aidan McBrien. But Soma will *not* fall under the Senate's thumb as long as I am the heir."

"The Senate demands you cease and desist. You will remove this barrier and allow us entry. Soma belongs to the Immortal government now."

"I'm afraid we aren't moving, Aidan."

She couldn't tear her eyes away from him. He looked so cold and indifferent. Nothing of the mischievous boy she'd loved remained in the jaded man before her now. Yet his eyes were glued to hers as if he couldn't make himself look away if he wanted to. *What have you been through?* Her thoughts hammered at the mental barrier standing between them.

I could ask you the same question, Lex.

His thoughts came to her like an old memory, swirling in her mind. Her knees shook, and she feared for a moment that she wouldn't be able to stay on her feet. His thoughts filled her with so much emotion—so many warring emotions, she couldn't stand it. Warmth spread throughout her entire body as her heart nearly beat out of her chest. All she wanted was to cross the distance separating them and finally feel his arms around her again. But she had a job to do.

"The royal family intends to disobey a direct order from the Senate?" he asked. "Do you have any idea of the consequences you will face if you do not yield to me now?"

"I will not yield and damn the consequences. The Senate has proven time and again that they have as little regard for young Immortals as Soma had." Her voice shook with rage. "I've watched them use and abuse those I love. The royals will not stand aside any longer. Soma *will* be a safe haven for our generation and those that come after us. I will not tolerate the abuse any more." *Least of all what they have done to you.*

"The Senate holds the same desire. There is no need for you to oppose us. We are all on the same side here. Stand down, Alexis. While you have the chance." *Please. You don't know what you're doing. I can imagine you must be thrilled to have your true family with you finally, but I fear they have led you astray.*

In case you forgot, I have a mind of my own. "Shall I ask your team if they feel confident in the Senate's desire to protect them?" Her hands rested on the hilts of her weapons, sheathed at her side. "You stand here with half an army of Syntrophos soldiers behind you, yet their other half is missing. I stand beside my own Syntrophos," Allie said. "I'd sooner come to you unarmed than to leave Darius behind for such a meeting as this. I can only assume the Senate has used the bond to manipulate you and your soldiers' allegiance."

"Our allegiance is to our government," Aidan said. "Not to a long dead nation or a queen who abandoned us to extinction thousands of years ago. We leave our Syntrophos behind to protect ourselves from those who would think to use us for our collective power."

"Like the Milan Initiative uses you?" she asked. "You are never allowed to leave with your Syntrophos unless you are escorted. Doesn't that sound familiar? A trick straight from the Coalition's rulebook; manipulating one Complement with the safety and wellbeing of the other. Or does it sound like Soma? Did you know that's what they did to Dean? For the last four years, your cousin has been a slave, Aidan. Bought and paid for through Soma. He managed to earn a certain level of freedom, but he and Tessa were never allowed to leave together. They love each other, and their owners used it against them. Sound familiar, Aidan?" Allie's voice rose in anger as she clenched her fists at her side, the spark of her judgment gift itching for release. But Allie had no guilty outlet for her rage against an unjust system. Not yet. But she would some day.

"Things need to change. The Senate sees that," Aidan said. *But you don't have to be the one to do it, Allie.*

"I don't care for their methods." *This is my choice. We can stand here arguing all day about how much you believe I am being manipulated, since you clearly don't think I'm capable of making sound decisions. Or you can come with me now. You and your Syntrophos soldiers. We will liberate your partners as a top priority.* His lack of faith in her hurt more than when he'd left her.

"That is not for you to decide. Stand aside now, and you will not be charged for your crimes against the Senate. They will take your position into consideration." *Leaving is not an option, Allie. Would you leave Darius if the situation were reversed? I know you think you are doing the right thing, but trust me, you're in way over your head.*

"Then we truly are against each other." Allie's heart shattered in her chest. Aidan would never see her as anything more than that silly girl who didn't know she was Immortal. "I will not allow you access to Soma."

"We will act by force if necessary. Your barrier can't keep us out forever." *I have a job to do. Please stand down. I don't think you have the full story.*

"As long as you stand with the Senate, you will not find entrance to Sterling Tower today or any other day. But if you seek refuge..." Her voice rose to address his soldiers. "If you seek asylum, then we can talk."

Do you have any idea how much I've missed you? How much your complete lake of faith is killing me right now? Her thoughts were a jumble of chaos. She was torn between her duty to her position and her heart. This whole thing started as one in the same, and somehow things had taken a drastic turn for the unexpected.

I've been with you everyday, Lex. Just because you haven't been able to hear me, doesn't mean I left you.

She wanted to cross the few feet separating them and kick his ass all the way home. But even more than that, her overwhelming desire was to hold him again. Even if just for a moment.

I'm afraid this will not end well for either of us, Aidan said. *I've tried like hell to protect you from all of this. And here you are, despite all my best efforts, right in the middle of it.*

Aidan, when will you ever learn? I don't need your protection. I don't need you making decisions for me. I just need you ... I need my equal standing here beside me. Not over there, standing against me.

"Stand down, Alexis," Aidan said again. "Or you will endanger everyone you're so eager to protect."

"I cannot." *Not even for you.*

Then we are at an impasse. "The Chief Justice will be in contact. The Senate intends to end the exploitation of young Immortals by entities such as Soma, including any *royal* who stands in our way."

"An admirable vow, but considering the Senate's involvement in the Soma slave market, I don't believe you," Allie said.

"The Senate has no official involvement with Soma. Any Senate representatives participating in the Soma slave market have been punished."

"My answer hasn't changed. I don't believe you. I have personally seen the slave market in action. I've seen Senate members purchasing young Immortals without batting an eye. Pardon me if I don't trust the government at their word. And quite frankly, I can't believe you would either. The Chief Justice will have to do much better than half-hearted promises if they expect us to work together. I am no threat to them or their administration. I have no wish to rule our world. I simply want to protect those who need it." *I need you to trust me, Aidan. Please, come with me now, and we will figure this out.*

I can't do that. I won't. "We have only the best of intentions," Aidan said. *Trust me, Allie.*

I don't think I know you anymore. She didn't know this version of him, nor what motivated him beyond his bond with Naomi and his need for revenge against Soma. "I don't trust the Senate's intentions. We are done here," Allie said. "You should go."

"Those are daring words," Aidan said. "Are you quite certain you understand what you're doing?" *You are crossing a line here. One I can't help you uncross. This could mean war.*

I don't need you to fix anything, Aidan. I need you to trust me. Allie stood ramrod straight as anger swept through her body. "I am Alexis Carmichael, the named heir of Indriell." Her voice took on a commanding tone even she didn't recognize. "Second natural daughter of the ancients, Ashar and Kassandre, former Chief of Justice. I am the child of prophecy, First Princess, and granddaughter of Queen Alísun and Alexander, the Scholar. I know *exactly* what I am doing, and you would do well to recognize my power, if not my authority. I am no child playing at war here. I am not the naive girl you met all those years ago, Aidan. I haven't been her in a very long time. I am the leader of Soma. You will be the one to back down today. Return to the Chief Justice and tell them the ball is in their court now. The Senate must cede the fate of Soma to the royals. If they choose war instead, so be it."

CHAPTER 28

"I can't feel my legs." Allie almost collapsed on her way back through the barrier. She shook with a mixture of anger and fear, finally letting it all hit her. Seeing Aidan again. The sweet relief of having him share her thoughts only to have him shut her out again. The fact that she was pretty sure she just started a war she wasn't sure she could win.

"Get her inside," Alísun demanded.

Darius and Livia shouldered Allie across the lobby full of onlookers and stepped onto the elevator to take her up to the penthouse where she'd been staying.

"You're scaring me, Allie," Darius whispered. "Was it seeing him? Did you hear his thoughts?"

"Yes."

"Is he really on board with the Senate?"

"Yes." She shuddered at the thought.

"That kid drank the Kool Aid," Livia said. "We can't trust him."

Darius shook his head. "We only got half of the conversation, Liv. What is he thinking, Allie?"

"I honestly don't know," Allie said miserably. "He tone says one thing, but his thoughts are more like the Aidan we know. He's with them a hundred percent. He won't leave Naomi, but

I think a small part of him does want to come home. I just ... I think we've lost him, Dare."

"He's gone then?" Darius tapped her forehead.

"Gone." Allie nodded, tears blurring her vision.

But Aidan had claimed he'd never really left her. Did that mean he could still hear her? *Aidan, please. You have to know I did this for you and all of your Syntrophos. To give you all a way out. You can come home.*

"Are you okay?" Darius asked, pressing a hot cup of coffee into her hands.

Allie sat on the plush red sofa and gazed around the pristine white penthouse suite that used to belong to her sister. Livia couldn't stand to be here now.

What just happened? She kept asking herself the same question.

"Allie, talk to me." Darius crouched in front of her.

"What have they done to him?" she asked, staring into his midnight blue eyes for answers she knew he didn't have.

"It's been a long time, Allie. Think of all the things we've been through since Aidan left. We aren't the same people we were then, and neither is my brother. He's a stubborn little bastard, but he has his reasons for backing the Senate. My guess is he wants them to take responsibility for Soma, so you don't have to. He thinks he's protecting you, shielding you from some responsibility he doesn't think you should have to shoulder."

"I love him, Darius. You know that."

"I know."

"But right now, I want to strangle him, hang him up by his toenails, and beat him with a sharp stick like a piñata. How many ways can I say it? How many times do I have to tell him he can't make decisions for me?"

"He's a fixer, Allie. He's always been the guy who takes care of his family and those he loves. Whether they want him to or not." Darius moved to sit on the sofa beside her. "I know you don't want to hear this, but you're a lot like him in that way."

"I care about people the way he does, but I don't bulldoze right over them without listening to what they want."

"Oh, yeah? When did you ask Aidan if he wanted to be rescued?"

"I—he ... Why wouldn't he want to come home?" Allie stammered.

"There's another side to his story, Allie. We can't know what's driving him; we probably don't have anywhere close to the full story. But you're doing the right thing with Soma. And we do need to give all of the Syntrophos of the Milan Initiative the *option* to leave. But we can't choose sides for them. Not even for my idiot brother."

"I really hate it when you're right."

"It happens a lot. I'm sure it's irritating." He smirked.

"All right, you get one." Allie smiled, putting her feet up on the ottoman. "It just feels like he has no faith in me. Like he will always see me as that fifteen-year-old, clueless, lonely girl that ran right into him on the trails of Kelleys Island a million years ago."

"Where you are concerned, Aidan will always react like an over-protective boyfriend first and your equal second."

"Where do we go from here, Dare?" Allie's eyes filled with angry tears. "I did all of this for him. I'm such a fool."

"You are not the fool here. Aidan takes that prize." Darius rubbed his hands across his face in frustration. "You know what needs to happen next, Allie. We have to move on without him."

"He left again," she whispered as she stared out of the floor to ceiling windows that often felt more like a prison than a luxury. A big part of her wanted to pack up and go back to school to the homey little cottage she shared with Darius and their friends. Where her adorable niece lived just across the street, so Allie got to see her everyday. She wanted that boring, normal life again. *The grass is always greener,* she mused.

"I think you should take a step back for a little while. Delegate some of your workload as we move forward. You don't need to be responsible for every single decision."

Allie nodded. She knew she had to slow down, or she'd never see this thing through. And she had to see it through. Soma was her responsibility now. She'd just never considered she'd be doing it without Aidan.

"Allie-girl?" Alexander knocked softly at the foyer entrance.

"Grandpa?" She stood to greet him. "What's wrong?"

"It's worse than we thought." Alexander crossed the room to her side. "Marcus isn't just in cahoots with the Chief Justice on the Milan Initiative. I've done some digging and it's not good."

Allie had never seen her grandfather so flustered before. "Sit down, Grandpa." Allie pulled him down on the sofa beside her. "What's he up to?"

"Marcus is a senator, Allie. He sits on the International Senate with his eyes and ears on every move the Chief Justice makes. They don't make a single decision without his approval."

CHAPTER 29

Standing in her cap and gown, Allie found herself alone among her classmates on graduation day. Darius and Sasha waited in line far behind her. With everything that had happened recently, this day wasn't the momentous occasion she'd been looking forward to for the last four years. She just wanted to get it over with, so she could get back to Atlanta and figure out what to do next. After she'd force herself to accept Aidan was on the wrong side, the burning need to take a stand against the Senate was stronger than ever before.

Allie absently followed the graduate in front of her, filing into the outdoor auditorium for the long morning of ceremony. Not for the first time, she wished she could have just received her diploma by mail and skipped the ceremony, but Lily and Carson deserved to have this day.

Allie crossed the green lawn and took her alphabetical seat among the other students with surnames beginning with "C." Her mind wasn't on the graduation or the dean's commencement speech. Releasing the spectral figures from her peripheral vision, she let them wander but didn't let them talk. She was back in control again, but she had to stay on top of them, taking the time to examine her visions as often as she could. She found that when she gave them the attention they deserved, focusing on one at a time, she began to see so much more than just the person. Little details began to surface. New faces and places emerged, giving her a much better look at what her gift was trying to tell her.

She saw Aidan first. He followed her often now, but it was odd seeing him like this after their real encounter recently. Her heart skipped a beat at the sight of him. In the privacy of her own thoughts, she studied him more carefully. In the intervening years, his jawline had hardened from the slight softness of boyhood he'd once had. His dark hair gleamed almost blue in the afternoon sunlight. His eyes smoldered with golden fire, his shoulders, wider than they were before, tensed with anger. He was so furious with her. But this wasn't him. Not really. He was lost to her now; the boy that had once been her high school sweetheart.

Allie rubbed her eyes, trying to clear the images from her vision. Strange, dark blue clouds rolled in like a storm suddenly brewing. But the sun still shone through, casting her world with an eerie green light. Thunder rumbled in the distance and yet the dean still droned on, her cue that this wasn't happening for anyone else.

She saw Aidan again. Her Aidan. The one she knew inside and out. It was the version of him just before he left. His dark eyes filled with anguish and despair as he paced across the lawn, his hands shoved deep in his pockets. Emma joined him, her arm around his waist, comforting him as they approached his parents. Emma spoke softly with them, while Aidan stood absently by, letting them make the decision of whether he would go to Germany or not. Somehow, Emma talked Naeemah and Gregg into letting him go. He left a few days later. He'd put on a brave front for her when he said goodbye, but as she watched him board the plane now, he looked utterly broken. It really had killed him to leave her.

So why did he do it? She shook her head, refusing to focus on him any longer. If she did, she would break down right here in the middle of her college graduation. Instead, she focused on the spectral figure of Livia. Her tall, dark, and regal sister. So much better suited for positions of authority than Allie. It was easy to think everything would be better with Livia in charge, but as Allie watched her and a future version of herself laughing with an older Lily and Carson, she realized how damaged her sister still was. Despite how far she'd come in the last years, Livia still had a long way to go. She deserved to take a backseat for once. Allie smiled as she watched herself and her sisters, one Immortal and one mortal, play with her mortal niece and nephew. She hadn't seen her sister Josceline much in the last few years, but they spoke often, and it warmed her to see a future where they were all together and happy. Carson rolled on the floor with his grandchildren, healthy and happy, looking younger than he had a right to look at his age in this future that was still a long way away. She'd once feared she wouldn't have her mortal family with her for long, and that she would be alone someday without a family of her own. But her Immortal family was there with her in this vision: Darius, Livia, Liam, and Kahlynn. Navid. Alísun and Alexander were there right alongside her mortal family. It was a good future. Aidan was there, too, looking more like the boy she remembered. Allie stared at them for a long time. The valedictorian was almost through her speech before Allie finally tore herself away from the happy picture. That future wasn't hers. Not yet.

The midnight blue clouds threatened to snuff out the sun as she took in the other figures swirling around her, vying for her attention.

She saw Gregg and Naeemah standing before the Senate, a panel of judges looking down on them with disapproval. A ghostly Allie stepped up beside them, Livia at her left and Darius at her right. Quinn stood proudly behind them with Sasha and Santi, but there were others. Many others. Alísun and Alexander stood with the McBriens. Her whole family was present, except Navid. He was a former Chief Justice who was supposed to be dead, so there was no way he could be there. The Senate watched the proceedings with confusion. The Chief Justice looked on from their high seats at the center of the courtroom, looks of disdain on their long faces.

And then Alexander and Alísun crossed to the center dais, standing opposite Naeemah and Gregg who were on trial for some unknown crime. Allie turned her focus to the ancient circular auditorium. Crumbling stone and faded frescos adorned the domed ceiling where an oculus opened to the starry night above. Hundreds of elected Senators sat in a semi-circle around the panel of the Chief Justice who sat with two vacant seats beside them. Seats Allie's mother and father once occupied. Others sat below them. High officials meant to assist the Chief Justice in their office. This was their government, broken as it was.

Why are those seats still vacant? It's been eighteen years. Allie tried to recall her lessons with Daniel. He explained it once, how the Immortal world moved so slowly. The next election wouldn't take place for another seven years. The office of the Chief Justice was traditionally held by four people. Two Complements, each representing one vote. The system was meant to check and balance each other. Nothing was decided until both parties could agree. Sarah and Charles Madison held only half of the office, yet they'd been trusted to take on the full responsibility of the Senate. *How much damage have they caused in the last two decades? And how much more can they cause in the next seven years?* To most Immortals, seven years was but a moment. To her, it was still a long time. She didn't trust the Madisons. They were working for Marcus, which meant his influence had also spread from the Coalition to Soma and now to the Senate itself. He was behind everything. The Chief Justice were his puppets. The vacant office needed to be filled immediately. The election couldn't wait any longer.

Allie scanned the courtroom, memorizing the faces of each senator. She didn't want to miss a single detail. And then she saw him. Sitting among the lower ranking senators at the back of the courtroom, with his unremarkable face, was Marcus Servius. The seat beside him where Livia's mother, Porcia, should have sat was vacant.

Seeing what her clairvoyant gift wanted her to see, the vision vanished, leaving Allie trying to figure out how the man got himself elected to the International Senate.

"Alexis Carmichael, graduating summa cum laude," the dean called.

It took Allie a moment to collect herself as she stood, shoving the remaining visions back into her peripheral vision. She took a shaky step toward her future, the next uncertain chapter of her life. She understood it now. The way some Immortals her age chose to stay in college for years and years. It was comfortable. It was normal and it was safe.

But what lay ahead of Allie was anything but safe.

Allie walked along the beach, her black graduation gown billowing behind her. She'd discarded her cap in the car on the drive home, but once they arrived back on Kelley's Island at the home she'd grown to love, Allie wandered down to the beach.

She'd promised Livia she wouldn't go far, but she needed some time to think. The rolled piece of parchment clutched tightly in her hand.

She found herself at the grotto. Darius and his family were still in the city, celebrating his and Sasha's big day. They were all supposed to be together today, but Allie had changed her mind at the last minute, preferring to be alone. She insisted that Darius go on without her.

Lily and Carson were back at the house, preparing some big last minute family barbecue with Liam and Livia. But they didn't know yet what plagued Allie's mind. The decision she had to make.

She sat at the cold, stone fire pit. She hadn't spent much time here in recent years. With school, she was too busy. But if she were honest, it was the memories keeping her away. Too many memories of Aidan haunted this place.

She stared at the piece of paper in her lap wondering what to do next. Retreat to Soma? Take her entire family with her? But how could she take her mortal family into one of the biggest seats of the Immortal world? How could she explain their presence at Soma?

Like so many times in the past, Allie wondered what good was the gift of clairvoyance if she couldn't see what was coming next? She released the visions again. She had to study them all, but there were still so many; she wasn't sure how she would ever learn to process them on her own.

She'd made the worst mistake of her adult life by allowing school to come first when she should have spent more time devoted to her training. Sweeping it all under the rug to deal with another day was never a solution. It had to stop now. And maybe one day, she would be prepared for the big things *before* they were sitting in her lap.

Allie studied a vision of Chief Justice Sarah Madison with

her prim, round face, watching her from a distance. Her Complement, Chief Justice Charles Madison, lingered behind his wife. They were Marcus's eyes and ears. It always came back to him. He was never in the picture, but he was always behind the scenes pulling his puppets' strings, making them dance to his tune. But if he truly was an elected Senator, he was keeping a very close watch on his most important puppets.

Allie watched them all. People she knew. Moments she recognized. Strangers. Simple moments that seemingly meant nothing—and wouldn't until they did. She saw fighting. War. Death and destruction right alongside peace, progress, and joyous moments of life.

"How did you do it, Kassandre?" she spoke to her mother. Her dead mother. "How did you see so much and make sense of it all?"

Kassandre and Navid had orchestrated every moment of their lives together, and every moment of their children's lives, right up until her death. For so long, Allie had held on to the hope that she would one day see her mother again. But it wasn't meant to be. She gave her life, so her daughters could have this one. This one future Kassandre saw for them that was the best of all the futures she'd seen.

"How did she do it? How did she know it was the right choice?"

She didn't. Allie realized. Even with five thousand years of experience behind her, Kassandre made her choices based on careful guesswork and intuition. That was what Allie had to do now.

She smiled as she caught a vision of Aidan making his way down the beach. His black pants rolled up as he walked barefoot in the shallows, the gentle waves lapping at his feet. He was different from the Aidans she'd seen lately. Less angry and scary. More like the boy she remembered.

He dissolved in a burst of green light as Darius charged down the beach. The bond ignited between them. Something was wrong.

"Darius?" Allie stood, her heart in her throat.

"I'm so glad you didn't come with us." He slammed into her side, pulling her tightly against his chest.

"What happened?" She pulled back, searching his eyes for answers.

"Mom has been arrested. They came for Dad, too, but he was with Sasha and Quinn, so they settled for Mom."

"Naeemah? Arrested? For what?" Her chest tightened with the burn of her power. This was all her fault. "For shielding me from them all these years?" Allie stared at the paper still clutched in her hand.

"It's a bullshit charge." Darius collapsed onto the stone sofa where Allie had been sitting. "Charges have been filed against them for harboring an unknown with *questionable* abilities. Somehow, they know about your judgment gift."

Allie sank down beside him, all the blood rushing from her face. *Marcus knows.* It was the thing that drove him and all of his ambitions. Thousands of years ago, Allie's ancestor, Queen Eiselynn, bonded with her commoner Complement, Ían, and jilted Marcus, known then as Lord Teigan. When Marcus attacked Ían, he retaliated and took Marcus's gift for himself. Since then, Marcus had obsessively hunted the royal line, looking for his gift to manifest in another. Allie's judgment gift was a combination of skills she'd inherited from her father, Navid, and her ancestor, Ían. And Marcus wanted it back.

"What's this?" Darius gestured at the rolled piece of paper in her hand. "Have you crushed your diploma?"

"No." Allie took a deep breath to still her racing heart. "This came for me a few hours ago, just after the ceremony."

"What is it?"

"A summons. I'm being called before the International Senate in Barcelona."

"You can't answer that summons, Allie."

"I have to. If they know about my judgment gift, I won't make it out of there a free woman. But I can't leave Naeemah to suffer this alone."

"What does that paper say about you, Allie?"

"I am a fugitive. There is a rather large bounty on my head if I don't show up for this."

"What have they charged you with?"

"Treason." Allie trembled at the thought of what faced her. This was serious.

"Dad will be the first to tell you to ignore this. We will find another solution for Mom. They can't hold her on something as trivial as neglecting to report a neighbor girl raised by mortals. They have no evidence that you are anything more to them than that."

"But if they know about my gift, they will make Naeemah suffer until I turn myself in."

"They might try, but they won't get far without any real evidence of what you can do."

"And the only evidence of that is still locked up in the crypt," Allie said bitterly. "Can they search the underground?"

"They don't know it exists. They'll never find him." Darius took the official summons from her, his eyes scanning the archaic looking document. "They haven't changed their methods in centuries. This bullshit is handwritten in calligraphy."

"Just another sign that they've grown stagnant and lazy," Allie said.

"What do you want to do?"

"That's why I'm here, trying to decide my next move. I don't have much time. The trial is in three days in Barcelona. I either need to run, taking everyone I love with me into Sterling Tower where they'll be relatively safe and out of the Senate's reach."

"Or?"

"Or, I go to this farce of a trial and make a deal with them to pardon Gregg and Naeemah."

"That's not a viable option, Allie. I hope you aren't considering it."

"I know but I am."

"After all the sacrifices everyone has made to get you into this position of power, you can't give up now."

"I know." But she knew what she had to do.

"You've seen something, haven't you?" Darius asked.

"I have." Allie nodded, gazing out across the lake at the beautiful sunset. She wished they could go back to simpler times when all they had before them was a lifetime of beautiful sunsets.

"You've already decided, so out with it."

"I have to answer this summons." She'd seen it in her visions. The charges against Naeemah and Gregg were a means to lure her out, likely orchestrated by Marcus himself. She had to go. It was time they met.

"You can't do this, Allie," Darius said.

"Trust me, it's the right decision. But I'm not going alone."

"Damn right, you're not. I'll be with you."

"I need Livia and Liam, too, of course, and Sasha and Quinn. Santi. My grandparents. Emma and Daniel. Gregg can't be there, but I need everyone else willing to stand with me to come to this summons."

"You know Dad won't stay behind."

"I know." She sighed. "But it's far too dangerous for him to be there."

"What do you intend to do once you get there? I don't want you sacrificing yourself for Mom. She wouldn't want that."

"I don't know yet. I just know I need to go to this thing, and I need numbers on my side. Once Gregg and Naeemah are released, I'll just have to trust my gift to show me what comes next."

CHAPTER 30

"I trust you, Allie," Gregg said, "but I don't like this."

Allie stared up at the sleek glass structure that was part of the Barcelona skyline. It blended seamlessly with the other nondescript buildings of the modern era in this ancient city. "That makes two of us, but they have Naeemah."

"She wouldn't want you sacrificing yourself for her."

"She's been like a mother to me. I can't leave her like that."

"She's not *like* a mother, Allie. Naeemah has a bond with you as her daughter. It's one-sided, and she never expects it to be anything more, but she's loved you as one of her own since you were sixteen years old."

"She's never said anything." It pained Allie to think of Naeemah living with a mother-child bond that was not reciprocated for all these years. But Allie had a mother. Bonding with Naeemah would be a betrayal of Lily. "All the more reason to walk in there and bargain for her freedom. I still don't like the idea of you being here. We're making it too easy for them to apprehend you."

Gregg blew out a breath as they made their way up the stone steps to the building that housed the International Senate. "I won't let you walk in there alone."

"I'm not alone." Allie gestured back at the others. Darius,

Livia, and Liam followed closely, with Sasha, Quinn, Santi, Alísun, and Alexander bringing up the rear. "You don't need to be here; we can do this without you."

"I can't abandon you any more than I can abandon my wife. I won't. And if this goes badly, then I will be with Naeemah."

"It shouldn't," Allie murmured. "I'm exactly where I need to be." The green aura of her clairvoyance shone all around them. It would all come to a head here.

"I can't say I'm not nervous about walking in there without a plan, but we're all behind you."

"They can't ... hurt you, can they?" She paused at the huge glass doors, trimmed in gold.

"They have the authority to execute criminals, but it is rare and only in extreme cases. We are likely looking at a hefty fine. Possibly a prison sentence of a few decades, which we will handle if we have to."

"Not if I can help it." Allie turned and stepped through the double doors. She was the one summoned here today. She would face it like an adult. But she wasn't about to let them take Naeemah and Gregg or anyone else for her sake. If anyone was going to jail today, it would be her. And it wouldn't be for nothing, either. Those back at Soma would see her as a martyr. It would only strengthen their cause, and they would carry on in her stead.

"This way," Gregg said, leading them across the grand lobby entrance to a pair of antique looking doors guarded by a bank of security officers. Allie showed her official summons to the bailiff. The other officers cast a skeptical glance at everyone behind her.

"Witnesses," she said by way of explanation.

"You sit with the observers. And no talking." The bailiff waved them through. "You're early. They'll call your case in about an hour."

Allie followed silently with Darius and Livia at her side. The others stepped into the ancient, crumbling domed building behind her. The green aura pulsed and shimmered, telling Allie she was right where she needed to be.

"They've built around the original Senate building time and again, keeping it protected and concealed." Gregg gestured at the open oculus in the ceiling. Late afternoon sunshine flooded the room, casting the center dais in a haze of golden light.

"So far, so good," she whispered. The full Senate was in session, and it looked exactly like the American Congressional court. hundreds of elected Senators sat in a semi-circle around a raised dais that housed multiple seats. Six of those seats occupied the lower dais for the four Chief Justice appointed secretaries and two seats for the Chairman of the Senate. A second raised dais sat elevated above them all, housing the four seats of the Chief Justice. Two of those seats were empty, but Sarah and Charles Madison currently occupied the other two.

Allie eyed the small man and woman seated on the lower dais below the seats her mother and father once held. *What would the secretary of a dead Chief Justice still be doing in their office? Whom did they serve?*

Allie sat down to await her case. She took the time to carefully examine each of the Senators, searching for Marcus. He was here. There was no way he would miss this.

As she scanned the faces, she sorted the familiar ones she recognized from Soma contracts. Too many faces were regular customers, but the majority was not. That boded well for her case. But still no Marcus. He blended in far too easily.

"Look," Darius said, gesturing across the room to the area reserved for criminals awaiting their trial.

Naeemah sat with a collar around her throat, and her hands secured in her lap with magnetic cuffs binding her wrists.

Without a word to her family, or an invitation from the Senate, Allie charged down the aisle to stand before the court. She wasn't going to sit and wait like a good girl. This had gone far enough.

"Do you even have a plan?" Darius asked frantically as he and Livia followed her.

"Following my gut here," she whispered. She didn't feel anxious or scared. Allie was angry. Angry they'd taken Naeemah from her family. Angry the two people responsible for governing the Immortal world were nothing more than puppets in Marcus Servius's pocket. Angry they dared to rule as a democracy when this was clearly a dictatorship. Angry they were all too stupid to even realize it.

"What is the meaning of this?" Sarah Madison asked from her perch high above everyone else. "Who is this child who dares to interrupt the Senate while in session?"

"I've been summoned," Allie said simply. Gregg came to stand behind her, giving her a nod of approval.

"You wait until you are called." Sarah sneered down her long nose. "I believe you were given a time and place for your trial. That time and place is not now. Bailiffs!" She snapped her fingers and a pair of bailiffs stepped forward to escort Allie to her seat.

Allie held up her hand to dismiss them. "I am not here for a trial."

The bailiffs paused, looking to their leader for direction.

"Very well, we shall do this the hard way. Greggory McBrien," Sarah said. "You and your Complement have been found guilty of neglecting your duty as Governor of your region. Take him into custody," the Chief Justice ordered.

"No," Allie cried.

"It's okay, Allie," Gregg said. "Follow your instincts, and do not worry about us."

He went willingly as the bailiffs read him his rights and placed a magnetic collar around his throat. She breathed a sigh of relief when they placed Gregg beside Naeemah. She desperately needed them to stay in the courtroom.

"Call special forces," Sarah said. "This young woman can't be trusted."

"And how do you know that? You don't know me. You accuse me of having *questionable* abilities, but you don't know me or my gifts. What right have you to take me into custody based on that alone? What right have you to find Naeemah and Gregg guilty without the benefit of an actual trial?"

"It is the court's prerogative to punish you for your crimes."

"Crimes worthy of the International Senate's time?" Allie turned to face the elected officials. She saw the questions in their eyes. The way they checked their dockets for information on her case. They were just as confused by this as she was.

As Allie turned back to face the Chief Justice, she heard the pounding of footsteps charging up the stairs behind the dais. She felt him before she saw him.

Special forces? Of course, she meant the Syntrophos of the Milan Initiative. But why did she have them here in plain sight? *Aidan?* She stared at him as he and his team of armed Syntrophos filed into the room. She wasn't at all prepared to see him again. Not like this. His raptor gaze was glued to her, his hand gripping the hilt of his sword like a vise. Like he was fighting with himself not to cross the room to her side. Whether to throttle her or kiss her, she couldn't tell.

Allie's heart twisted in agony with the desire to go to him. But they were not on the same side. She tore her eyes away from Aidan. She had to have her head in this and not focused on why he was here.

"Look, they aren't separated this time," Darius whispered.

Naomi stood beside Aidan, reluctant, but ready to do the

bidding of the court. Four more Syntrophos pairs lined up behind them.

Only the court couldn't see what they were with their bonds concealed.

Why did you come, Allie?

She shivered at the sensation of Aidan's thoughts in her mind. Once such a burden, it was now like a sweet reward. *You expect me to leave your mother here, alone?*

I had hoped you'd let me handle this.

How was I supposed to know you'd even be here? That you'd even know what was happening?

"Guards, take this young woman into custody immediately," Sarah ordered.

Allie flinched as Aidan and Naomi moved to do as she said. "That won't be necessary." Allie stepped toward the podium. "You won't be arresting me today."

Allie don't. You don't know what she's capable of.

I think I do. Please, for once in your life, trust me?

"Who are you to presume so much?" Sarah snapped.

"You know exactly who I am, Sarah. Let's dispense with the pretenses."

"Very well, Alexis Carmichael, by showing yourself here today, you have agreed to the terms outlined in your summons." Sarah stood. "Your presence is an admission of guilt. We are done."

"You misunderstand, Sarah. I am not here admitting guilt for anything. I am here to negotiate the release of Naeemah El Sadawii and Greggory McBrien, Governor of the Great Lakes Region of North America."

"Negotiate?" Sarah smirked. "That is not an option, my dear. We were told you wouldn't show," she muttered irritably. "And if you did, you'd come quietly."

My bad, Aidan said.

"We don't negotiate with children," Sarah said. "Besides, their case has been decided. And you will address me as Chief Justice Sarah Madison."

"Come now, you and my parents were good friends once," Allie said disdainfully. "Surely, we are all on a first name basis here."

"I do not know your parents, child. Stop wasting the court's time," Sarah said.

"My parents once sat right beside you, ruling as the Senate was meant to be ruled with proper checks and balances."

"You dare to speak of the dead with such lies?"

Allie turned to face the Senate, frantically looking for Marcus. He was here somewhere. "How dare you allow this government to become a dictatorship? My parents died *eighteen* years ago, and you still haven't elected a Chief Justice to replace them? You all are so careless with time. You see it as an endless commodity. No need to act now, we'll have another election in a few decades. Yet how can you not see how much damage can be done in that time? You've lost control of our government and in your complacency, you don't even realize it."

"Who are you, young lady?" A senator seated to her left asked.

"I am Alexis Carmichael. Don't I look like my mother, Kassandre?" She turned, smiling as she saw the light of recognition register in his face. "It's the hair." She brushed her long locks over her shoulder. "But I have my father's eyes."

"Kassandre and Ashar had a natural child more than two centuries ago," Charles Madison spoke for the first time. "She was the image of her father, with her mother's eyes. Do you expect us to believe you are their second natural child?" he snarled.

"Yes," Allie said simply.

"We have heard enough of this nonsense," Charles said.

"I don't think we have," Aidan said. "She has done nothing wrong."

A collective gasp swept the courtroom. All eyes turned to Aidan.

"Who are you to question this court?" Sarah said. "I have been told your training is complete, but I will not tolerate this kind of insubordination in my courtroom, young man."

I'm stalling here. Keep looking for whatever it is you're looking for. "See something, say something." Aidan shrugged. "Our trainers have taught us to seek justice. That is our job as special forces to the Chief Justice, isn't it? I am no one, but I am not seeing justice in this courtroom today."

With all eyes on Aidan, Allie continued her search of the crowd.

What are you looking for? Aidan asked.

An empty seat that shouldn't be empty. Marcus would be alone. The seat meant for his wife would be vacant. Porcia left him years ago.

"I apologize, Madame," Aidan said. "Perhaps I have overstepped in my desire to serve this court." *Left Center, about midway down.*

Allie followed his directions. She almost missed him again. He was so commonplace her eyes wanted to slid right over him. It was the empty chair that led her to him. When her eyes finally landed on Marcus Servius, he smiled.

Allie leaned back and whispered instructions to her sister to have someone keep their eyes on him at all times. They couldn't afford to let Marcus slip away.

"I am afraid we agree with the head of your special forces." A handsome ancient stood from his seat on the lower dais. "Has this young woman committed a crime so heinous that she does not deserve a trial? As Chairman of the Senate, we must remind you, once again, to follow protocol." The man took his seat beside his Complement who shared the position of Senate Chair with him. "We ask that her formal charges be read for the court's approval, since they are not recorded on today's docket."

"She was raised as an unknown and has failed to register with the Senate," Sarah said simply, although that was not what Allie's summons claimed. "We have received multiple reports that she possesses questionable abilities."

"That is all?" the Chairman asked. "That does not sound like a crime that would interest the International Senate, much less the Chief Justice. Alexis's local authorities should be handling her case. As I see, they are in custody." He gestured at Naeemah and Gregg. "I must ask the court to be more specific concerning their crimes of neglect."

"Their case has been closed," Charles Madison said.

"Perhaps we were too hasty. Please, tell us what specific crimes the governor has committed."

"They have harbored this young woman, in full knowledge that she was an unknown."

"The governor adopted Alexis then?"

"No, but they took on the responsibility of training her," Sarah Madison said. "Which is why this court has charged them with neglect of their official duties."

"I see." The Chairman nodded. "That is a huge oversight on their part, but does the crime warrant sentencing when a fine would be more appropriate?"

"The Chief Justice does not believe a fine is severe enough punishment for this crime and asks the court to support their decision."

"Very well. The Chair requests permission to question the girl."

Sarah looked like she wanted to deny the request, but she

had little choice but to comply. With a nod, she gave her permission.

Allie jumped on the opportunity to lead the Chairman's line of questioning her way. "The Chief Justice has failed to inform you that I have also taken over the institution known as Soma," Allie said. "My summons claims charges of treason have been filed against me, but perhaps the Chief Justice wishes that aspect of my *crimes* to remain secret."

Shocked whispers swept the room.

"So you are the one making great claims to the throne of Indriell?" the Chairman asked.

"It's no secret that Soma is corrupt," Allie said. "And it's no secret that the Senate is their best customer." Allie glared around the room. "I know who you are. I've seen your files. I stepped forward as the named heir of Indriell to put an end to the corruption I saw running rampant within our own government. Our children deserve better than to be bought and sold by those who should know better."

"You take it upon yourself to police the Senate?" he asked.

"Chairman...?"

"Thomas," he supplied. "Edward Thomas."

"Chairman Thomas," Allie began. "I am the granddaughter of Queen Alísun of Indriell, and Alexander the Scholar. It is my right and my duty as a royal to intercede when I see so many of my generation suffering at the hands of those older and wiser."

"You make a daring claim, young lady. Have you the means to back it up?"

"I do. Grandmother, Grandfather, could you please join us?"

Murmured conversation flew across the Senate as Alísun and Alexander came to stand behind Allie at the podium. Allie felt the ice queen's presence more than she ever had before.

She felt the sheer omniscience of her grandfather, overwhelming in its intensity. There was no doubt these two were exactly who they claimed to be. Allie struggled to find that sense of oneness with her people that always brought on her own princess mojo. But she wasn't one with the people in this room. Instead, she brought up memories of her time with the kids of Soma. The mantle of power fell heavy on her shoulders. She was getting used to the weight of it.

The room grew silent as Alísun and Allie settled their gaze on the Chairman. He gave a visible shiver at their scrutiny.

"My granddaughter speaks the truth," Alísun said. "You can surely sense the mantle of authority she now wears. She is my named heir and first princess. You would do well to listen to her. She is wise beyond her years."

"This farce of a trial has gone far enough," Sarah Madison said. "Guards, take the girl into custody as I have commanded or face charges for your insubordination."

Allie held her breath as each of the Syntrophos looked to Aidan for direction. With a nod from him, they all settled back to attention.

"Respectfully, we will not," Aidan said.

"She is guilty of treason, and I will charge you all with accessory to her high crimes if you do not follow orders now!"

"High crimes? Treason? I have not finished questioning the accused." Chairman Thomas raised his hand. "I find little evidence of treason, despite her claims to Indriell or what amounts to a corporate takeover of Soma. If anything, we should be thanking her for dealing with that accursed institution. Soma was never under our jurisdiction and she has not made a bid for the power of the Senate. So I ask you, how can her actions amount to treason? If this woman is to face punishment, she will have a fair trial first."

"We have heard quite enough," Charles said. "The girl is guilty of treason for daring to call herself first princess."

"The court has not yet decided what that means," Chairman Thomas said. "The Chief Justice will remember they work for the Senate who represent the people of this democracy. They do not have supreme authority to sentence anyone for their crimes without evidence of those crimes. The Chair asks the court to revaluate the charges against Ms. Alexis Carmichael. I move that the court disregard her failure to register with the Senate in light of who she is. She was obviously trying to protect her identity and her privacy. Any further accusations against Ms. Carmichael will come *after* the court has questioned her. What say you?" The Chairman turned to the Senate for a vote.

Allie breathed a sigh of relief at the overwhelming response of "Aye" from the court.

Sarah and Charles settled back nervously in their chairs.

"The court wishes to fully understand the identity of Ms. Carmichael as the named heir of Indriell as well as her intentions." Chairman Thomas addressed the court.

"Queen Alísun, you stand here today, a relic of the ancient world come to life again." Chairwoman Thomas stood, speaking for the first time. "I can hardly believe it, but clearly the last queen of Indriell we all thought to be dead stands before us again with the Scholar at her side. This is an unprecedented moment in our history. You claim this child, your granddaughter, is the second natural daughter of the ancients, Kassandre and Ashar?"

The queen nodded. "We do."

"Then by default, you also claim she is the child of prophecy? The *son* we've waited and wondered about for millennia? How do we know this isn't a manipulation of the prophecy?"

"I am the one who foretold of Alexis's birth. I recorded the original prophecy with a false interpretation to protect her," Alísun said.

"Then how can we know for certain what the true prophecy means?" Chairman Thomas asked.

"It is a sad day when the nature of prophecy is no longer understood by those who profess to lead us." Alísun stepped forward. "Do you not realize what you have standing before you? I am a prophetess. The knowledge of every prophecy I've ever spoken lies within my gift. If the court wishes to see the original prophecy concerning Alexis, I am prepared to share that knowledge with everyone present."

Chapter 31

Allie wasn't sure she wanted to hear the true prophecy her grandmother gave so many thousands of years before her birth.

"It would please the court," Chairwoman Thomas said. "Proceed."

"This is ridiculous," Sarah Madison protested. "These people have manipulated their way into a powerful position, taking over Soma, and making claims they cannot hope to prove. Let this end now."

"The court wishes to get to the bottom of this," Chairman Thomas said. "We will hear the whole story. Including the original prophecy as given by the queen."

"The queen?" Sarah harrumphed, leaning back in her seat.

Alísun ignored Sarah's remark as she approached the podium to stand beside Allie. "Please take your seats and try to relax as I share the prophecy. This will not be comfortable." She raised her eyes toward the oculus above them, the fading light of evening casting them all in shadow.

The silver of her eyes grew opaque, like opals. A cool breeze flew in from the oculus causing those inside to shiver. Alísun held out her hands for Allie and Livia. "Stand with me, my girls. I am sorry to have to show you this."

Allie and Livia quickly took their grandmother's hands,

standing solemnly beside her. Darius stumbled to sit on the steps behind them. A blast of power shot through the room, snapping Allie's head back. Tightness coiled in her chest, and a sense of doom settled all around them like a mist. Murmurs of distress rose from concerned voices but were silenced as a shadow, thick as night, fell upon the room. No one could move. No one could speak. Terrified eyes gazed above.

Silvery swirling figures took shape, dancing across the domed ceiling. The sound of her grandmother's otherworldly voice echoed across the chamber as she quoted the prophecy Allie knew by heart. But something was lost in the translation from Alísun's original prophetic vision and the simple words she ultimately recorded on paper.

The ethereal figures took on the forms of the ancient queens: Allie's ancestors. Queens Ashlynn, Celyn, Alyvia, Fáelynn, Eiselynn, and a younger Alísun with a baby Kassandre in her arms, all looked down on the Senate with disappointment and anger—anger for their laziness and complacency.

The queens faded, leaving only Alísun and her young daughter, Kassandre, standing beside her father, Alexander the Scholar.

Tears slid down Allie's face as she watched her mother grow up a happy child, her beautiful red hair as vibrant as Allie's. Alexander chased his young daughter with a spark of laughter in his eyes. A shadow of his voice called out for his "Kassie-girl."

Kassandre grew into a strong woman with her Complement, Ashar, by her side. Allie choked on a sob, seeing how happy her father was with the woman he loved. But she cried out in anguish when an innocent young Livia joined them. Her sister was a beautiful child, surrounded by a family who adored her. But a moment later, a faceless man ripped Livia from her parent's arms and disappeared with her in a puff of smoke. Several lifetimes would pass before they saw their daughter again.

"Livia," Allie sobbed her sister's name, grasping for her free hand. Livia shook with sorrow and rage as she watched her parents mourn the loss of their child.

More than two hundred years later, Kassandre and Ashar grew strong again. Allie watched in awe as her brave mother, the only daughter of Indriell to never be queen, became Chief Justice of the modern Immortal world alongside her Complement.

The figure of Kassandre drifted away from Ashar as she grew heavy with her second pregnancy, hiding it from the Senate. Kassandre removed herself from her duties for a short while until after the birth of her secret child. Allie trembled, sinking to her knees when she saw a new figure join Kassandre. Her face was blurred in shadow, but Allie would recognize the woman who raised her anywhere. Lily Carmichael helped Kassandre through the birth of her second daughter. Kassandre sobbed in agony as she kissed the redheaded child on the head and left her with Lily and Carson Carmichael.

Allie rested her head against her grandmother's knee, clutching her hand like a lifeline.

"Allie-girl!" The ghost of Kassandre's voice echoed across the domed ceiling. Kassandre and Ashar raced down the beach toward a toddler-Allie, sweeping her up in a tight embrace. "How we've missed you, my love." She buried her nose in Allie's hair, turning to greet Lily and Carson, thanking them for caring for their daughter.

Allie's shoulders shook as she sobbed at the sight of both of her mothers and fathers.

"Stay strong for our girls," Kassandre spoke softly to her Complement. "Watch over Allie. She will be lonely. She'll need you more than she knows. And help Alivia forgive herself. She is a fighter. She will survive it all and come out stronger for it, but she will be hard on herself. And promise me, if you can ever learn to love again, my darling Ashar, find whatever happiness you can." The life in Kassandre's eyes grew dim as blood bloomed across her chest. Kassandre and Ashar vanished like smoke on the wind.

A young Allie stood alone and lonely as the years went by until Ashar returned for her, taking her to a safe place to become the woman she was destined to be.

An ominous darkness lay behind Allie, an oppressive void representing an uncertain future that no other prophecy had ever foretold. A faceless man grew strong in the darkness. He moved with stealth through the years, seeking to destroy everything the modern Immortal world had built. This faceless man *was* the great darkness.

But Allie shone as a beacon of light in that void. Shadowed young Immortals came to stand with her. Strong and powerful, they were united with the strength of their ancestors. They shielded Allie with an aura of power and protection. *They* were the pathway through the abyss. They would find the light of the future together. The uncertainty frightened the older generations, but it excited these brave, young warriors.

Only they would have the strength and power to fight the darkness and move their people forward. Their biggest obstacle wasn't the unknown: it was their parents and grandparents. It was their leaders and teachers who told them time and again that they didn't matter because they were too young. Allie stood as their champion. To stop her was to let the darkness win —a darkness that already held sway within the world.

Allie's head fell forward as the prophetic moment faded into nothing. Silence echoed across the ancient chamber. She took a deep, shuddering breath, and the sound of movement returned. Quiet murmured conversation hummed all around her, but she couldn't find the strength to stand.

Stand up, Alexis Ann. You're the strongest person I know. The prophecy isn't just about you; it's about all of us. Get up and show them who you are.

Allie nodded, settling her eyes on Aidan. Reaching for her grandmother's hand, she got back on her feet. Livia sat motionless behind her, eyes rounded with shock.

"Seeing is believing," Allie said with more confidence than she felt.

Alísun clung to Allie's hand and turned to face Livia. "My girls are strong," she whispered. "Strong like their mother."

"I think we can all agree that Alexis Carmichael is the undisputed heir of Indriell and the child of prophecy," Chairwoman Thomas said with an unsteady voice. "Yet the court needs to determine what that means in terms of her authority in the modern world."

"Really, Chairwoman Thomas?" Sarah scoffed. "That is quite a leap."

"Have you ever witnessed a prophet speak, Sarah?" she asked. "I have. My father was a prophet with nothing resembling the talent the queen possesses, but I know a true prophecy when I see one. No one here can deny what we just witnessed was indeed the original prophecy. Not even you."

CHAPTER 32

"Are you prepared for what comes next?" Chief Justice Sarah Madison asked the Senate. "It is Soma today, but what happens when this girl desires more power? We cannot allow her the kind of authority the royals are suggesting."

"Do not put words in my mouth," Allie said. "I have no desire to rule. Perhaps the court should ask me why I seized Soma in the first place?"

"You have the floor," Chairman Thomas said.

"I never wanted anything from you," Allie said. "I just wanted to be left alone to run Soma as an independent safe haven for young students to come and learn without the threat of being used for their talents."

"While you train your students to support your bid for power wherever you can?" Charles Madison accused.

"No more interruptions," Chairman Thomas said. "Let the heir speak."

"I initiated the takeover of Soma before Chief Justice Sarah and Charles Madison could do so," Allie announced to the wild murmurs spreading across the room. "I couldn't allow Soma to become a government institution. We must provide a place for our children that has no ties to any government."

"How do you know the Chief Justice meant to seize Soma?" Chairman Thomas asked.

"Move to strike the question," Charles said. "This child is skating on thin ice with her accusations."

"Denied. The Chair would like to hear her answer," Edward said. "Please continue, Alexis."

"The Milan Initiative," Allie said. "A top secret organization meant to take over Soma with the aid of a Syntrophos army Sarah and Charles have built."

"Syntrophos?" outraged cries rang out among the Senate.

"What do you mean, Syntrophos?" Chairman Thomas asked.

Allie glanced at Aidan and his team. *Will you show them?* she asked.

"She means us. The special forces team," Aidan said. He turned and nodded to his soldiers, who were all loyal to him. "Show them."

Aidan and Naomi were the first to drop the protective facade that shielded their bond from the Senate. The others followed, one by one until all five Syntrophos couples stood proudly, allowing the Senate to experience the bond for themselves. Allie and Darius followed suit, as did Sasha and Quinn. Collectively, their power surged together. Their bonds ignited among all the Syntrophos, feeding off one another, leaving no doubt in the minds of those who witnessed it that a Syntrophos army was something to be feared.

"The Syntrophos bond is alive and well among our generation. I suppose you can thank me for that," Allie said sadly. "You just saw my grandmother's prophecy of how I would 'gather my equals.' This bond unites us all. But my fellow Syntrophos here today have been hunted and drafted into the Milan Initiative. Aidan McBrien's family was threatened unless he agreed to enter the initiative. They also threatened him with my safety." Allie turned her gaze to him. "We believe he agreed, so he could protect his family. To protect me, at first. But as time passed, he also took on the responsibility for the others. He stayed with the initiative for them."

I knew you would get it.

"Aidan and the others have been trained for the sole purpose of seizing control of Sterling Tower on the orders of the Chief Justice."

"She lies," Charles said, outraged.

"I can prove it." Allie raised her voice over Charles's blustering.

"How?" the Chairman asked, darting a glare at the dais.

"If the Senate would allow my mentor, Emma Renard, to question the Chief Justice, all will be revealed."

"Emma Renard? She is an officer of this court, is she not? Lieutenant governor of the Great Lakes Region of North America, I believe," Chairwoman Thomas said.

"And a powerful truth seeker," Allie added.

"We will not be subjected to such an insult," Sarah bellowed. "This has gone far enough."

"We will put it to a vote," the Chairman said. "All those in favor of the questioning?"

The ayes and nays rang out among the Senators, but the ayes were easily the majority.

"Emma Renard will address the Senate. Let it be on record, the Chief Justice, Sarah and Charles Madison, will take the stand for questioning, but they have not been officially charged. This is not a formal trial." He gestured for them to remove themselves from their seats of office to take the witness stand.

Allie watched them move slowly to stand before the Senate. Each wore a mask of confidence. But Allie knew they were no match for her mentor.

"What am I asking?" Emma approached the podium where Allie stood.

"Just a few questions." Allie handed Emma a piece of paper. She'd written her questions before they arrived.

"Clairvoyant indeed," she murmured. "Your mother would be proud."

"Ladies and Gentlemen of the Senate, you are familiar with my gift?" Emma turned to face the court. "Let it be known, what you will hear is the undisputed truth, on my oath as an officer of this court."

"Chief Justice, Sarah Madison," Emma began. "What is the purpose for the Milan Initiative?" Emma read from the paper Allie gave her.

"To strengthen the Senate's forces, that is all," Sarah replied.

Emma's diamond-clear eyes shone bright in the dim light of the evening. "Why have you hunted the Syntrophos to build this army? An army you have created on the Senate's dime without their knowledge or permission. Why?"

"They are a necessity," Sarah said, clamping her mouth shut to say no more than necessary. But Emma was much stronger than Sarah.

"For what reason, precisely?"

"We have trained them to infiltrate Soma in the guise of students. Once inside, they are to take over in the Senate's name." She clapped her hand over her mouth.

"And do you have Senate approval for such a task force? Chief Justice Charles Madison?" Emma asked.

"No." He choked on the word.

"Did you ever intend to inform the Senate of this army or of this takeover?" Emma demanded.

"No. We do not need their approval for matters of security." Charles's eyes grew wide with fright. He had no means of protecting himself against Emma's gift.

Cries of indignation arose from the Senate body.

"You routinely disregard the Senate's permissions for such endeavors," Emma continued, ignoring the outrage of the court. "Who orchestrated the capture of Alivia, first born of the ancients, Kassandre and Ashar?

"The Coalition," Charles said. "Everyone knows that; it was two hundred years ago."

"But it wasn't the Coalition, was it? Alivia was taken by one, Marcus Servius when she was just four years old and you helped him do it, didn't you?"

"Yes." Charles stared down at his hands, unable to resist Emma.

"And the assassination of Chief Justice Kassandre and Ashar? Who is responsible for their deaths?"

"The Coalition," Sarah forced herself to say.

"They are an easy scapegoat. But let's try that again?" Emma asked. "The truth this time."

"W-we gave the order," Sarah said through gritted teeth.

Allie's rage ignited like hot lava in her blood. She stood beside Emma, silently, her fists clenched at her sides. She'd always been able to control her judgment gift. No one had deserved it since the night she used it against Michael to save Aidan. But Sarah and Charles deserved her wrath, and she thirsted to give it to them. But she couldn't put her gift on display here. Not if she ever wanted to walk out of this courtroom again.

"Relax, Allie," Darius whispered beside her, taking her hand in his. "Draw on my strength."

Livia silently took her other hand, offering her strength as well.

A strange calm suddenly fell over her. Allie could feel the

rage rippling under her skin, but it didn't overwhelm her. She embraced her rage, letting it give her the focus she needed.

"And who do you work for?" Allie asked, her voice laced with acid.

"Answer the heir," Emma demanded.

"The ancient, Lord Teigan, betrothed to Queen Eiselynn before she ruined the Immortal world forever." Sarah's voice rang out like a death knoll. Her own. "He will claim what is his by right!" she screamed. "And we will be by his side when he brings the Immortal world into the light of day once more, banishing the mortals to death by fire as she should have ordered thousands of years ago." She shot Queen Alísun a hateful glare as she collapsed in her seat.

"We will not have this." Charles stood. "I demand this entire testimony be stricken from the record."

"Denied," Chairman Thomas said.

"And where is this Lord Teigan now?" Emma asked.

Allie turned, looking for the empty seat. He was still there, sitting quietly, completely unnerved by the proceedings. He gave her a smile and a little wave.

"Keep your eyes on him," Allie whispered to Darius and Livia.

"I do not know," Sarah said through gritted teeth.

"Rephrase the question," Emma said. "Where is Marcus Servius? Charles?" She turned to the more susceptible of the two.

"He sits there!" Charles Madison stood and pointed at the man in question. "He is Senator Robert Sinclair."

Loud murmuring rose to a din as Emma continued, "Senator Robert Sinclair, also known as Marcus Servius, the man who abducted the young Alivia, also known as the ancient, Lord Teigan, correct?"

"That is correct," Charles said.

Allie's eyes darted to the vacant chair, but now there were two. He was gone. She searched frantically for him. "Don't let him leave." She pointed at the bearded man walking up the stone steps to the exit.

Senators rushed from their seats, blocking her view. Allie charged up the stairs, Livia and Darius behind her, but it was too late. Marcus had slipped away.

"Bailiffs, search the building for him," Chairwoman Thomas ordered.

Three uniformed men ran from the chamber, issuing orders to the guards outside the room.

"You won't find him," Allie said. "He disappears as fast a smoke in the wind. With his common features and extraordinary gift for evasion, he is already gone.

"Madame Under Secretary, please issue a warrant for the arrest of the man known as Senator Robert Sinclair, Marcus Servius, and the ancient Lord Teigan," Chairman Thomas said. "I put forth a vote to the Senate," he continued, turning to face the courtroom, "to remove the Chief Justice Sarah Madison and Charles Madison from office and charge them with high crimes of treason against the International Senate they have sworn to serve. What say you?"

Allie breathed a sigh of relief at the unanimous sounds of agreement from the Senate body.

"Bailiff, take Sarah and Charles Madison into custody to await their trial," Chairwoman Thomas said with formality.

"You cannot do this. You don't have the power to remove the only seated Chief Justice," Charles snarled.

"That is for the Senate to decide. You have been stripped of your office and will receive a formal trial," Chairwoman Thomas said as the remaining bailiffs rushed to arrest the Chief Justice, leading them from the room.

Allie stepped forward. She needed to do this next part

quickly. "I ask the court to release the Governor Naeemah El Sadawii and Greggory McBrien immediately and dismiss the charges brought against them. They have no ties to the royal family and should not be held accountable today, or any time in the future, for my actions. Please allow them to continue to loyally serve this court as they always have."

"In light of today's events, your requests are granted," Chairman Thomas said.

Aidan didn't wait for direction. He crossed the room and freed his parents.

We need to get out of here, Allie. I still don't trust any of them. Aidan escorted Naeemah and Gregg across the chamber to sit with the rest of their family. His face a mask, hiding his true feelings.

Agreed. Get all of our people behind me.

"The court apologizes to you and your family," Chairman Thomas said. "But it seems we find ourselves leaderless. We cannot adjourn until we have appointed a temporary Chief Justice today. For the first time ever, we have a queen in our midst." He turned to Alísun. "Will you and the Scholar step in to lead us until arrangements can be made for an election?"

"We will not," Alísun said. "It is not our decision to make. It has been a very long time since the queens ruled our people. But when a queen names her heir, the heir becomes the highest authority of the Immortal world. This decision falls to Alexis."

"I am afraid we cannot allow an Unproven child to make such a decision," the Chairman said.

"You mistakenly discredit youth." Alísun shook her head sadly. "In my day, we revered it. Respected the voice of our children for they would be the ones leading us when we grew old. Alexis is more than capable of appointing a trusted substitute," Alísun said. "Her gift will guide her. She is the highest authority in this room, and the decision should fall to her."

"We cannot accept your recommendation," the Chairman said. "The Senate will decide."

"I will decide." Allie let her rage fill her, building like a storm inside her. She was in control. No one present deserved her judgment. The mantle of Indriell swirled around her as she stepped forward. "You will do as I say and you will respect my authority." She paced in front of the Senate, her eyes blazing with fury and the strength of her power. "I do not wish to govern, but I will if you continue to push me."

Silence echoed in the chamber.

"Chairman Thomas," Allie approached Edward and his wife. "May I take your hand?"

"Of-of course." Both the Thomas's extended their hands to her, wary of Allie's show of strength.

Allie studied them with her gift, examining their character. At their core, they were good, honest people who had grown discontent with the ways of the current administration. They thirsted for change, but they also thirsted for power, which gave her pause. They also feared her and had a grudging respect for her and her family. They would be a good choice, perhaps the best choice given her limited options. "You will take on the role of *temporary* Chief Justice."

"If the court agrees, it would be our honor to serve," he said with a respectful nod.

Allie turned to the raised dais where the under secretaries sat. Darius, Livia, Aidan, and Naomi followed her. She studied the Madisons' secretary. A bonded couple that had held some of the highest positions in the Senate before taking their current appointment. They intended to pursue the high seat of office in the next election. But they were loyal to Marcus. She could see it in their greedy black souls. He paid them well for their loyalty. "You are dismissed from your post," Allie said. "They will stand trial as well."

Aidan gestured for two of his team to arrest the under secretary.

Allie approached the secretary who served her parents. “How long after they died did you take control of their office?”

“W-what?” The woman stammered, her eyes huge with fright. “We carried on in their stead as is customary given the circumstances.”

“You vote based on what you believe they would have wanted?”

“We do,” the man said, lifting his chin in defiance.

Allie didn’t like them, but she could see how they had done the best they could in a difficult situation. “You will serve as secretary to the temporary Chief Justice. And you will no longer speak for my parents.”

“Who shall take the remaining seats?” Chairwoman Thomas asked.

Allie wanted to appoint Gregg and Naeemah, but she knew they wouldn’t want the position. And she needed them near, needed their guidance.

“The people must choose.” Allie turned to face the Senate. “I ask the court to make arrangements for public elections to be held within the year. The people deserve the right to elect two new Chiefs of Justice who will then appoint a new Chairman of the assembly.”

"That is not enough time," the secretary insisted. "We will need at least a year to plan the election and a year for the candidates to campaign."

"You people drag your feet when you need to take action.” Allie slammed her fist down on the dais railing. “I don't care what you have to do to make it happen. Make the announcements, and give the candidates four months to campaign, and then we will have an election *this* year. If you fail to take action, then I will return and take action for you.”

"And what do you intend to do as first princess?" Chairman Thomas asked. "What authority are you assuming here?"

"I have no desire to participate in the Senate unless I have to. Don't make me have to." Allie glared at the silent senators. "Take your positions seriously or I will clean house. Otherwise, I will remain in my position as the leader of Soma, free of government interference." Allie stepped up to the podium, turning to address the assembly. "I ask that every member of this Senate, from the high-ranking officials seated here today right down to the lieutenant governors who police the cities, to set their slaves free. Any person who has been purchased from Soma will be freed one way or another. I will be following up, and if I find you have not complied with this simple request, I will remove the slave from your home and you will be charged with crimes of human trafficking." Allie stared at the Senators seated before her. "I will not tolerate corruption."

"While you and the royal family have the full support of the Senate as well as our respect," the Chairman said, "we simply must determine the legal extent of your authority in the modern world." He took a step toward her. "We would like nothing more than to foster a positive relationship with the royals, but the parameters of your authority and ours must be clear in the eyes of the law."

"That matter has already been decided," Alísun said. "My heir has stepped forward and everyone in this chamber has already accepted her authority, whether you realize it or not. The matter is closed."

"It is not closed," Chairwoman Thomas said. "While we believe the heir deserves a voice in this chamber, the weight of that voice must be discussed at length."

"The royal family will decide the extent of my authority," Allie announced. "No one else has that right. The queen has never abdicated. Her sovereignty remains just as it was when she was named queen thousands of years ago. You are here today in your positions of power because she allowed it. And we are here, displaying the mantle of our authority because you have allowed yourselves to become corrupt in your thirst for more power."

"Perhaps you are right," the Chairman said. "But I am confident we will reach an agreement both parties can be happy with." He stepped down from the dais. "We invite you to stay here in the city. We can reconvene later this week to make the necessary decisions. You and your family are more than welcome to stay in the hotel suites here for our distinguished guests."

That's our cue to leave, Lex. Aidan stepped between Allie and the Chairman as his soldiers fell into a V formation around Allie and her family.

"That won't be necessary," Allie said, backing away from the Chairman. "We will be leaving now."

"I'm afraid we cannot allow you to leave until these matters have been decided." The Chairman raised his hand, causing all the doors to the chamber to slam shut, their locks clicking into place.

Time to go. Aidan and his soldiers started backing up. "Samantha. Bennett." Aidan nodded for two of his team to break formation.

The two raced to the top of the chamber. Raising their hands together, Samantha and Bennett demolished the locked door. Splinters and debris rained down where the door once stood.

"Stop them," Chairman Thomas called.

Senators rose from their seats to intercept, but they were too slow to react.

"Now." Naomi nodded at pair of female Syntrophos.

The two grasped hands and an icy blue mist formed a wall

around Allie and her people, closing them off from the Senate's reach.

"Quinn, Darius," Aidan said. "A little help?"

Quinn and Sasha joined hands, cloaking everyone under the veil of mist with Quinn's invisibility, and Darius threw up his soundproofing barrier, so they could no longer be heard or seen.

"All right, everyone, we're walking out of here now," Aidan said. "Go, quickly."

The Senate erupted in chaos when Allie and all of the Syntrophos disappeared.

"Seal the building," the Chairman cried. "Do not let them leave. Especially the Syntrophos. They cannot be trusted."

How are we getting out of here if the building is on lockdown? Allie asked.

Same way we're walking through this doorway. Aidan ushered her through the crumbling debris of the chamber doors and into the lobby. Darius and Livia closed in tightly behind her.

Is everyone with us? Allie asked, frantically looking over her shoulder.

My team will get us all out of here.

Samantha and Bennett charged across the lobby, using their gift to demolish the glass facade of the building at street level.

Shards of glass no bigger than grains of sand exploded out of the building, causing the guards to panic, desperately searching for a threat they couldn't see or hear. Mortal men and women on the sidewalks screamed at the explosion, cowering behind cars, searching for a source of the violence.

Allie and Aidan shot from the building with their hands clasped.

"Where will we go?" Allie asked, searching up and down the street for a way out.

"This way." Aidan turned, dragging her to the cars waiting along the curb.

"You planned this?" Allie asked.

"I had a feeling we'd end up on the same page at some point." Aidan skidded to a stop beside a white delivery van.

Allie had wondered why only five of the Syntrophos pairs were present in the courtroom when Naomi had said there were eight. The other three were waiting to drive them out of here.

"Get in," Aidan shoved Darius and Livia into the back of the van. Alísun and Alex were right behind them.

Allie tugged Aidan's hand as she stepped into the van, but he pulled her back.

"You were amazing." With one arm around her waist and his other hand splayed across her back, Aidan kissed her. And then he shoved her into the back of the van and slammed the door in her face.

Chapter 33

Allie sat at the base of the old laurel tree along the cliff side near Naeemah's house. Her arms resting on her knees, she let it all go. The tension of the last weeks and the stress of what still lay ahead of her.

After escaping the Senate, Aidan and his team had escorted them to the airport, where he left. Again. Allie never got a chance to really speak with him. After he'd shoved her into the van, he'd shut his mind off to hers. Again. That was two weeks ago.

It hurt to think about that one frantic kiss, but that was all she could focus on. It was like a knife in the gut every time she thought about it.

"Same page," Allie muttered. They were never on the same page. *But what did it mean? Was it goodbye?* But then Aidan had sent a pair of his Syntrophos with her, so that couldn't be it.

Neela and Ivy followed Allie wherever she went. Even now, they stood on the hillside, waiting and watching for any harm that might come to her. But they refused to divulge any information about Aidan's whereabouts or his intentions. It was infuriating.

Allie would be leaving for Soma soon, and they would surely follow. The move would be permanent this time. Allie had to make a clean break from Naeemah and Gregg, at least for now. She couldn't risk them losing their position as governor for associating too closely with her.

Lily and Carson would stay in Cleveland. Allie dreaded distancing herself further from her mortal family, but it was better for them if she did. Gregg promised he would keep his people watching over them. This time tomorrow she would officially be the head of Soma. She had great plans for the future, but she still couldn't understand why Aidan refused to be part of it.

Her visions wandered the hillside aimlessly. She was devoted to studying them more carefully, looking for clues of what might be coming for her next. Each was like a little mystery; once solved the vision evaporated, often replaced with something new and even more confusing.

Nothing was ever easy. There was always something. The Coalition, secret sisters, attacks on the family, blood moons, Syntrophos, captives, broken hearts, ancient grandparents, betrayals, heirs, and prophecies. That was her life, and she needed to get better at recognizing the things her gift tried to tell her.

Her visions were stronger now. More ominous. A dark vision of Emma followed her everywhere she went. Always there, like a harbinger of bad news, babbling in rapid French Allie couldn't even decipher. Sarah and Charles Madison's phantoms came to Allie just hours after the trial, but they faded into oblivion once news of their treason became widespread knowledge.

Allie saw Aidan's Syntrophos army, scattered at different points across the world. Sometimes together, sometimes not. Sometimes, they all remained with him. Sometimes, it seemed like their numbers were only half of what they were. She couldn't seem to land on an explanation for their behavior.

A vivid image of Soma in the distant future rested at the bottom of the grassy hillside. Still protected by Quinn's barrier, but it was Soma as she dreamed it could become. She saw Aidan with her. Their family together again. She just couldn't see the path that would lead them there. Like Harry staring into the mirror of Erised, she saw what she wanted but had no idea how to achieve it.

She smiled at a vision of Aidan making his way up the hillside, his black hair shimmering blue in the afternoon sun. He was her future Aidan. The version of him she saw with her at Soma. He was more like the boy she fell in love with a million years ago, but also the guarded man he had become in his absence. It gave her comfort, knowing the Aidan she loved might still be there, stuck in some future she couldn't see how to get to yet. But she would figure it out.

The vision of him paused on the grassy slope near the laurel tree where she sat, as if uncertain of how he'd come to be there. She heard his breath rushing in and out of his lungs, the rasp of the grass against his jeans. Allie sat up straighter, feeling uncertain if he was really a vision or not.

"Allie?" His voice was soft and low. A question.

Allie closed her eyes, pushing all of the visions away, silencing them and shoving them back where they belonged. She gasped when his shadow fell over her.

"Open your eyes, Alexis Ann," he said, crouching before her. "I want to see those weird, green eyes again."

"You're not here," she whispered, shaking her head and shutting her eyes tight. "You can't be." She didn't want to hope he was real. She couldn't face the heartbreak that would come the moment she opened her eyes.

"But I am." She felt his warmth as he sat beside her just as he had when they met here as teenagers a lifetime ago. "Why don't you trust what you see?"

Allie opened her eyes. *Is he really here, or have I finally lost touch with reality?*

"I'm really here." He took her hand. "Tell me why you think I'm not."

"The visions." She waved her hand in the direction of the hillside. "They're everywhere."

"All the time?" He frowned.

She nodded, still not believing what her eyes and her body were telling her. "Are you back?" she managed to whisper.

"I'm home." His smile was hesitant.

Allie flew into his arms, not trusting her own sanity until she felt his embrace and his breath in her hair.

"You're really here?" She leaned back, running her hands up the length of his arms. "For how long?"

"I'm not leaving again."

Allie hugged him tighter. "I swear, Aidan Loukas McBrien, if you ever slam a car door in my face like that again, I will tear your face off." Her words came out as a strangled sob.

"I'm sorry about that." His fingertips brushed the hair back from her face. "You have no idea how much I wanted to come home with you after the trial." He held her at arms' length, his hands cupping her face, and his thumb caressing the length of the tattoo along her throat. "But I had to take care of my people first. They depend on me."

"You brought them with you?"

"Not all of them. Not yet. I gave them the choice to leave and return to their lives but they all chose to take a brief visit home to take care of their families. They will make their way to us in time. It's the way of the Syntrophos. We stick together." Aidan's hands wandered down her arms, grasping her hands again. "To set the record straight, when we came for you at Soma, I never once questioned your position as first princess and the named heir of Indriell. But I was so angry. I had a plan

I'd been working toward for a long time, and I had to rethink things when you beat me to the punch. I convinced myself you were being used and manipulated. It was just so unlike you to reach for that kind of power. Then you told me off right before you turned away, leaving me and my soldiers gaping like morons. That was when I knew you really were the mastermind behind everything happening at Soma."

"I was doing it for you, you big dummy." She sniffed.

"I didn't think you'd still ... that you'd put yourself out there just for me."

"It wasn't just for you. I did this for all of us. But bringing you home was my main motivation. It wasn't until much later—when Darius pointed it out to me—that I realized all along I was telling myself I was going to rescue you when I'd never even considered that might not be what you wanted. Not like I could have asked, but I shouldn't have made that decision for you."

"We have to stop doing that to each other." Aidan smiled.

"Yeah." Allie sighed. "It's a lot harder than it sounds."

"I would get down on one knee, but I'm pretty sure you'd kick me in the nuts if I did." Aidan gave a wry grin. "Alexis Ann." He reached to brush a stray curl from her face. "You have my loyalty and my fealty."

"Aidan, don't." She squeezed his hand. She couldn't stand this. Not from him. "You are my equal. You don't have—"

"Of course, I do. I pledge my life and my service—and that of my army, no matter how big or small it may prove to be—to the heir and future queen of Indriell, however she chooses to reign. I will be her equal and her confidant. If she'll have me?"

"Why did you leave, Aidan? Before all of this madness started." She needed to know.

"Lots of reasons. None you'll like."

"Try me?"

"At first it was the Darius thing. I knew that was going to be hard on you and even harder with me here. So I planned to take myself out of the picture for a few months."

"And then?"

"And then Naomi happened." He shrugged. "And it became even more complicated and more clear to me that we needed the time apart. But in the end, she needed me more than you did. You had Darius. She didn't have anyone."

"I wish you would have discussed it with me first." Allie stared down at their entwined hands. It was a long time ago, and she didn't want to dredge up old things that were better off left buried, but she needed some kind of closure to that part of their lives.

"I know. It was stupid and selfish. I only hope that one day you can understand what my eighteen-year-old head was thinking when I made those choices—not just for us but for myself. I hope you'll understand that I was doing what I thought was best for Naomi and me. And the time apart ... that wasn't just about you."

"The time apart was never the issue. I came to understand just how much we needed it, too. It was your silence that killed me."

"I never really left you, Lex. I was always right here." He tapped her forehead. "For the last four years, whenever you've thought of me or spoke to me, I heard you. And it tore me apart not to respond."

Allie's eyes filled with tears as she realized just how close he had remained all these years. "One of these days, I'm going to kick your ass for that." She managed a watery smile.

"You never answered my question," Aidan said, brushing the tears from her eye with his thumb. "Will you have me, my queen ... to be?" His smile was uncertain, as if she might reject him. "It would be my honor to serve the royal family."

She titled her head back, meeting his gaze. "Aidan, I don't want you in my service. I want you as my equal and my friend. Besides, you have an army." She flashed him a wide grin.

"There's the smart ass I remember." He pulled her into his arms, holding her tight.

CHAPTER 34

"Your tattoos have changed." Allie ran her hand across Aidan's shoulder. They were alone at last in her penthouse room at Sterling Tower. The last week had been a whirlwind of activity, getting settled into a routine. But Aidan had been by her side the whole time. This was the first night they'd had together like old times and she was nervous.

"One of my Syntrophos has a gift like Erin's. She made some changes for me over the years." Aidan ran his hand down Allie's arm, his hum of contentment echoed in her ear, making her smile.

"The cuneiform symbols are gone. I remember those from the first day we met. I don't think I ever knew what those meant?"

"They were numbers," he said.

"Like a tally?"

"Exactly."

"What were you tallying on your body?" She leaned back so she could see his face. His eyes filled with amusement.

"I forgot how insanely wild your hair gets." He smoothed her crazy hair out of her face.

"Don't change the subject, mister. What were you using your body to keep track of?" She frowned down at him.

"Days."

She made a sound of annoyance deep in her throat and he laughed.

"It's ancient history now, but at the time, I was keeping track of how many days I'd gone without hurting anyone in my family with my fire gift."

"Oh, Aidan." She hit him with a pillow. "You were such a drama queen."

He laughed, the sound so familiar and still somehow different. More grown up. More ... man than boy.

"I was a bit broody in those days," he agreed. "The night Kayla was hurt at the bonfire, I begged Erin to come and wipe them all away. I couldn't look at the evidence of my failure. She took them away and banned me from her tattoo service for being a melodramatic bitch baby." He chuckled at the memory of his spunky cousin. "She eventually let me back in when I told her you'd notice my vanishing tatts."

"I recognize the Egyptian symbols for luck, life, and protection." She traced the intricate lines of the Eyes of Ra across his collarbone, symbols of his mother's Egyptian heritage. "But what does this one mean? I don't remember seeing this." She traced the ring around his nipple, resting on a straight line.

Aidan smiled and grabbed her hand. "That is the Egyptian Shen, which means Eternity."

"I love it. I need one just like it. What are these?" She pointed at the ancient symbols in rows down his left arm.

"Inspirations." He rose up on his elbow, pointing at the top symbol. "This is Sanskrit for warrior. And these mean strength, balance, energy, and patience."

"And this set over here?" She moved her hand over his heart.

He swallowed, his Adam's apple bobbing. "Those mean love, friendship, loyalty, and compassion. Also in Sanskrit."

"For Naomi?" She glanced back up, trying to put a clamp on the surge of unreasonable jealousy.

He nodded. "For Naomi."

"And these?" She moved on to the symbols beside Naomi's. These were the only colorful tattoos he had. All in red.

"Cuneiform," he said. "These are the symbols for sun." He pointed. "Strength, love, and divine light."

"And these tree-looking things?" She traced the simple lines, close to his heart.

"Orchard," he whispered. "The last one means brave hero."

"These are mine?" She lifted her gaze to meet his.

"Yes. You saved me that night." He placed his hand over hers.

Allie leaned forward, pressing her lips against his chest and over the symbols he'd placed there for her.

She inched her way up, placing kisses over each of his tattoos, even the ones for Naomi. Lingering over the symbol for eternity, she explored him in a way she never had before. As her lips met his, the heat of her power burned hot in her chest. She'd missed him. Missed the intimacy she'd only ever shared with him.

"Allie." Aidan groaned in frustration as he eased her off him, placing a chaste kiss on her forehead.

"What?" Allie asked, her heart growing cold at the sudden rejection.

"Don't look at me like that, Lex." Aidan rolled onto his side, facing her. "Trust me, I want to be with you like this again more than I want air."

"But?"

"It's been years. I don't want to mess this up again. If we're doing this ... if we're going to really be together, I want to get it right this time. Let's not rush into anything while we're getting to know each other again."

Allie nodded. "You're right. I don't want to mess this up either." She moved back to her side of the bed.

"Too much has changed, Allie. I'm not sure we can pick things up right where we left them."

"It's healthier to start over." She reached for his hand but kept her eyes on the ceiling.

"What are you thinking?" He gazed down at her with a worried frown.

"If you'd let me back in, you'd know what I was thinking." She pressed her fingertip against his forehead. She wasn't mad. Or hurt. She knew he was absolutely right about not rushing into anything they weren't ready for. But she felt ... sad. She couldn't even explain it. Not in words.

"I'm not keeping you out for any specific reason, Lex. Don't you like your privacy? Don't you remember how awful it was not having any?"

"Awful." She nodded. Sure, there were moments when it was bad. But she never remembered it being awful. She loved having Aidan back, and she was all in for taking it slow. But without their connection, it was like he wasn't really back. Not all the way.

Allie waited until Aidan's breath fell into the regular rhythm of sleep before she slipped out of bed. She hadn't seen Darius all night, and she ached to be near him.

She tiptoed down the hall to his room, but he wasn't alone. Naomi's giggle was like a hot poker, rousing the jealous green monster that had taken up residence inside Allie since her arrival at Sterling Tower. She and Aidan had moved into the penthouse with Allie and Darius, but she was supposed to be sleeping on the pullout in the study, not in Darius's room.

Allie retreated down the hall and stepped onto the enormous balcony running the length of the building. She could still hear them, talking and laughing. They had the sliding glass panels open to the patio, letting in the unseasonably warm evening air.

Allie leaned against the railing, watching the Atlanta lights twinkling and listening to the nightlife drift up from the streets below.

"What are you doing?" Aidan whispered as he came to join her, his bare chest warm at her back.

"Couldn't sleep." She pulled his arms around her waist, snuggling back against him.

"I woke up and you weren't there. I didn't like it. I thought for a minute that I'd just dreamed I was here with you."

Allie turned, wrapping her arms around his middle. She reached up on her tiptoes to kiss his nose. "You don't have to worry about that."

"I dreamed about you constantly." He smiled. "You haunted me, Allie."

"Back atcha, big guy."

"Big guy?"

"You're huge. Or hadn't you noticed," she teased. "You were always freakishly tall, but you've got the bulk to back it up now."

"Freakishly tall? Maybe you're freakishly short." He pressed a kiss to the top of her head.

"Do you hate this as much as I do?" She looked up at him.

"Yep." His mouth drew into a firm line. "Don't like it one bit, but it's not for us to get in their way. They hate what we have just as much. It's the most difficult thing about being Syntrophos at this age."

"You think it will get easier when we're older?" she asked.

She couldn't imagine ever not being jealous of anyone Darius might love.

"When we bond with our Complements, we will find balance in both of our relationships. Until then, it will be difficult."

"Right." Allie frowned at the idea.

"What do you know of your Complement, Allie?" Aidan whispered.

"Nothing." She shrugged.

"Still?" He stared down at her in confusion. "You've never seen or felt anything about him?"

"Emma always said that part will be hard for me. I see and feel so much through my gift and intuition; I don't know if I would recognize those little glimpses for what they're supposed to be."

He sighed. "That makes sense."

"What do you know of yours?"

"Lots of little things. Nothing important."

"What's it like when you know you've seen something about her?"

"It's like a little reward." He smiled. "I could see how you might dismiss it as something related to your clairvoyance. Sometimes, I see a hint of her face, but it's hard to really see anything recognizable. Or I feel her mood. See different versions of her at different stages of her life. Nothing that tells me who she really is. But it's a comfort knowing she's out there somewhere living her life."

"I don't like the thought of you having a Complement."

"Let's not let that come between us now."

"I won't. I still don't have to like it, though." She smiled up at him.

"Still stubborn. Still with the mortal brain." He returned her smile, brushing an errant curl from her face.

"Always."

"And until we all complete our partner bonds, we're going to have to deal with the wild jealousy as best we can." Aidan scowled toward the room where his brother and his Syntrophos were.

"I want to go in there and tear her face off," Allie said cheerfully.

"Please don't. I like her face."

"Ugh. You would."

"This isn't going to be easy. Jealousy ran rampant among the Syntrophos training with the Initiative. But we dealt with it and learned to be respectful of the relationships forming around us."

"You have a lot of experience with the Syntrophos bond. Would you consider teaching a class? We could all use as much insight as we can get."

"I was actually thinking about taking some classes myself this fall."

"College?"

"Yeah, I never finished."

"What about music school?"

"Maybe in another life." He smiled. "I'm out of practice. I kind of thought I'd start with a degree in education and maybe next time, when things settle down, I can pursue the music dream."

"You will still play, won't you?" It bothered her to think he'd give up on music all together.

"Music is in my blood. I'll always play."

"Good. And what about teaching that Syntrophos class?

"Madame director, your mind is always on business, isn't it?" His voice took on a familiar teasing tone.

"'Fraid so."

"I suppose I'd have to teach my brother, too?"

"Yes, you big goof." Allie gave him a playful punch.

"You know we can hear you guys, right?" Darius leaned out on the patio. "Might as well come inside and hang out with us before faces get unnecessarily torn off for no reason."

"Was he always such a smart ass?" Aidan took Allie's hand.

"Always." Allie laughed. "It's what I love about him."

"Ugh. You would."

CHAPTER 35

"Allie-girl." Alexander stepped into her office. "Navid says there is a young girl outside asking for entrance."

"Bring her in, Grandpa. We don't turn anyone away." Allie looked back at her desk. New students arrived on a daily basis. They were nearly at full capacity, but Allie refused to send anyone away.

"She is asking for you. She won't come in until you come out to talk to her."

"Who is it?" She looked up from her work.

"It's Chloe Long."

"Chloe!" Allie jumped from her desk and charged out of her office. She hadn't seen Chloe in more than two years. The death of Ming Lao had changed her. Allie had seen the hard road that lay ahead of her friend, and she'd tried to help Chloe through her loss, but she didn't want it. Chloe drifted away from her family and friends. And when she graduated high school, she disappeared without a trace. Liam tried to keep tabs on her, but she never stayed anywhere long enough for him to find her. Jin Jing had spent the last few years chasing his daughter's shadow.

For Chloe to show up out of the blue was a miracle.

Allie raced into the lobby where Navid waited for her. "Take me to her."

"She's changed, Allie," he said gently. "Prepare yourself, she's not the girl you once knew. Losing someone the way she did ... it breaks something inside you. She'll never be the same."

"Take me to her, please?" Allie didn't care who Chloe was now. If she came here, she needed help, and Allie would give her whatever she needed.

"Just be cautious. She's probably second guessing her decision to come here, so try not to spook her." Navid opened a rift in the barrier and Allie rushed inside. She walked carefully, following Navid's steps, ignoring the voices calling to her from the dreamworld. She'd done this a thousand times now. She knew to keep a straight and narrow path to the other side. The way was slow and steady. And it killed her to think Chloe might leave before she could get to her.

"Careful, Allie," Navid said as he breached the rift into the world outside of Sterling Tower.

"Chloe." Allie managed to keep her voice steady as she approached the girl who vaguely resembled the one she once knew. Chloe was taller, curvier. Her long, dark hair was pulled back in an elaborate style with streaks of blue highlights, a pair of expensive looking headphones holding her hair back from her face. Her eye makeup was dark and thick, her eyebrow pierced, and her arms tattooed.

"Allie." She nodded.

"It's good to see you," she said.

"It's been a while." Chloe shifted nervously on her feet. "I hear you're some kind of princess now."

"Something like that," Allie said dryly. "Would you like to come inside? See what we're about?"

"You train people here? People with modern gifts?"

"We do. And we guarantee your safety while you are here. The only way in and out is through Quinn's barrier." She gestured over her shoulder.

"Yeah. I forgot he's a dream walker, right?"

"Right." Allie nodded. "Why don't we just sit here?" She gestured at the bench along the sidewalk, which was a new addition to the front of Sterling Tower, just for this reason. "You can tell me about whatever you're struggling with."

"It's too much," Chloe said, taking the seat Allie offered. "I can't handle it anymore."

"What is it? Your path of least resistance?" She could imagine how that particular gift might become overwhelming. Chloe could see the decisions people struggled with, and she could see the path they should choose. It was a branch of Clairvoyance and likely a manifestation of her father's probabilities gift she'd inherited from him.

"Yes. I forgot you called it that." She gave a lukewarm smile. Something told Allie that Chloe hadn't smiled much in recent years. "It was always more of an intuition when I was a kid. Now, it's evolving into a physical manifestation of my gift where I can actually see all the decisions the people around me struggle with, and how all those decisions are connected. And the sheer volume of the voices is more than I can handle. I used to be able to silence them, but I can't seem to control it anymore. I'm back to wearing headphones all the time now."

"So it's more information than you can possibly process at once?" Allie asked.

"Yes. That's it exactly. I haven't had a mentor in a long time, but I've always been able to handle my progress on my own. Until now."

"Graham and I are in a class that would probably help you."

"Graham's here?" Her voice shook with emotion. She and Graham were once close friends.

"He just arrived a few weeks ago after his graduation from MIT. We're all here, actually. Right where we need to be. And we'd love to have you join us. Graham and I are both struggling with the same thing you are. Our gifts are overloading us with too much information that's made it almost impossible to function. My visions are constant. I see them everywhere I go. Even now, they are swarming all around you, demanding my attention. Some days I can hardly handle it. But I'm coping. We have a new teacher who is helping us learn to process what our gifts are trying to tell us faster, so we aren't crippled by what we see and hear."

"That sounds like exactly what I need." Chloe leaned forward, her elbows on her knees. "But can I really come back? To the family?"

"Of course, you can. But here, it is mostly just old friends. The family comes and goes frequently, but Soma is a place for the young."

"Dad's going to come find me here if I stay too long."

"And we would let him in with open arms. But you don't have to see him if you don't want to."

"It's too hard. Seeing him without Mom."

"I actually understand how difficult that is for you. The man who greeted you is my natural father, Navid. My mother was killed the same way your mother was. I never knew her the way you knew and loved Ming Lao, but knowing I won't ever have that chance is painful."

"It still hurts, Allie. So much," she whispered.

"I know. But maybe we can offer you a respite from the pain. And if Jin shows up, then maybe my father could help him, too." Allie knew she needed to tell Chloe about Livia, but she feared if she did, she'd never see her friend again. She would have to send Livia away for a while. Until Chloe found some healing. "Will you come inside with me?"

Chloe nodded. "I can't promise I'll stay."

Allie draped her arm around Chloe. "You can leave whenever you want. All you have to do is ask."

Epilogue

Four months later

"Don't linger, Graham," Gabe said. "You, too, Allie. Watch Chloe, how her eyes move rapidly. She's taking in everything at once, cataloguing it for later. This is what we must do when our gifts bombard us with too much information."

"Right, sorry. I was distracted by something impossible to ignore." Allie flushed a shade of red to match her hair. A rather delightful vision of Aidan swimming demanded a long pause. All wet and ... yummy. And not constantly turning her down.

"Keep moving," Gabe said. "Catch up and don't miss anything. It's important, Allie."

"Right." She scanned through the visions drifting around the room. There were more than ever now that she lived inside Sterling Tower where the things they did and learned were shaping the future of all their lives. She catalogued everything she saw and heard, sorting through the faces, sounds, random snatches of conversation, and even the clothes her visions wore. She placed single words, noises, and phrases that tended to crop up often into small, manageable bits of information like Gabe taught her. That way she could sift through it all later, keeping the relevant bits and discarding the junk. A familiar process, but on a much larger scale. Allie spent the better part of her training time these days dedicated to the process.

Gabe was a lifesaver for her and Graham and now Chloe and a few others, too. Jayesh found him among the Soma trainers from before the takeover—one of many who stayed. He was brilliant with the kind of gifts that overwhelmed students. His own gift was similar to Graham's tech gift. He was bombarded with computer code wherever he went, and he'd had to learn how to translate and process all of that information, so he could use it to his advantage. Now, he was one of the leading techs at Soma, and his classes filled up quickly.

They were all making such progress; it astounded her every day when she heard the stories of the students in residence here.

"Good job, everyone," Gabe said. "I have another class this afternoon, so I need to run. But keep practicing, and we'll meet again next week. If you need me before then, catch me during my office hours."

"Bye, Gabe, thanks!" Allie waved as he left them to their practice. It was Allie's idea to structure the new Soma to be more like a college with scheduled classes, qualified instructors, and various levels the students could work toward. That was one thing she liked about the old Soma. The reward system. She'd made changes to the system, so it focused on the accolades and pride for a job well done.

"See you next time, Allie," Chloe called as she left with Graham for their next class. It was good to see them so close again.

Allie made her way back to her office for her meeting with Emma. Her mentor spent a lot of time traveling back and forth from Cleveland to Atlanta. And Allie made the trip home as often as she could. It was important for her to still see her family on a regular basis. She missed her mom and dad, as well as her niece. Livia still couldn't bring herself to let Kahlynn spend time in Atlanta, but Allie thought she might eventually see how much good Soma could do for Kahlynn's training when she was a little older.

"Emma." Allie smiled as she greeted her mentor with a hug. "I hope I haven't kept you waiting long?"

"No, we just got here. Daniel's off looking for Quinn and his girls."

"Daniel's back again? I just saw him two days ago." Allie stored her yoga mat and gym bag in her private bathroom.

I swear that man's favorite thing these days is chartering people back and forth in his new jet."

"Well, it sure makes the commute a lot easier."

"Two hours here and back and I'm home for dinner with Parker." She took her seat on the gray suede sofa.

"How do I know when I've seen or felt something about my Complement?" Allie kicked off her shoes and sank down on the sofa beside her mentor. The question just rolled off her tongue before she could even consider it.

"Way to get the ball rolling," Emma said. "We've talked about this before, Allie. It's going to be difficult for you to recognize. I'm not even sure you ever will. What's brought this on? Do you think you've seen something?"

"No, it's just something Aidan said about the way he can sense her mood sometimes and gets a flash of all the different versions of her. I just ... I don't know if I've seen that myself or not."

"Her?"

"His Complement. He seems to be able to recognize her so easily. I guess I'm just feeling the need to prepare myself for the inevitable. Sometimes, I think he's so open to the idea that when she does come around, he's going to fall so hard and so fast."

"Well, she has to find him first. And that might take her a good long time. And when she does, she might not be ready to see him yet."

"That would make him crazy." Allie laughed at the idea.

"I imagine so," Emma said, picking at a loose thread on a throw pillow.

Her expression reminded Allie of a vision she'd meant to ask her mentor about.

"I saw a vision of Aidan during my graduation ceremony," Allie began. "It was years ago, right before he left for Germany. He came to you for help."

Emma nodded. "He did."

"What was that about?" Allie played with the hem of her yoga pants, avoiding Emma's gaze.

"He needed some help convincing his parents to let him go to school in Germany. I saw how much it meant to him, so I agreed."

"He was hurting." Allie looked up.

"He wasn't in a good place, Allie. He came to me in confidence. I won't break that confidence now."

"It's okay. I was just curious."

"Just be patient with him. Coming back to his family and starting over, it's a lot for any twenty-three year old kid. I imagine he's struggling to pick up the pieces. And I imagine you two are probably struggling to find your place as a couple. Try not to rush into anything too serious too soon."

"Oh, no, you have your scary mentor face on." Allie leaned back in her chair. "Don't rock my boat, Emma. I'm in such a good place right now."

"That's probably why," Emma said softly.

"Why what?"

"It's time, Allie."

"For what?" She swallowed, her throat going dry.

"Time for your Proving."

"What?" Allie's heart skipped in her chest as panic set in. "I'm not even twenty-two yet."

"I've been watching you so closely this year, and I'm sure of it."

"How can I possibly be ready?"

"All the signs are there, Allie. The way you took on the Senate all by yourself. How you were prepared with those questions ahead of time, reacting to events as they unfolded around you. You were confident and completely in control of your judgment gift, embracing the mantle of authority Alísun passed on to you. The way you've really learned to trust in your gift and your intuition, even when you can't see the forest for the trees. The sheer amount of progress you've made with your visions. First on your own and even more so with Gabe. The work you've done here at Soma in such a short amount of time is remarkable. You are ready."

"I don't feel ready." Allie's blood ran cold with fear. "Not even a little bit."

"We have to get you prepared for this." Emma bent toward her, taking Allie's hands in hers. "And that means I have to tell you what a Proving is really all about."

Allie nodded, too scared to speak.

"You remember how difficult your Awakening was, how you had to battle to gain control of your power before it ended?"

"I'll never forget the struggle," Allie said.

"We were so worried to prepare you for it. Afraid it might send you into an early Awakening. You've seen how hard Lennox has had to work to come back from that. It's been a long road for her, but she's recovering, and the harder she works, the easier it will get for her."

"Why are we talking about early Awakenings? If I'm

Proving early, as we always suspected I would, shouldn't it be like Darius's?"

"Yes, but that's not the point I'm trying to make." Emma sighed. "An early Awakening is a difficult thing to come back from, but it is possible. But a failed Proving ... that you can never recover from."

"What does that mean? A failed Proving?"

"When you fail to pass your Proving, your power will slowly begin to die. You will always be Immortal, but an Immortal with no power and no means to protect yourself. These Immortals tend to live in small colonies together, isolated from the rest of us. It's not something people talk about."

"And why is this the first I'm hearing of it?" Allie's hands trembled as her mentor held them tightly.

"The early years of an Awakening are hard enough. We do not tell our children of this possibility until they are near their Proving. It's an effective means to help young Immortals focus on one hurdle at a time."

"That's a big hurdle."

"During your Proving, you will come face to face with your demons. All your fears of inadequacy, self-judgment, and all of your failures. You will not pass your Proving until you come to terms with who you are at the very core of your being. And for most, it's a deeply disturbing and humbling experience. It's why Darius didn't want to see you at first. He couldn't face you."

Allie held on to Emma's hands as if they'd keep her rooted in this moment, so she didn't have to move forward. She could almost hear the clock ticking.

"And on top of all that, you will have to conquer your power, each of your gifts, and master the art of being a Syntrophos."

Allie took a deep breath, trying to still her racing pulse. "And how long do I have to prepare for this impossible task?"

"Your Proving will take place within the year."

What happened in the four years Allie and Aidan spent apart? What led Aidan and Naomi to make the decision to join the Milan Initiative? Find out in the dual point of view novel, Betrayal (book 5), coming soon.

DON'T FORGET YOUR FREE BOOK!

In Heir, find out what happens for Allie and her friends four years after the end of Judgment and Captive. And then download your FREE copy of SCHOLAR and discover everything there is to know about the Immortals of Indriell. **Loyal subscribers will also receive bonus chapters and a short story.**

Visit **bit.ly/ScholarOffer** to download now

Also by Melissa A. Craven

Immortals of Indriell Series:

Emerge (Book 1) | Catalyst (An Immortals of Indriell Short Story) | Edge (Book 0) | Judgment (Book 2) | Scholar (An Immortals of Indriell Series Companion) | Volunteer (An Immortals of Indriell Short Story) | Captive (Book 3) |Assignment: An Immortals of Indriell Novella | Heir (Book 4) Betrayal (Book 5) | Runaway (Book 6) | Proving (Book 7)

Queens of the Fae Series

Fae's Deception (Book 1)

Fae's Defiance (Book 2)

Fae's Destruction (Book 3)

Crimes of the Fae Series

Fae's Prisoner (Book 1)

Fae's Power (Book 2)

Fae's Promise (Book 3)

HISTORY OF THE INDRIELL QUEENS

Long ago, before the most primitive of mortal man existed, a mighty race of humans inhabited the earth.

In those days, the Power was pristine and the forest city of Indriell was the greatest in all the world. Governed by the beautiful Indriell Queens, the city prospered. Queen Fáelynn reigned for centuries, preceded by her mother, the Dowager Queen Alyvia and her mother, Celyn, and her mother, Ashlyn. All royal daughters of Indriell, ruling in an unbroken line of succession stretching back further than living memory.

As Queen Fáelynn's reign drew to an end, she prepared to pass the kingdom to her only daughter, the Lady Eiselynn, first princess, fifth of her line.

She was a shy but powerful young woman who dreaded the day she would be named and forced to marry Lord Teigan. He was her equal in skill, but a man she could never love.

One morning, she rode through the meadows and came upon a young farmer. She watched as he called upon the power to plow his fields. He was not strong, but the intricacy with which he handled his task was breathtaking to watch.

She absently mimicked his simple manipulation, reaching out to his more refined touch. He saw her and inclined his head in respect, but continued working. Mesmerized, her curiosity grew and he responded to her curiosity with his own. He was confused when she fumbled with the simple chore.

As their power mingled, she felt a jolt of surprise from the contact that was far more intimate than anything she had ever experienced. His eyes widened in disbelief when her strength bolstered his, while his delicate simplicity corrected her firmer hand.

In that moment, she reached for him, knowing he was the one she would choose—had she a choice. She could see the same realization burning deep within his silvery eyes. As their power flowed, isolating them from the world, an unbreakable bond formed between them. It was as if they had always belonged together.

For months, they met privately and their love grew strong. She knew Ían could be a compassionate ruler. Despite his limitations, he was capable of the most astounding feats. Somehow—impossibly—he was learning. She wanted to present him to the council as her equal, but she feared their response. As months passed, the queen grew suspicious and sent Lord Teigan to follow the princess.

As Eiselynn retreated to their special meeting place, she was unaware that her betrothed and his manservant, Tomás, followed. When she eagerly leapt into the arms of her beloved, Teigan was furious to witness her betrayal. Heedless of the bond that united the lovers, he attempted to drag her home. Enraged, Ían stepped between them and a brawl ensued.

A powerful connection formed between the angry men. Ían felt a surge of strength rise within him but his opponent recoiled from the invasion, as if an agonizing pain reverberated through his mind. When the extraordinary link subsided, Ían rose, profoundly altered. Somehow, he had taken a portion of Teigan's ability for his own. He swiftly brought the stunned man to his knees, thrilling at the strength that now made him Eiselynn's equal.

As they fled, Teigan demanded his servant's silence, but the incident intrigued Tomás. He had lived in subjugation all his life, treated like a simpleminded child, never allowed to make his own decisions, while Ían had simply taken what he desired.

That night, Tomás discovered he was very much like Ían—he could learn.

For months, he practiced until he was prepared to choose his first victim. He preyed on those weaker than himself, and never failed to defeat them.

Tomás took a few select individuals into his confidence and taught his secrets. For years, they worked together, traveling outside the city to select their targets, growing evermore powerful. They called themselves the "Enlightened" and were determined to usher in an Age of Reason.

Eiselynn and Ían were married and ruled together for many long years. The duel faded from memory and Indriell prospered under their reign, until the attacks on the nobility began. They immediately recognized the signs and grew nervous when murmurings of the Enlightened grew louder.

Soon it was unsafe to walk the streets of Indriell as this influential group called for the complete destruction of the nobility, claiming it was time for tradition to die in the name of reason and logic. Time to progress into an age where those who proved capable of learning and growing could be given the opportunity to reach beyond their common birth to become more than the simple minded servants of those born to better circumstances.

As this Age of Reason gained momentum, the nation fell to the Enlightened. Eiselynn and Ían were hidden safely among their advisers, but the world was now at war.

New weapons were created with the power, causing strange imbalances in nature. An odd illness spread among those exposed to these destructive magnetic forces.

For a century, there was little peace among the nation as the Enlightened fought for dominance in the name of their cause. Ían and Eiselynn chose to fight against the overwhelming, unnatural strength of the few Enlightened who had long ago become drunk with a power that was not their own.

Years of war and violence took a toll, and the human race was in danger of extinction. The earth suffered greatly from the effects of such reckless warfare. Destructive earthquakes fractured the land, creating huge oceans. Lakes and rivers dried up, leaving famine and hunger in their wake. Even time was disrupted by the corruption of the power that was once so pristine. The slow tranquil days of the past, when the sun traveled leisurely across the sky, were no more. Now the sun and moon passed swiftly on their journeys, causing confusion among the living.

Tomás took the throne for himself, murdering Eiselynn and Ían in a mad display of violent executions, but their young daughter, Alísun, survived to carry on in her parents' stead.

In her grief, young Queen Alísun led her forces to victory, capturing the remaining Enlightened and ending the Great War. She was just a child; a child who knew nothing of the power that should have been her birthright.

Out of the ashes, the beautiful forest cities of Indriell were rebuilt and life moved on, but many of Alísun's generation remained feeble. Her advisers feared the years of violence had destroyed the gift.

On the dawn of her sixteenth year, Alísun's power awakened in a violent, sudden onset. A rare few of her generation suffered similarly and were limited in ways that baffled their parents, but many remained untouched by their heritage.

Alísun, and those like her, found a way to flourish despite their limitations, but the afflicted children were an anomaly and their lives were taken before they lived a single century.

For years, the births of mortal children escalated while the births of normal children declined. Alísun feared if this epidemic were left to spread, it would eventually leave them extinct.

She chose to banish the afflicted to the furthest corners of the world and within a few short years, the disease died out among those left behind and they finally began to grow in number.

Meanwhile, the banished mortals struggled under harsh conditions as they learned to survive on their own. Life was difficult for them and a hatred for their Immortal brethren was born.

As memory began to fade and young mortals no longer recalled their gifted ancestors, a select few Elders vowed to keep the hatred alive.

In time, the mortal race thrived as they learned a rudimentary way to survive as hunters and gatherers. Immortals withdrew from their once great cities to live among their cave dwelling brothers and sisters, watching over them in secret, protecting them with their powerful gifts. Those who hated the Immortals, hunted them, using their own weapons against them.

As Indriell dissolved into the stuff of legends, the reign of the Great Queens came to an end with Queen Alísun, the greatest of them all. Thousands of years have passed and the Immortal race still thrives, despite the damage caused by one man's misguided pursuit of Enlightenment.

The power is corrupted and will remain so until a new generation is born with the strength of their ancestors, led by one with an unsullied, natural connection with the power. His heart will guide him, giving him the restraint to wield his power wisely. He will gather his equals and together they will stand against those who persist in the corruption of the natural order. He will be strong and fierce in his beliefs, and steadfast in his love. Born the second child of the seventh daughter of his line, he alone will possess the skills and the knowledge to heal what has been broken. He alone will have the courage to judge unbiased and mete out the ultimate punishment. Until the time of his birth, may we prepare the way and hope for the future of all the races of men.

—Book of the Indriell Queens – ca. 6000 B.C.E.

About Melissa A. Craven

Melissa A. Craven (the "A" stands for Ann—in case you were wondering) writes Young Adult Fantasy with crossover appeal to other genres and audiences of all ages. She believes in stories that make you think and she loves twisty plots, and playing with foreshadowing, leaving clues and hints for the careful reader. She draws inspiration from her background in architecture and interior design to help her with the small details in world building and scene settings. Melissa is also the indie manager and a staff reviewer at YABooksCentral.com. You can follow her reviews and her contributions to the YABC blog at the link below. And if you love Sweet Romance and Contemporary Fiction, you can find Melissa's books in those genres under her pen name, Ann Maree Craven.

Join Melissa's Underground on Facebook
Or visit her at Melissaacraven.com

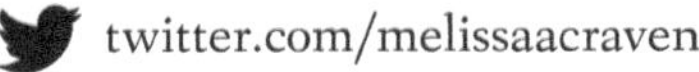

instagram.com/melissaacraven

bookbub.com/authors/melissa-a-craven

Acknowledgments

I have been waiting three years to write Heir and it was a blast. Yet, the journey to create this book was a super fast one and quite a personal challenge. I've never written a book as fast as I wrote Heir. I gave myself four months from concept to completion and actually pulled it off, despite the complete mind screw of jumping four years ahead in the story.

My biggest thank you is to my sister, Angela for putting up with my constant "Let me just finish this book and then I'll do (insert whatever task Melissa has been putting off), I promise." Now that it's done, I have a lot of promises to fulfill.

To my family, I could literally never do this without you. A special thanks to my mother, Debby for her hilarious text messages of "I need more chapters" and "are you done yet?" and "WHERE is Aidan?" And for saying Heir is my best book yet. (To be fair, she says that every time and she's my mom.) To my Dad. The Heir is dedicated to the very special man who never fails to support me and my crazy endeavors. Thank you for constantly showing me and my sister that we'll *never* know what it's like to have one of those fathers who just doesn't care. And for teaching me the subtle art of sarcasm ;)

To Jenny, you are the best, best friend I could ask for. Thank you for your encouragement, and for the way we will always pick up right where we left off, no matter how much time has passed or how busy life gets. And for game night. Game night is important.

A huge thank you to my editors. Chase Night and Rebecca Jaycox. I feel like I've finally cultivated my dream team. Chase, you're a tough critic and sometimes I hate you lol, but you're always right and you always get me there in the end. Rebecca, you're amazing in the way you pick up on my weaknesses and slay those adverbs we both hate. And you've saved my rear end on more than one occasion when I've had zero time left in my schedule and feel like panicking. You *always* come through.

To Daqri Combs at Covers by Combs for the very special redesign on all the series covers. I love your work and appreciate your guidance.

A big thank you to the city of Cleveland and to Kelleys Island especially. The island as it is portrayed in the book is purely fictional, but is based on the real Kelleys Island near Sandusky, Ohio.

To all of my author friends across the world, thank you for your constant support, encouragement and sense of community. The indie community is an amazing place and it is such a comfort knowing I am not doing this alone. And to Michelle Lynn, my author BFF, Co-Author and venting buddy, you are the BEST! I can't wait for our upcoming collaboration!

To C.J. Redwine, Author of The Shadow Queen and my YABC mentor. Thank you for bringing me on as the site indie manager and for providing ALL the books. The experience has been invaluable and I look forward to the future of YABooks-Central.com

And most importantly, to my ever growing audience of readers who have waited patiently for each book, thank you from the bottom of my heart for your enthusiasm and loyalty. I promise there will be much more to look forward to in the years to come.

Finally, I thank God for the constant reminder that I am doing what I'm supposed to be doing. Over the past years, circumstances *always* bring me back to writing—my favorite thing to do in the whole world.

www.ingramcontent.com/pod-product-compliance
Lightning Source LLC
Chambersburg PA
CBHW030526310726
48979CB00010B/1815/J
* 9 7 8 1 9 7 0 0 5 2 1 5 2 *